# A ROCKY MOUNTAIN REUNION

DEBRA MOSER

Recycling programs for this product may not exist in your area

ISBN-13: 978-1-335-46041-7

A Rocky Mountain Reunion



For questions and comments about the quality of this book, please contact us at CustomerService@Harlequin.com.

Harlequin Enterprises ULC
22 Adelaide St. West, 41st Floor
Toronto, Ontario M5H 4E3, Canada
www.Harlequin.com

HarperCollins Publishers
Macken House, 39/40 Mayor Street Uppe
Dublin 1, D01 C9W8, Ireland
www.HarperCollins.com

**Printed in U.S.A.**

## “I shouldn’t have started this...”

Hawk gently took her hands in his. “I don’t have room for more distractions in my life right now and you’ve made it clear you’re going back to Michigan.”

Meg pulled her hands free. “You know, I’ve thought about this moment since our ride together the day you and Lame Eagle found me leading Molasses. Never once did I imagine you’d immediately tell me you regretted it.” She pushed off the swing.

“Meggie.” He followed her and stretched out his hand to take hers. In the deepening twilight, headlights, bright and steady, shone on the road. He lowered his hand and looked at her. Tiny creases were etched across her forehead. He wanted to tell her he didn’t regret it—at all.

What Hawk regretted was wanting more...and knowing he couldn’t have it.

Dear Reader,

I love reading stories about families, small-town communities and the bonds created within each. Of course, when the story includes falling in love, it's even better.

In *A Rocky Mountain Reunion* Meg Farrell, a bit of an outsider on the family's ranch due to her asthma, comes back to Bent Fork for a visit. Her changing feelings for family, the small community of Tyler, Colorado, and her childhood crush, Joe Hawk, give her cause to think maybe she does belong after all.

Hawk, half Native American Ute and half stubborn Minnesotan, is struggling to clear his ranch of debt caused by his long absent father and keep the promise of honoring his ancestral land. A promise made more challenging when Meg finds fossils on Sitting River and wants to excavate.

Finding themselves together again and again, Meg and Hawk build bonds of belonging, not only within their families, but for each other.

I hope you will find a place in your heart for the high-country ranchers of Colorado. They certainly have a place in mine.

*Debra*

**Debra Moser** writes about families, small-town communities and the bonds created within each. She lives in Colorado and loves waking to see blue skies, sunshine and snow blanketing the mountain peaks before morning coffee with her childhood sweetheart. Her stories have twice finaled in the Romance Writers of America Golden Heart Contest. When she's not writing, Debra enjoys diving into genealogy research or a good book. Time with family and all their activities, from hockey, skiing, and soccer to walks, games, and impromptu meals are her most treasured moments.

Visit the Author Profile page
at Harlequin.com for more titles.

This book is dedicated to my mother, who fostered my creativity and loved me unconditionally

# *CHAPTER ONE*

SHE HEARD THE SOUND and flinched—the crack of a rifle. Meg froze mid-stride on the rocky path.

*Where did that come from?*

Eyes wide and ears alert, she scanned the area in front of her. Nothing.

The climbing switchback trail twisted around boulders and threaded through pine and aspen trees until it leveled off at the top of the ridge. Nothing but a lot of Colorado Rocky Mountain majesty and solitude. And someone with a rifle.

Another crack shattered the stillness. Meg dropped to the ground. She seized two rocks, sidled off the trail and crouched behind a boulder. Her ears perked for any sound and her mind raced with questions.

Who fired the shots? Poacher? Hunter? Where were they?

Her father had mentioned seeing signs of trespassing on their ranch. Tire tracks in an area of Bent Fork that the family covered on horseback. A neatly set ring of blackened stones full of ash and supporting a makeshift spit.

The sun-heated rock warmed her back. The wind, blowing cool off the snowcapped peaks, rustled the glossy leaves of the nearby aspen trees. A Steller's jay squawked from a tall pine just off the path. Meg wished she had the jay's vantage point. She wished she were back in Michigan starting work as head of the Earth Sciences Department at the new Mayfield Museum of Science and Nature. One didn't feel compelled to hide behind rocks in a museum. One tended to study them.

Meg gripped the stones, held her breath and waited. No one at home knew she'd be up on the ridge today. She had no plan when she'd saddled Calypso after breakfast and left the chatter of family. Less than twenty-four hours back home and all she'd wanted was a quiet ride. A chance to feel the wind, see the peaks, move in the silence and meld into the magic of the mountains and maybe spot a potential area that might yield fossils.

She'd expected to hear birdsong, cattle mooing and the wind in the trees. She hadn't expected to hear rifle shots.

"Meggie?"

Meg freed the breath she'd been holding. A poacher wasn't likely to call out her name.

"Meggie?"

She knew that voice. She knew the man it belonged to. The man who, years ago, had fueled her then-budding teenage imagination of a hero. She relaxed her grip on the stones and crept from behind the boulder and came face-to-face with the man…and a gun.

He stood stone-still a few yards down the path resting a rifle in the crook of his arm. The brim of his wheat-colored Stetson sat low on his forehead, shading his face, and, with the late morning sun behind him, he appeared like an avenging spirit dropped from the heavens.

She knew the proud stance, from the long denim-clad legs, well muscled from a lifetime of riding, to the shoulders wide enough to carry his dual heritage and all that came with being half Ute from his father's family and whatever ancestry his mother possessed aside from her proud claim of being a hardy Minnesotan.

His hair hung longer than the last time she'd seen him, but not nearly as long as when he'd first arrived on the neighboring ranch. At fourteen, Joe Hawk had worn angst and rebellion like a battle shield. The thick braid that had hung from under his oversize Stetson had dared anyone to question the heritage he claimed.

He'd been the hero of her daydreams. Over the years, on visits home from college, the sight of him working on the Sitting River Ranch at his grandfather's side without complaint, the friendship with her brothers, the gentle playfulness he showed her nieces opened a part of her heart that had held wishes of a future she couldn't reconcile. Hawk belonged heart and soul to Sitting River. His future wove itself daily into the very soil, water, wind and history that created his home.

Her future? Didn't.

Her future waited in Michigan at the Mayfield Museum. An opportunity to use the benefits of her geology and paleontology background. A future she'd planned for as loneliness and the sense of not belonging had grown.

She stepped forward and braced her stance wide and solid on the trail. "You fired those shots? You nearly scared the life out of me. Why didn't you say something? Call out. Anything."

"Meggie, I—"

"Didn't you see me?"

Hawk put a finger to his lips. "Shh. Listen."

A whimpering followed by a deep throaty growl came from among the pines to her right. She glanced up at Hawk. "Two animals?"

He nodded. "One predator, one prey."

The whimpering came again. Meg edged toward the trees. Hawk caught her arm. "Where are you going?"

"To help the one that's not the predator."

"That predator could be the mountain lion I've been tracking. Or a coyote wanting a meal. It's nature, Meggie. Best to leave it alone."

Meg pulled free. "I can't do that." She glanced at his rifle. "Come with me or give me your rifle."

He tucked the gun close to his body.

"I know how to safely use a rifle, Hawk." She

held up her hands still clutching the stones. "I am going over there. It's either with these rocks or the rifle. Your call."

Hawk shook his head and blew out a heavy sigh. He waved her behind him and raised the rifle. They crept several yards into the clump of pines. Hawk stopped and lifted his hand.

Meg peered around him. A coyote stood on the trunk of a fallen pine, front legs braced wide, head down and the skin around its long narrow snout drawn back in a snarl.

The whimpering came again, softer and broken. Meg tightened her grip on the stones and followed the line of the coyote's snout until she spotted the other animal.

It lay in the dirt on its side. A similar size and light and dark brown coloring but its face lacked the sharpness of a coyote.

"It's a dog," she whispered.

Another whimper rose from the dog. The coyote's snarl shifted to a confident growl. Meg stepped from behind Hawk, drew back her arm and flung one of the stones.

The rock caught the coyote on its shoulder. The animal yelped, leaped from the tree trunk and fled. Meg bent and picked up another rock. Better safe than sorry played a big part of living in the Rocky Mountain high country. She hoped the coyote wouldn't return, but wild animals, especially hungry wild animals, were unpredictable.

She edged her way toward the dog. "It's okay, fella," she murmured. "Just stay calm. Okay. How about we both just stay nice and calm."

"Meggie, wait."

She stepped closer to the dog. Blood oozed from its right haunch. "That's a nasty wound you have there." Her next step prompted a growl from the injured animal. "I'm not going to hurt you. I just want to help." The dog stilled. Labored breathing replaced the whimpers.

"That's a good boy. You are a boy, aren't you?" Meg took a quick look and nodded. "And such a handsome fellow, too. I bet someone's missing you." She slid forward one more step. The dog stiffened. His nose twitched and the soft whimpers she'd heard from him earlier became a rolling guttural mew. He tipped his nose into the air and flared his nostrils. He sensed something, smelled something.

Meg whirled. She expected to see the coyote back for another attempt at an easy meal. Instead, Hawk stood a few feet away, rifle at the ready.

She swung her gaze from the gun to the bleeding wound on the dog's haunch and back to Hawk. The dog emitted another low groan. She stepped in front of the injured animal and with a growl of her own, flung a stone.

Hawk ducked. "What the—"

"You shot that poor dog." She threw the other stone.

This time Hawk's reflexes weren't quick enough.

The rock grazed the left side of his face, scraping a raw, thin line across his cheek.

Meg bent and grabbed two more stones.

Hawk let the rifle hang from its shoulder strap and reached her before she could hurl another. "Enough." He caught her wrists. "Enough." He eased the stones from her hands and tossed them aside.

Meg planted her palms on his chest and shoved.

He staggered back a pace and balanced. "I didn't shoot anything."

Hands on hips and head cocked to one side, Meg stared at him. "You're the one with the rifle."

"I heard the shots. But I didn't shoot my rifle."

"Then who?"

Hawk stared down at her. "I don't know but I intend to find out." He nodded at the dog. "Are you sure it's been shot?"

"His haunch is bleeding badly."

"Could be the coyote already had a go at him." Hawk moved closer and surveyed the animal from head to tail. "I want to check his hindquarter. Will you hold his head?"

Meg sat in the dirt between Hawk and the dog's head. "It's okay, fella. He's a rancher. That means he has at least a modicum of veterinary knowledge. You're going to be just fine. I promise." She stretched out a hand and stroked the soft fur between his ears and the dog settled. "Okay. Do your thing. But if he snaps at me, you get to play vet on your own."

"He's lucky it was a coyote after him. Even given his size, I'd say forty pounds, maybe more, he's lucky. When Larry and I checked the East-ridge watering trough this morning, I spotted cat tracks around the trough and found one of my calves with a gnawed leg."

"Mountain lion, not coyote?"

"Trust me. I know the difference." He squatted next to the dog and pushed aside the fur. "A bullet didn't do this. It's a nasty gash and it needs stitched."

"A gash?"

"I also know the difference between a bullet wound and slashed hide." Hawk pulled a bandanna from his back pocket.

"But we heard shots."

"You didn't see anyone? Hear anyone?"

"No. Nothing. Only the two shots."

He searched his front pockets and came up empty. "I want to stop the bleeding. Do you have a bandanna or a handkerchief?"

She pulled a large white handkerchief from each front pocket of her khaki pants and a red bandanna from each of the back pockets. "Here."

"Four?" He took the cloths. "You carry four hankies?"

"They come in handy for marking areas of interest during a fossil search and for wiping a sweaty face and—"

"I get it. They're required paleontology equipment." He knotted her four together and folded his into a thick wad and wrapped the cloths around the dog.

She shifted closer to the dog's head and continued to stroke the fur behind his ears. "It's going to be okay, fella. I promise I'll stay with you until everything is okay. Hawk? He is going to be okay, isn't he?"

"Even if I can stop the bleeding, this gash still needs a vet's attention. Do you have a pickup, or did you ride out?"

"I rode out on Calypso. She's tethered at the foot of the trailhead. It's easier to spot fossils on foot. Don't you have your pickup?"

Hawk shook his head. "I sent Larry on to Big House with the calf while I followed the cat tracks."

"You've been following those tracks on foot? Up here?" Meg shivered. Rocky Mountain resident cats weren't sweet fluffy kittens. They were mountain lions. Predators. She'd seen their leftovers. It wasn't a pretty sight.

"I'll get Calypso. You can ride two-up in the saddle with the dog. Larry and I set the ridge trailhead as a rendezvous spot. He should be there soon and then I'll take the dog to Dr. Wallace."

"*We'll* take him to Dr. Wallace."

"You sure you want to come along?"

"I'm sure."

Hawk stood, pulled the rifle and strap over his

head and handed the rifle to her. "Here. Keep this close."

Meg took the rifle, checked that the safety was on and placed it on the ground beside her. "Hurry."

Hawk tugged the brim of his hat. "Yes, ma'am. I'll be right back."

True to his word, he promptly returned leading her pinto. Calypso lowered her head and nuzzled Meg's shoulder. "Sorry about the climb girl, but it's for a good cause." She rose, handed the rifle to Hawk and brushed dirt and dust from her pants. "Okay, let's do this." She climbed into the saddle and scooted back against the cantle. "Ready."

Hawk lifted the dog and gently draped him over the saddle. "He's heavier than I thought. Make that fifty pounds."

Meg crooned and stroked the thick fur. She felt around the dog's neck. "No tag but he belongs to someone. Blood-matted fur aside, he's been groomed."

"Dr. Wallace can scan for an ID chip."

The dog lifted his head. Meg draped her arms over the animal's body. "Just relax. You'll like Dr. Wallace. He always has a pocket full of doggy treats." She looked down at Hawk. "I think you should lead Calypso so I can keep both hands on him."

Hawk led the pinto along the trail while Meg hummed. Occasionally the dog whimpered and lifted his head. She calmed him with gentle pats and assurances of reaching the end soon.

"Are you sure Larry will be at the trailhead?"

"Better be. The walk to Big House from here would be the end of boots I can't afford to replace." The dog kicked against the saddle. "Keep humming. He seems to like that."

"Mom used to hum to me when I sat propped up in bed with asthma issues. She'd sit in the rocking chair beside my bed and hum and rock while the floorboards creaked with every back-and-forth motion. I found the sounds comforting. I knew in those soothing moments I'd breathe easily again."

"Healing songs. Lame Eagle sang healing songs."

"Your grandfather had many gifts."

"Yes, he did." Hawk tugged the brim of his hat low on his forehead. "Hard to believe he's been gone almost a year."

"I miss him, too."

Silence, heavy with memories, hung over them. Meg shifted as far back in the saddle as she could to give the dog more room. She'd ridden two-up before but never with a dog. The last time she'd shared a saddle had been with the man walking beside her.

"Hawk, do you remember the day you and Lame Eagle found me near the junction of Fendels Creek and the Meyer Ridge runoff? I was walking a lame horse."

Hawk glanced up at her with brows puckered. "Fendels Creek and Meyer Ridge runoff? I remember you pulling an old nag alongside the creek."

Meg smiled at his reference to Molasses. The name had suited the oldest, slowest, laziest animal on Bent Fork Ranch at the time and usually Meg's ride when she had a chance to be on horseback. Astride that horse there could be no threat of an overexerting ride that might trigger an asthma attack. That day the ride had been just the two of them, Meg Farrell and Molasses in the great outdoors.

Meg closed her eyes and lifted her face. "Freedom."

"What?"

"I'd felt so independent that day. It was the first time I'd ridden on my own since smoke from a wildfire kept me indoors for days."

"Lucky for you Lame Eagle and I came along. I remember you rode up with me and Lame Eagle pulled the mare."

Fleeting memories of that ride flashed in her mind. His arms around her as he held the reins. She'd sat in front of him with tumultuous butterflies crowding her stomach. Her teenage crush had flared to life that day. She chuckled. "I guess I was a bit of a nuisance."

"You didn't cause me any trouble. At least not then."

Meg latched on to the "not then" and looked down at him. "But I do now?"

"Do what?"

"Cause you trouble."

"What do you think? You accused me of shooting at you. Then, you accused me of shooting a dog. You threw rocks at me and gashed my cheek. And now I'm walking you, the dog and your horse down a fairly steep switchback trail with the hope of finding my foreman and my pickup at the end of the trail so I can take the dog to the vet before he bleeds to death. I should be out stabilizing old fence posts before my cows figure out a few gentle huffs will blow the fence over and they can look for better grazing elsewhere."

"Wow. A mountain lion pestering your cattle, cows plotting their escape, fences and boots in need of repair. I think the dog and I are the least of your problems."

Hawk chuckled. "Well, problem or not, you are better company and nicer to look at than my cattle."

Calypso picked up her pace. Hawk tugged the reins and held out a hand to steady the dog.

"Easy, girl," Meg crooned. "She senses something. Maybe the coyote or the cat?"

"Look." Hawk pointed down the trail.

Meg looked past his extended arm. No coyote or mountain lion in sight. Only beauty. The icy cold snowmelt of Fendels Creek meandered across the wide valley floor dotted with wildflowers and meadow grasses. Beyond the valley, Meyer Ridge and Silver Slip Peak poked their snow-covered tops into a clear blue Colorado sky. Meg sighed. "Beautiful. I hope I never get tired of looking at these mountains."

"Not the scenery. Larry."

A few yards from the base of the trail, under the shade of the tall cottonwood trees, sat a charcoal-gray pickup bearing the Sitting River Ranch logo, a white block-lettered SR sitting above a wavy blue line. Larry perched on the lowered tailgate eating a massive sandwich with his right hand while a navy sling cradled his left arm.

Hawk hailed his foreman.

Larry placed his half-eaten sandwich on a piece of foil, wiped his mouth on his sleeve and hopped off the tailgate. "Whatcha got there?"

Meg nudged Hawk with her booted foot. "Will you take the dog so I can climb down?"

Hawk slid an arm under the dog's haunch and shoulder and eased him off the saddle. "A hurt dog. We think he had a run-in with a coyote."

"There's no thinking about it," Meg said. "I saw the coyote."

"Mornin', Meggie." Larry slowly stretched out his free hand and scratched between the dog's ears. "Hey there, fella. Whatcha thinkin' takin' on a coyote? You're a people dog. You shouldn't be messing with coyotes. He's a nice mix. Some retriever, maybe some shepherd or a little collie. Mostly a strong mix." He looked at Hawk. "Hurt bad?"

"There are some nasty gashes along his back and left side and the right hindquarter needs stitched." Hawk settled the dog in the back of the pickup.

"We're taking him to Dr. Wallace." Meg climbed

in and pushed aside a shovel, a post digger and large metal toolbox to reach one of the horse blankets piled under the cab window. She draped it over the dog.

"You both going?" Larry asked.

"I promised I would stay with him." Meg tucked the blanket a little tighter around the dog. "Can you get Calypso to Bent Fork for me? Or, if you'd rather take her to Sitting River, I'm sure someone will come for her."

"I'll ride her to your folks' place. Emma's already there helping set up for tonight's Willow River Festival committee meeting and that way my wife and I can drive back together after the meeting." He tugged the stubble covering his chin. "She says there's lots to do." He closed the tailgate and followed Hawk around the pickup. "I heard the committee has plans for you. And Meggie, now that she's home."

"Me?" Meg shook her head. "I don't think so. I have four whole weeks before I have to be back in Michigan to set up for the museum's grand opening and I intend to spend the bulk of this visit fossil hunting."

Hawk climbed into the driver's seat and started the truck. "All set back there?"

Meg raised the blanket and looked at the dog's haunch. Blood seeped through the makeshift bandage. "Yes. And hurry."

# *CHAPTER TWO*

"WHAT'S TAKING SO LONG?" Meg poured another cup of coffee.

Hawk grimaced at the pot of dark liquid. "How can you drink that stuff? It looks thicker than molasses."

"It's only my second cup."

"It shouldn't be much longer." He patted the seat next to him. "Try and relax."

"I can't." Meg continued her back-and-forth trek across the tiled floor of the small waiting room. "Dr. Wallace said he'd be right out and that was an hour ago."

"Pacing isn't going to hurry him along. And coffee isn't going to calm your worries."

Meg lowered herself onto the padded bench. "The bleeding hadn't stopped."

"No, but it had slowed." He touched a finger to his cheek and inspected the end. A faint hint of blood spotted the tip. "I can't believe you threw rocks at me."

"It's just a scratch." She rose, pulled several tissues from the box on the check-in desk and dampened them at the water fountain. "You were pointing a gun at the dog, and I thought, even if briefly and incorrectly, that you'd shot the dog thinking it was a coyote." She crooked her index finger and thumb around his chin and turned his head to the side. "This shouldn't hurt one bit," she said, dabbing at the scratch.

"Who knew your fascination with rocks would jump from hobby to geology to paleontology to warfare?"

"I'm sorry, Hawk. I didn't aim at you. I just threw." She lowered her gaze to the exposed brown skin of his throat before beginning a slow, steady climb past the sharp plane of his jaw. His lips were cast from different molds. His upper lip, slightly narrower than his full lower lip, stretched just beyond the outline of its mate. The left side had a tendency to tip up when he was amused. "Shouldn't even leave a scar on that handsome face of yours."

"Handsome, huh?"

*Very.* She'd always thought him good-looking and now age had sculpted his young attractive features into rugged and handsome. *Very handsome.* A familiar sizzle peppered her insides. Time to focus on something other than his looks and her old teenage crush. Lingering on those thoughts served no purpose. She couldn't risk old feelings resurfacing and morphing into something complicated when she knew she wasn't staying.

She gave his cheek another pat. "What happened to Larry's arm?"

"He cut it on a rusty nail while pulling down some ancient fencing that's needed repairs for some time. The cut required a few stitches, and Larry needed a tetanus booster." Hawk chuckled. "You should've heard him when he got the shot. Hollered like a two-year-old denied a lollipop."

"He's okay, isn't he? You don't typically sling an arm because of a few stitches and a tetanus booster."

"He's fine. The sling is to help with a shoulder issue. If the shoulder doesn't improve, he'll need surgery. Neither one of us is looking forward to that."

"I'm sorry."

"I'm sorry his wife is playing doctor. Emma made a poultice for his shoulder that smells like boiled bat droppings." He wrinkled his nose. "Larry's a great foreman and Emma is a wonderful housekeeper, but some of her medicinal concoctions have me questioning the decision to have them live in Big House with me."

"They're not in Little House anymore?" Meg pressed the tissue against his cheek. "Is there something wrong with Little House?"

Hawk flinched.

"Sorry."

"It's okay." He turned away from her tender

ministrations. "There's nothing wrong with Little House."

"I'm glad. It's lovely. Although I prefer Big House with its wide steps leading to the wraparound veranda, the rocking chairs, the big windows and the bright yellow door always open and welcoming. And the swing. I really love the swing. It begs for a person to sit and revel in the awesomeness of the area. A spot perfect for sitting, talking, singing, storytelling."

"And on occasion, sleeping."

Meg smiled. "You or Lame Eagle?"

"Lame Eagle when, according to him, he didn't see my grandmother's point of view. And me when I failed to understand my grandfather's *no* was meant to teach and always said with love."

She crumpled the tissues and tossed them into the waste bin. "You really should have Dr. Wallace look at that while we're here."

"I will. Once he's finished with the dog."

Meg refilled her mug. "The poor little guy. He looked so weak. I promised him he'd be okay. What if he's not?"

"That's the thing about promises."

"What's that?"

"You shouldn't make them if you can't keep them."

Meg resumed her pacing. Hawk's words stayed with her, rolling across her mind with each turn across the floor. He was right about promises. She had no way of making sure the dog would be okay.

Her words were only meant to soothe and reassure the injured animal…and maybe herself.

She drank the last of her coffee and reached for another refill. Pot in one hand, mug in the other, she frowned at the dark liquid. "I like my coffee black, but another cup of this might require cream *and* sugar *and* maybe chocolate."

"I can make some fresh, Meggie."

Meg spun and nearly dropped the pot. Dr. Wallace stood wiping his hands on a thick towel.

"That's been cooking all day."

"Is he okay? Please tell me he's okay."

Dr. Wallace slung the towel over his shoulder and took the coffee pot from her. "He's going to be fine."

She blew out a long sigh. "Thank goodness."

"There are no internal injuries. I stitched the gash on his haunch and another cut on his leg. I also scanned for an ID chip. Nothing."

"Has anyone reported a lost dog?" Hawk asked.

"No."

"With no ID, what happens now?"

"Well, I want to keep him overnight. I don't know how long he's been on his own, but he's badly dehydrated. I've started him on fluids, and I want to see how he moves in the morning. You should be able to pick him up tomorrow after eleven. Call before you come for him just in case something changes."

"Pick him up." Hawk held up his hands. "Sorry, Doc. He's not our dog."

"I don't have the space or the staff to care for strays. You can take him to the local shelter. It's small and they may not have room, either. If that's the case, there's a good shelter over in Gunnison."

"He's not a stray," Meg said. "He's well-groomed and friendly. He belongs to someone."

Dr. Wallace nodded. "I agree he's been someone's pet. However, that someone may have decided they didn't want a pet anymore and dropped him on the side of the road to fend for himself."

"That's cruel."

"Yes, and unfortunately, it happens far too often." He turned to Hawk. "Now, I'd like to take a look at that cut."

Hawk rubbed his jaw. "It's fine. Just a scratch."

"Scratch or not, it needs cleaning."

Dusk sat on the mountaintops by the time Hawk pulled his pickup to a stop in front of the Bent Fork homestead. Meg slid out of the passenger seat, closed the door and leaned her forearms on the open window. "Thanks for the ride and the help with the dog. I know you had more important things to do today."

"Helping my recently returned home neighbor is almost as important as tending to my cattle."

"And tracking mountain lions?"

"Only the one attacking my livestock."

Meg frowned. "How can you be sure it was the right one?"

"Good question." Hawk held out his right hand, palm up. "There's a slight mounded impression on the right front pad. Probably scar tissue from an old wound."

She nodded. "Hmm."

"Now, a question for you. What were you doing up on the ridge besides rescuing a stray dog and throwing rocks at me?"

Meg looked over her shoulder. A blend of male and female chatter drifted through the open living room windows. Early arrivals for the Willow River Festival planning meeting. "I could say I was looking for fossils."

"Were you?"

"I'm a paleontologist. I'm always on the lookout for fossils."

"Find anything?"

She glanced again at the house. "Yes." She leaned in. "Peace and quiet."

Hawk chuckled. "You were hiding."

"Guilty. Mom and Ruby started event conversation early this morning. They pulled out clipboards and charts and talked about needing volunteers to do a million things, including something with crepe paper rosettes."

"That's why you insisted on going to the vet's office."

She shook her head. "I went with you to Dr. Wallace's office because I promised the dog I would."

"Do you always keep your promises?"

"I try." She sighed. "I promised the dog everything would be okay. I'll call Dr. Wallace tomorrow. Maybe the dog's owner will have claimed him. If not, you could take that beautiful boy home as a companion for Maiku." She smiled, wide and hopeful.

"Sorry, Meggie. I can't have a nonworking dog on my ranch."

"You have Maiku."

"Who belonged to my grandfather and since his passing Maiku has taken to following me just like he dogged Lame Eagle."

Meg pursed her lips. "Poor pup. I'll ask around and see if someone wants the handsome fellow."

"That's a start. Have you promised to help with the festival?"

"Not yet." She offered him a wide smile. "You want to come in? Wc can volunteer to do something with rosettes."

"Couldn't even if I wanted to. I still have fence posts that need shoring up until I can get the wire fencing and I need to gather repair supplies to take up to the Meyer Ridge storm shelter tomorrow."

"Snow damage?"

"Yep. Winter pack was heavy. Good for water supplies, not good for my storm shelter's roof."

"Be careful and stay away from mountains lions."

"I can't promise that, Meggie. This one's harming my cattle and my cattle are what's keeping Sitting River afloat right now. Besides, tomorrow I'll be out on Wickiup. He has a great nose. He'll sense something long before I see it."

Meg took another look over her shoulder. "I should go. Are you coming back later?"

"And get roped into doing something with paper rosettes? I'd rather face an angry mountain lion."

"Or be subjected to one of Emma's home remedies."

He made a face.

Meg chuckled. "Coward." She stepped away from the truck and started up the steps. At the top step, she paused. "Just so you know, Ruby made rhubarb pie for tonight." Everyone knew the Farrells' live-in housekeeper made the best rhubarb pie in the county.

He'd be there. She hoped.

# *CHAPTER THREE*

HAWK STOOD WITH one booted foot on the first step leading to the Farrells' front porch. Voices drifted through open windows and the screened door. The festival committees were still going strong. He dreaded facing them. He wasn't sure he'd hold up under a fevered plea for help.

He shouldn't have come.

Sitting River demanded every waking minute of his time right now and then some. With Larry less than 100 percent and the Lander boys, his part-time helpers, off for a rodeo competition, the number of less urgent chores being pushed aside were mounting and becoming more urgent.

The thought of hiring extra hands had crossed his mind more than once during the last twelve months. He could barely afford to pay the part-time help he had, let alone adding more. And the Reeds. Larry and Emma had told him over and over that their pay need not be a priority. He'd paid them anyway. They'd earned every cent and more. He just didn't have more to offer.

The vet visit had taken time. He and Meggie had

left the office with the doctor reminding them that the dog couldn't stay beyond needed care. Someone would have to pick up the animal if the owner didn't appear.

It wouldn't be him. Meggie had tried to convince him Sitting River would be the perfect place for the dog. He loved dogs. Emma loved dogs. Larry loved dogs. They were a perfect match. She'd asked him to think about taking the dog, and as much as he would like to, he couldn't. A non-trained working dog on his ranch would be a mini disaster he didn't need.

He needed to talk to Meggie about the animal. To talk to Meggie meant he had to go inside. Going inside meant he would encounter the committees. As much as he dreaded telling them no, he dreaded telling Meggie he couldn't take the dog even more.

He shouldn't have come.

He stepped down and turned to leave.

"Hey, Hawk. Where're you going?"

Hawk turned back. Andrew Farrell, third born of the four Farrell boys and only six days older than himself, an inch taller, carrying a few extra pounds of muscle and blessed with a generous spirit, stepped onto the porch, letting the screened door slap into place behind him. He crossed to the side rail and dumped the contents of a tall glass. "Yuck."

"Ruby's punch?"

Andrew met Hawk at the foot of the steps and

sat. "The woman makes a fantastic rhubarb pie, and her pot roast is amazing, but her punch is downright nasty."

Hawk joined Andrew on the step. "Are the committee members still rounding up volunteers?"

"Let's just say you won't be allowed to leave Bent Fork until you've volunteered for something. Diana Maine, the new committee chair, expects the whole town to volunteer in one way or another."

"I hear there's plenty to do."

"Speaking of plenty to do, Meggie mentioned you had problems with the Meyer Ridge storm shelter."

"And Split Rock shelter."

"How bad is Split Rock?"

"Lightning snapped a pine that damaged the chimney shell. I need more stone, lumber, time and a foreman with two good arms."

"Yeah. She also mentioned Larry's accident." Andrew pointed to the scratch on Hawk's cheek. "Looks like you had one, too."

Hawk traced the scratch and grinned. "That was no accident. Your sister threw rocks at me because she thought I'd shot a dog."

"I would too if I thought you'd shot a helpless puppy."

Hawk looked across the rough-cut grass already browning due to lack of rain. "You weren't near Meyer Ridge today, were you?"

"No. John and I were moving hay bales to the fairgrounds. Why?"

"I heard shots near the ridge." Hawk leaned forward and braced his forearms on his knees. "And someone, maybe that same someone has been in my storm shelter."

"Any idea who?"

"No. When I came across Meggie, I thought it might have been her, but she only had a handful of rocks."

"Ah, Meggie and her rocks. You're not the only guy she's thrown rocks at besides her four brothers. I remember when she hurled rocks at the Miller boy."

"Caleb?"

"Uh-huh. He tried to kiss her. Meggie took care of him. At least I didn't have to get all big brother and chase him off."

Hawk eased back and rested his elbows on the step behind him. "Heaven help any male who shows interest in Meggie Farrell."

He himself had more than once fought the temptation to kiss her. The urge quickly faltered when he allowed the thought that his action might change the relationship he valued between himself and Meggie and potentially with her brother Andrew, his best friend.

Occasionally, on her visits back to Bent Fork, he'd gotten the impression she wouldn't throw stones at him if he'd attempted to kiss her. He'd held back on pursuing such fancies knowing Meggie Farrell wanted to create a life for herself away from Colorado. Away from Colorado meant away from him, his ranch, his life.

"Yeah, between the eagle-eyed protection of four older brothers, plus the hovering of Mom and Ruby, the kid has been pretty sheltered. Still, hovering over Meggie with her asthma usually kept Mom too busy to notice what we boys were into." Andrew mimicked Hawk's position. "I feel sorry for her. Just a little."

"I'd say you and your brothers owe your sister big-time."

"I'll thank her someday. Right now, I want to thank you again for letting me lease those Sitting River acres. Dad doesn't think much of my hybrid grain idea. In his mind, using Bent Fork acreage for an 'agricultural experiment' is a waste of valuable grazing land. I still think it's a valid concept and I think I can make it pay off."

"I'm counting on it." Andrew was right about Lansford Farrell. The man knew cattle and horses, but he didn't have the patience to work with Mother Earth and her offerings.

Hawk had trust in his land. The decision to lease even a few acres of Sitting River to his best friend and neighbor hadn't been an easy one but the very thought of selling Sitting River acreage made his gut clinch. He had finally stopped looking at Andrew's plan as subtle charity and stepped in to share the work. Taking help didn't sit easily on his shoulders, but he'd carry the discomfort if it put him closer to freeing his ranch from the debt it held.

"I'll need to put a pole barn up there," Andrew continued. "I talked with Aaron Collins today about renting a small excavator and something to haul it up to the site we agreed on."

Hawk cast his friend a sideways glance. "A barn? An excavator?"

"I'll need a place for storing equipment and—"

"A permanent structure?"

"I'll be solely responsible for it."

Hawk leaned forward and anchored his hands on his knees. "Let me think about it for a day or two."

"Okay, but I want to start this project as soon as I can."

Laughter erupted from inside the house. Hawk stood. "Sounds like someone's having fun. Let's get in there before Ruby's pie is gone. We can talk business later. I want to see if anyone has seen or heard evidence of a stranger wandering around."

"We've seen tire tracks in areas where we usually go on horseback. Mostly close to the boundary line between Sitting River and Bent Fork. I'll keep my eyes open." Andrew rose. "What happened with the dog?"

"We took him to Dr. Wallace. He's resting comfortably with a few stitches and fluids."

"Then what?"

"Don't know. He's domesticated but had no tags or ID chip. Meggie's going to talk with Dr. Wallace tomorrow about finding the dog a home."

Andrew picked up his empty glass. "Before we get pie, let's find something worth drinking. And maybe while you're trying *not* to get roped into volunteering, you can find someone who wants your dog."

Hawk followed his friend up the steps. "He's not my dog."

MEG TUGGED THE belt of her terry robe tighter and leaned against the windowsill. Twilight replaced the clear light of day, and stars, faint in the space between the setting of the sun and the brightening of the moon, became more visible. She loved the night sky. So much yet to be discovered. Just like the secrets hiding under the layers and layers of the earth.

A soft knock sounded on the door. "Meggie?"

"Come in, Mom."

Joanna Farrell stepped into the room. Her gaze went directly to her daughter. "You're not dressed."

"I just need a few more minutes."

"Diana wants everyone gathered to go over setup plans." She stepped to the bed and tugged the edge of the handsewn quilt and smoothed invisible wrinkles.

"Mom, why do I need to be there? I'll most likely be in Michigan setting up exhibits at the museum during the festival."

"Yes. Your new job."

Her mother joined her at the window, straightened the narrow cushion on the window seat and sat. With the back of her hand, Joanna pushed open the curtain. "I haven't seen so many cars on this property since your grandmother passed away."

Meg looked out the window. Cars and trucks lined the long gravel driveway and spread onto the rough grass in front of the equipment garage. "Seems like there are plenty of volunteers."

"Yes. Diana has gathered quite a group. She's making all sorts of promises for a spectacular festival."

Meg smiled. Joanna Farrell was a rancher's wife, a rancher's partner who worked hard, in the home and out. She was as comfortable mucking a barn stall in rubber boots and denims as she was sipping tea dressed in pearls and silk. Gray had invaded the dark hair she kept short and "manageable," and the faint lines around her blue eyes and small mouth added more life to her face than age. A woman who bore the joys and sorrows of life without complaint.

Her mother's fingers worried the nickel-sized nugget of turquoise suspended from the silver chain hanging around her neck. A chunk of opaque, blue-green mineral Joanna Farrell called her worry stone. Tonight worry weighed on Bent Fork's matriarch.

"Mom, has something happened to Keith?"

Her mother put her hand to her heart. "Oh,

no, no, no. Thank goodness. No. Your brother is fine. Heidi heard from him early this morning. He's fine. In fact, he told her his discharge may be moved up to September." She let the curtain drop. "They want to start looking for a place of their own."

"Is that a problem?" Meg adored her sister-in-law and admired Heidi's show of confidence for Keith's safe return, especially in the presence of her daughter.

"I'm thrilled and thankful my son may be coming home sooner than expected. I feel like he's been deployed forever, and it must feel worse for Heidi and little Ava. I told Heidi they could stay on at Bent Fork indefinitely. There's plenty of room and we love having everyone here. But you know young people. They don't want to hang around their parents once they reach a certain age. They want to see the world, have adventures, join the military, take jobs that move them across the country."

Meg covered her mother's hand with her own. "They won't go far, Mom."

"Unlike my only daughter, who's choosing to stay in Michigan."

"It's where my job is located."

"Grand Rapids is a big city. You don't like big cities."

"Grand Rapids isn't nearly the size of Chicago or New York. Neither of which I want to visit again anytime soon. Sensory overload shatters my ability to focus after a day or two in larger cities. I'll be fine in Grand Rapids."

Her mother patted Meg's cheek and rose. "I know you will." She started toward the door, stopped and picked up the yellow shirt Meg had worn earlier.

"Sorry." Meg reached for the shirt. "I meant to put it in the hamper."

"What's this?" Her mother held the shirt at arm's length.

Meg saw the smear of blood. "It's not mine." She raised her hands. "Honest. I found a dog up on Meyer Ridge this morning. He'd been in a scrape with a coyote, so we took him to Dr. Wallace. It must be his blood."

"We?"

"Hawk and I." She took the stained shirt from her mother and stuffed it into the hamper.

"I wish you'd be more careful when you're roaming around looking for rocks and bones."

"I am careful." Meg caught the corner of her bottom lip between her teeth. Inhale. "Please don't fuss." Exhale.

"I'm your mother. A mother worries about her children regardless of their ages." She glanced at the terry robe. "I'll tell everyone you'll be right down." She stopped at the door. "You will be right down, won't you?"

"Of course. I just need…" She needed to climb

out the window and head up into the mountains before the festival team guilted her into volunteering the time she wanted to use for fossil hunting. She would have little opportunity for fieldwork once the museum opened, and she would miss the joy of searching, hoping with every step and overturned stone to find something extraordinary. Inhale. Exhale. "I just need a few minutes."

"Five minutes." Her mother paused at the door, her hand on the glass knob. "And, Meggie, no khakis with their profusion of pockets. Please."

"Yes, ma'am." Meg closed the door behind her mother and looked longingly at the cargo pants she wore like a uniform hanging in the closet before pushing them aside and selecting a dress. Colors, from the softest seashell pink to coral and deep rose, shimmered as the fabric moved. She had logged extra hours at the library cataloging maps and shelving mountains of books just to afford the dress. And it was worth every penny.

Tossing aside her robe, she slid the dress over her head. The hem skirted the top of her knees and swirled gracefully around her legs when she moved. She added her grandmother's pearl earrings before slipping her feet into delicate coral-colored sandals. She wanted to look her best and told herself it had nothing to do with Hawk.

The reflection in the mirror revealed someone she barely recognized. Someone feminine and confident instead of her usual dusty, sweaty, grimy self. It also showed wayward wisps of hair that refused to be bound by the elastic band. She tucked the strands behind her ears and twirled.

Maybe it did have a little to do with Hawk.

"Meggie."

Someone beat a jaunty knock on the heavy oak door. She pulled the door open. The youngest of her four brothers stood in the hallway wearing dark jeans and a crisp white shirt with a plaid clip-on bow tie dangling from one collar point. He pushed his russet-colored hair off his forehead and whistled. "Wow."

"Thanks. You look pretty wow yourself. John Farrell wearing a tie."

"I'm not wearing it yet. I can't get it straight."

"No surprise. You've never been able to draw a straight line. Even with a ruler."

"But I'm really good with other tools," he said with a grin.

Meg plucked the tie from the collar point and clipped it properly in place. "There. So, who's the lucky girl?"

"Beth Lawrence and—"

"Mary Margaret!" Her father bellowed from the foot of the staircase. "Shake a leg, girl."

Meg rolled her eyes. "Everyone is in such a rush."

"According to Ruby, Mrs. Maine keeps the committee meetings on a strict schedule, and you don't want to cause a deviation from her timetable. She's a lot like the drill sergeant Keith complained about."

"She can't be that bad."

"Wanna bet?"

"Against you. No thanks." She adjusted the bow tie. "Perfect. Tell Dad I'll be right down."

She closed the door, leaned against the dense wood and breathed easily in and out. Not something she could always do in this room. She scanned her childhood domain. The curtains of pink and purple stars that had framed the dormer windows for as long as she could remember had recently been replaced with simple drapes the color of pale white sage that matched the quilt her mother had smoothed earlier and complemented the dark sage-, ivory- and pale gray-striped pillow shams on the bed and cushions on the window seat.

A plush dark gray rug covered a large portion of the wooden floorboards. Two stuffed armchairs in the same stripe as the pillows and cushions sat on either side of a small three-tiered table holding magazines, books, heavy glass coasters and a reading lamp. Framed photos of scenic areas around the family ranch had replaced her posters of dinosaurs. Simple changes had altered the look of the room. The changes hadn't altered her childhood memories of the space.

Those memories assaulted her, swirled around her and started to squeeze the breath from her. As a child, her asthma had been serious, even life-threatening at times. During those early years, the family followed medical directions and did what they believed best for her. They protected her from household dust to the slightest swirl of breeze-whipped topsoil. Cat and dog fur to horse-hair. Days too hot and nights too cool. Even her activities had been limited.

Over the years, she'd learned to manage her issues with asthma. Most of the time. Still, in this room a mood of frailty weighed on her.

Meg took a deep breath through her nose and exhaled. Inhale. Exhale. A practice she used to calm anxiety and help during asthmatic stress. She took another deep breath and pushed away from the paneled door. Time to join the crowd.

The old glass knob felt cool and soothing under her fingers and less of a barrier than she remembered. She glanced back into the room and smiled. Some things had changed. Something needed to change. It wasn't her room anymore and it certainly didn't define her as a frail asthmatic child anymore. She drew another breath, deep and easy, and stepped into the hall.

The mingling of dozens of voices filled the lower level. She hoped the crowd included one particular person. Even if he came smelling of boiled bat droppings.

# CHAPTER FOUR

"THERE YOU ARE."

Despite time and hard work, her father stood straight and sure at the foot of the stairs. Touches of gray streaked the hair at his temples and threaded through the rest of his thick dark brown hair. He had replaced his work denims and cotton shirt for khaki pants and a pale blue polo shirt. Years of outdoor work and age had left their mark on his face, adding wrinkles to his tanned skin. To a daughter's eyes, Lansford Farrell's wrinkles were laugh lines.

"You didn't need to wait for me."

"I didn't need to." He dropped a kiss on the top of her head. "I did need to get away from the chaos in there."

"Chaos?"

"This year's committee head has a very different vision of what Tyler's Willow River Festival should look like." His forehead creased into a perplexed frown. "I don't know what Diana Maine is thinking. She's talking about elaborately decorated floats and giant balloon structures."

"I heard she had the role of event chair for this year."

"Took charge of everything. Doesn't matter what it is. She wants to be in charge of it. She's arrogant, bossy, domineering, overbearing, dictatorial, controlling and stubborn."

"What did you do, search the internet for synonyms under Mrs. Maine?"

"As soon as I heard she got the go-ahead."

Meg chuckled and slid her arm through her father's. "We could sneak out the back."

"Or you could join the rest of us in the living room." Joanna Farrell stood in the doorway, arms crossed and lips pursed. "There's work to be done and we need everyone's help if we're going to make this year's festival a success."

"In spite of Diana's over-the-top ideas?" Lansford asked.

"Or because of them. Give her a chance. She's using her experience of working on such events in New York to make ours even better."

Lansford reached for his wife's hand. "Just because she has lived and worked in the big city doesn't mean she knows how to produce something for *our* community. The Willow River Festival is more than just fireworks and pretty decorations. Tyler wouldn't exist if it weren't for the Willow River. The town would have burnt to the ground the day of its inauguration had that river not flowed nearby." He closed his fingers over hers. "I wish she'd listen to you. You've done such a great job over the last few years as committee chair."

The look on her mother's face softened. "I've been trying to help her understand. She's just such a—"

"Bulldozer," suggested her husband.

"We could still sneak out the back," Meg offered.

Her father tipped his head toward the back of the house. "I'm game."

"Enough, you two."

"Now, Jo, we're just kidding."

"I'm not," Meg said.

"Meggie." Ruby Turner charged down the hallway. "Professor Nelson is here to see you and he says it's urgent, so I put him in the back office for some privacy."

Meg frowned. "Professor Nelson? What does he want?"

"Well—" Ruby balled her fists and stuck them on her wide hips "—it certainly isn't to help with the celebration. When Mrs. Maine pointed out that everyone in the community should be helping, he told her he had more important things to do with his valuable time. Then he marched right past her and told me he needed to speak with you, privately, and that it was extremely important."

Her mother held up her finger. "I've heard he's been pressing the community college for a course on fossils. You took his geology class at TCC, and now with your degree in paleontology, maybe he wants to discuss ideas with you."

"She won't find out standing here." Her father turned his wife in the direction of the living room. "Come on, let's see what Diana has planned for us. The sooner the meeting is over, the sooner we can have pie."

Ruby followed Meg down the hallway. "I think your professor has a mighty high opinion of himself." She jutted her chin toward the door. "He makes Diana Maine seem like the friendliest person in town. You be careful in there."

"Thanks, Ruby. I promise I'll stay on my toes." She gave the woman a solemn nod and opened the office door.

The man in front of her father's desk turned. Thin, graying hair lay slick across the top of his scalp. He inclined his head and large, thick glasses slipped down his sliver of a nose.

"Professor Nelson."

"Ah, Miss Farrell, Meggie. I knew you would remember me. My students always remember me." He extended his hand.

Meg slid her fingers across his outstretched palm, pulling away before he could engage in his habitual finger-jiggling greeting.

"It's good of you to grant me a few moments of your time. I won't keep you long. I'm sure you are eager to get out there and volunteer, being the kind and generous person that you are." He placed a hand to his chest. "I am personally too busy to be involved in such extravagant plans for a single ordinary day."

"A single day." Meg's eyebrows rose. "It's not just an ordinary day, Professor. It's the day we celebrate Tyler becoming an incorporated town in the state of Colorado. It's the day to remember that during that ceremony a fire erupted in the mill and the whole town formed a bucket brigade to move water from the Willow River to extinguish the fire. It's a day to remember bravery and loyalty and how the people of Tyler saved their town. It's not just another day."

"Ah, man's history. It is so insignificant compared to that of the dinosaurs." With a twitch of his upper lip and nose, he kept the dark-rimmed glasses perched in place and peered over the top. "I am glad you took my recommendation to pursue paleontology. I witnessed your passion for fossils the first time you held my prized allosaurus claw. I knew then you were destined to search for more prehistoric treasures." He sighed heavily. "I had the same desire once, but times being as they were, and finances that…well, that weren't, forced me to stay with geology." He leaned close and wagged a finger. "And now you've been employed by the new Mayfield Museum of Science and Nature."

"I didn't know you'd heard about my job there."

"Oh yes. I keep up with the happenings in the

field of paleontology. Even insignificant events like the position you've been given."

"A position I've earned," Meg amended.

"I had the pleasure of meeting Dr. Vanover at a conference several years ago. When I heard she had employed one of my former students, I contacted her to offer my congratulations."

Meg folded her arms. "Professor, will you get to the point. *My* time, like everyone else's, is also valuable."

"Of course. You must be so eager to join the throng of party planners." He cleared his throat. "Now, where was I?"

"Paleontology as a hobby of yours."

"Yes, yes. My teaching focus, as you well know, is geology at Tyler Community College. This minor occupation has allowed me to develop a critical area of pursuit. My hobby." He paused, bobbed his head and offered a thin-lipped smile. "I know it sounds mundane, a mere hobby, but hobbies can have their rewards."

"I'm sure they can."

"Yes, yes. I apologize again for keeping you from your opportunities to do important work for the community, but timing is critical you know."

"No, I don't know."

"As I said, I keep in touch with the world of paleontology. I have recently learned that an expedition in Canada—" he leaned toward her and whispered "—has unearthed eggs."

"Eggs?"

"Yes. Beautifully preserved, beautifully whole eggs." He cupped his hands as if he held something precious and droned on. "Can't you picture them? Secure in their ancient nests, hidden for millions of years until we, the explorers of history, cast away the layers of time to discover prehistoric life in its most primal state."

Meg *could* picture the sight. A nest of fossilized eggs. The moment of discovery. The process to determine what creature had deposited the eggs. She could imagine a giant beast standing over the nest, nurturing and guarding until… What happened? Why weren't they allowed to hatch? Could there be other nests, other fossils?

"That's why I came to see you." He gave her a knowing smile.

"Because a site in Canada found eggs?"

"Precisely."

Meg frowned. "Professor, what does any of this have to do with me?"

"Everything. You could not have arrived at a more opportune moment." He sniffed his glasses into place and smiled again. "You see, I've become quite the expert on fossilized eggs, if I must say so myself. Once I heard they had discovered nests of fossilized ovum, I offered my expertise. They accepted my offer with tremendous enthusiasm despite the fact that I unfortunately have no official qualifications in the field of paleontology."

"Congratulations."

He, placed a hand on his chest, bowed slightly. "I knew you would recognize my achievement and understand the importance."

"I'm sorry, Professor. I'm afraid I don't."

"Of course, your arrival and your generous spirit secure this marvelous opportunity for me. So, I am pleased to be equally generous and offer you a wonderful opportunity." He steepled his fingertips. "An opportunity that will allow you to develop new skills and experience new accomplishments."

"New skills and accomplishments?"

"I certainly wouldn't entrust my class to just anyone. You were my best student, and I am very pleased to leave my class in your capable hands."

"What? Your class. In *my* hands?"

The professor beamed. "Of course."

Meg shook her head. "Thank you for the offer, Professor, but I can't accept it. I'm going back to Michigan in a few weeks to set up exhibits and the paleo lab and—"

"Yes, yes, all important work. However, teaching has wonderful rewards and experiences. Intellectual, emotional and philanthropic."

"I get it. You can't volunteer at the dig site in Canada unless someone takes your class."

He pressed his palms together and gave a triumphant clap. "I knew you would see the importance of my presence at the dig."

"I'm sorry, Professor Nelson. I cannot agree to taking on your class."

"But, but," he stammered. "I need you to reconsider before you dismiss the request. Students have already signed up and paid their fees. They are so excited and looking forward to learning more about the geological formations of our planet."

Meg turned her face from the man and looked out the window. The Rocky Mountains, majestic in their creation, dominated the distance. Up and down the Front Range, one could see sharp, steep summits, broader worn peaks, layers upon layers of multiple kinds of rocks, minerals, volcanic ash, lava, ancient seabeds and the remains of both miniscule and massive creatures. The mountains held a great fascination for her and, according to the professor, for his upcoming class.

"I only have four weeks before I need to be at the museum. Your class, as I recall, runs for eight weeks."

He clasped his hands behind his back and nodded. "Yes, eight weeks. You could shorten it if necessary. The students are all residents of Tyler and I'm sure they would be very understanding of any changes you would need to make."

Meg knew a great many of the town's residents. Like most living in Colorado's high country, they were hardworking ranchers, farmers, and dedicated community members. "All I can promise right now is that I'll think about it. When does your class start?"

"In six days."

"Six days!"

"Everything you'll need is prepared and sitting in my office. Mrs. Burlew will give you access." He smiled. "You will thank me later for giving you this opportunity."

MEG FOUND HER father leaning against the doorframe of the overflowing living room. Every available spot on the two leather sofas held a body. The overstuffed chair next to the fireplace, usually claimed by her father, supported the substantial frame of his best friend, Ed Ball. Side chairs, pulled from corners, and additional seats from other parts of the house littered the highly polished oak floor. Even the window seats were occupied.

"How's it going?"

Her father groaned.

"That bad?"

"We're at a temporary standstill. There's no agreement on where to put the booths for crafts or a place for food prep or a location for tables and chairs for eating. The only unanimous decision has been where to stage the musical performances. That decision had nothing to do with an agreement and everything to do with the accessibility of electricity and a large enough area for the musicians and equipment." He tipped his head toward the wide stone fireplace. "It wasn't where she wanted it."

Meg glanced at the woman sitting in her mother's wingback chair. She looked out of place dressed in a dark pin-striped pantsuit and pointy-toed four-inch black heels. She sat stiff-backed with her narrow face and narrowed eyes directed at the crowd. Her head, covered with cropped salon-enhanced red hair, shook back and forth while one fingertip coated in red lacquer tapped rhythmically on the clipboard she gripped.

"I assume the woman sitting in Mom's chair clacking on the clipboard is Mrs. Maine."

"The one and only."

"She doesn't look happy."

"She moved in with her cousin a few months ago from New York and doesn't quite relate to a Colorado ranching community. She doesn't comprehend the space we'll need for animals and their needs. Nor does she understand how many pieces of heavy equipment will be driving around during the event. She's never attended a rodeo. Has no idea what barrel racing means, and *she* wants to ride with the mayor in the first float."

"Tyler High's valedictorian always rides with the mayor."

"Yep."

"Mom knows all that. Hasn't she explained it to Mrs. Maine?"

Lansford slid her a sideways glance. “What do you think?”

“I think Mom tried and Mrs. Maine ignored the advice of the woman who’s been handling our festival successfully for years.”

“Uh-huh. How did your meeting with the professor go?”

“Puzzling. I think he needs a reality check. He also needs to learn to ask first before he makes plans for someone else.”

“Do you need me to talk to him?”

Meg shook her head. “I’ll handle it.”

“Was it truly urgent?”

“It was to him.”

Her father leaned close. “Are you sure you don’t want me to talk to him?”

She slid her arm through the crook of her father’s and squeezed. “I love you for caring, Dad. But I’ve got this.” Meg spotted her mother among the volunteers flipping through the pages of a three-ringed binder. “How’s Mom really handling not being in charge this year?”

Lansford looked across the room at his wife. “She looks like she’s searching for information Diana requested, but notice her chin.”

Her mother had tucked her chin close to her chest. Meg smiled. “I know that gesture. She’s struggling to keep from throwing that binder in the fireplace or she’s considering hitting Mrs. Maine over the head with it.” Meg took in the pinch on her mother's face and how close her shoulders were to her ears. "Did Mom voluntarily hand over the reins?"

"Yes. She felt she needed to be more focused at home. Having Heidi and Ava living with us while Keith is deployed eases a lot of burdens for them, financially and emotionally. Your mom and Ruby have been taking turns watching Ava and getting her to and from kindergarten while Heidi works her shifts at the clinic."

Meg knew through regular calls home that her brother's family had moved into the Farrell homestead. She hadn't heard about Heidi's job change until she'd arrived on Bent Fork. "I bet it's been a good move. Heidi's switch from the hospital to the clinic saves on gas and drive time. And I bet Ava loves being closer to her cousins."

"She does. We seem to have all of our granddaughters here quite a lot lately. With Alison carrying twins and needing extra bed rest, Caroline and Molly spend more time here with Ava. Caroline's in first grade now so that's another run into town at the end of every school day if Alison isn't up to making the trip. Fortunately, Connor isn't traveling back and forth to Houston like he did when they were expecting Molly."

He paused and Meg followed his gaze around the room until it landed on Connor. The oldest of the Farrell sons and the first to marry, move off

Bent Fork, have children and work full-time at something other than the family ranch.

"Your brother's a good husband and a good father. I would like to see him resign from the accounting firm and be a good rancher. I'm not going to be around forever."

"Bah. I absolutely forbid either you or Mom to even think about not being around forever."

"I'll do my best."

"Your best at what, dear?"

They turned in unison. Joanna Farrell stood behind them, binder in hand and eyebrows arched.

"About getting things moving along. I'm hungry."

Joanna thrust the binder against his chest, kissed his cheek and nudged him into the crowded living room. "Your turn."

He didn't waste any time. "Listen up, everyone," he shouted above the chatter. "I suggest we take a break and have something to eat."

Diana tapped her clipboard with a pointed nail. "Now, Lansford, I know there's a lovely array of snacks for us and—"

"Snacks?" Ruby rose from the straight-backed chair near a food-laden table. "Snacks? Some of us have been cooking all day to provide the *snacks* for this meeting."

Diana offered Ruby a tight smile. "May I continue? In the past, a break at this critical juncture might have worked. However, we have far too much to accomplish, and the days are passing. Taking a break will only delay our progress."

"I'm with Lansford," Tom Pierman spoke up. "Feed the body and good things happen to the brain. Don't know what. Don't care what. I smell Emma Reed's chili and I'm hungry."

Laughter rose above Diana's protests. Most of the volunteers headed for the food tables. Others went in the direction of the beverage table, where everything from water to wine awaited the thirsty.

"Meggie." Tom came toward her carrying a large bowl of Emma's chili topped with onions, cheese and sour cream. "I'm sure you've been told you're the spitting imagine of your mother at this age. Joanna was—" he paused and winked at Lansford standing nearby "—and still is, a beautiful woman."

"Thanks, Mr. Pierman." Meg smiled. "Gives me hope for the future."

Her father looked at the heaped bowl of chili his friend held. "Did you leave any for the rest of us?"

"A little but I'd hurry if you want some. Andrew and Hawk just walked in. I've seen those boys eat."

Meg glanced over Tom's shoulder. Her brother made for the beverage table. Hawk paused to shake hands and exchange a few words with several committee attendees before catching her eye.

He wore new denims that had not yet succumbed to the rigors of ranching and a black button-down shirt. He must have left his Stetson on the front seat of his pickup. With the hat on his head, Joe Hawk looked strong and sure. Without it, he was everything her youthful imagination had sparked and still drew her like a moth to the flame. Meg tucked a few unruly strands of hair behind her ears and worked her way toward him.

"Hi."

Hawk looked her up and down. "Wow. I haven't seen you in a dress since your graduation from TCC. Looks nice."

*Nice.* Her brother's whistle had flattered her more. At least Hawk had noticed she wasn't in her typical khakis and sweat-stained T-shirt. She'd take that. "Have you heard anything from Dr. Wallace?"

"No. Have you?"

"No. Maybe the dog's owner has claimed him."

"I admire the positive attitude."

"Sometimes a positive attitude is the only way to go."

"There you are, Joe Hawk." Ruby pushed a loaded tray under his nose. "This is headed for the dessert table. Helen Pierman also made a rhubarb pie but if you want a slice of mine, you'd better get it now."

"Ruby Turner, you are an angel." He took a plate holding a generous slice of pie and kissed her plump cheek with a resounding smack. "I've been looking forward to this since Meggie told me you'd made pie." He guided a large bite into his mouth. "Mmm. You should open your own shop."

The woman chuckled. It started as a deep rumble and left her lips like a burst of firecrackers. "A shop would be too much to worry about. I'm just an old, worn-out housekeeper."

Meg slipped her arm through Ruby's. "You are not old. You are not worn-out. And you are not just a housekeeper. You're family. You've been family since before I came along."

"See why we miss this girl when she goes away? And why we're so glad she's home where she belongs." Taking the now-empty plate from Hawk, she nudged Meg. "I heard Mrs. Maine assigned the two of you to do float work."

"Really?" Meg stared into the living room, where Diana Maine sat bolt upright in the wingback chair flipping through a stack of papers. "Why do people keep making plans for me without asking me?"

"Hey, Hawk." Andrew and John pushed their way between Hawk and Meggie. John snatched a piece of pie from the tray. "Dad and Larry are out on the front porch. Larry's been telling Dad about the Split Rock shelter. Said you could use an extra hand with the chimney work."

Hawk nodded.

"Well, I could use an extra hand or two for some repairs on our north shelter," John continued. "I can—"

"You can make yourself useful and take these pies to the dessert table," Ruby said.

"Here." Andrew took the tray. "I'll take it. Don't say any more until I get back. I want to hear details about the Split Rock damage and how Hawk tried to shoot a helpless dog."

"You what?" Ruby swatted Hawk's upper arm. "Joe Hawk, your grandfather would roll over in his grave if he knew you did such a thing."

Meg held up a hand. "In Hawk's defense, he did not shoot the dog. No one shot the dog. Although we both heard shots." She studied her brothers. "Were either of you near Meyer Ridge today?"

"You can't blame us," John said. "We were busy trucking hay bales out to the fairgrounds. The way I heard it, Meggie hurled rocks at Hawk to keep him from shooting a wounded dog he thought was a coyote."

Hawk swung around to Meggie.

She raised her hands, palms out. "I told Mom we found an injured dog and took it down to Dr. Wallace. That's it."

Andrew returned dangling the empty tray at his side. "Are you talking about the dog?"

Meg took the empty tray from her brother. "Somebody's been exaggerating the incident."

Everyone looked at Andrew.

"Would I tell people my best friend got beat up by my little sister to keep him from shooting a helpless, injured puppy he thought was a coyote? That would be downright embarrassing." He looked at Meg. "Dr. Wallace called. He wants to keep the dog for another day. He said to feel free to call if you have questions. He also said you were overwrought with concern. Was that for the dog or Hawk?"

"He did not say I was overwrought."

"No, but he did say you were worried."

"It appears I had cause to be worried if he's keeping the dog for another day. That can't be good."

"It's just precautionary," her brother assured her. "I'm going to get something cold to drink. Anyone care to join me?"

Hawk glanced at Meggie, then back to Andrew. "I'll join you in a minute."

"Aw, come on," John said. "Meggie doesn't mind. Do you, Meggie?"

Meg shook her head. "Go on. They'll nag until you give in."

"Now, then," John grinned. "Let's get out of here before we're roped into more volunteering."

"More?" Andrew asked.

"Yeah, I've already been put on the banner and flag-hanging committee, and I took the liberty of adding all your names."

Hawk shook his head. "I am *not* hanging anything. I *do* know the difference between a dog and a coyote. I did *not* shoot the dog."

# *CHAPTER FIVE*

MEG WATCHED THEM walk away, all laughing at something John had said to Hawk. Two of her four brothers. Despite their pranks, despite how they infuriated her with their protectiveness and hurt her with their dismissive attitudes, she loved them and actually missed them when she was away.

And Hawk.

Joe Hawk confused her. From the first time she saw him, standing next to his grandfather with an oversize Stetson on his head, a lost and lonely soul needing a place to belong, to the confident man whose Stetson now sat true on his head as he faced each day.

One night, recovering from a serious asthmatic episode, propped up in bed *not* sleeping, she'd imagined her destiny bound with Hawk's. A life of love, laughter, family and working the ranch side by side until an inevitable asthma attack would prevent her from being the partner he needed. Her asthma, mostly manageable, still flared on occasion, forcing her to monitor some of her activities, including her fieldwork. That lonely-night image still worked itself into her thoughts from time to time.

"Ruby, is Hawk seeing anyone?"

"Not that I know about. Andrew and John push a girl his way from time to time. I occasionally overhear them discussing a date for Hawk and a meeting place. According to Andrew, Hawk rarely sees the same girl more than a couple of times."

"I wonder what he's waiting for."

"The right one."

"Hmm." *The right one.* Was there a right one? Her parents certainly appeared to have found the right one. Two of her brothers happily shared their lives with the women they believed right for them. She slid a glance past Ruby through the wide windows to where Hawk leaned against the porch rail sipping from a tall glass of amber liquid and laughing with Andrew. *The right one.* How was one to know?

Meg held up the tray she'd taken from Andrew. "I'll put this away," she said and headed for the kitchen.

The maple panels of the swinging kitchen door shone honey gold. Meg bumped open the door and backed her way into the heart of the Farrell home.

Scents of fresh baking permeated the room. The oak trestle table, tucked into the bump-out bay window, nearly groaned from the results of volunteers' cooking. The center island held an assortment of dishes, cups, glasses and utensils.

Meg made room on the table for the tray, hooked

her foot on a leg of the bench, pulled it out and sat. This room held the essence of the Farrell family. Warm, welcoming, complete. It smelled like home. It looked like home. Home where she, according to Ruby, belonged.

Did she belong here? She had gone to school, graduated, done her due diligence and could declare herself a paleontologist. She had a new job waiting for her in Michigan. She'd wanted to fit in, to be a part of all that needed doing around the ranch. Her asthma had limited her participation. So much so that she had rarely felt like she'd belonged.

The kitchen door stopped its back-and-forth swinging and dimmed the droning voices of the crowd. She should go back and join the volunteers and offer to help somewhere. She should, but night sounds from myriad Colorado wildlife drifted through the open windows and beckoned.

Meg slid off the bench, crossed the wide-planked floor and stepped onto the screened-in porch. It held everything from a line of boots to a wall of pegs laden with heavy Chesterfields and a variety of hats. A bin of work gloves sat between a dark-stained wicker chair and a low bench that offered seating for removing muddy boots. A heavy wrought-iron stand held large and small umbrellas.

She stepped past the work gear to the screened door. Beyond the wire mesh, night waited. Stars covered nearly every inch of exposed sky hanging above the treetops and mountain peaks. Stars looked so much bigger, brighter and closer here than in Grand Rapids or Ann Arbor. City lights dimmed the brilliant display. Here in the high country, they teased you into thinking you could reach up and stir them around.

Ursa Major, the Great Bear, one of her favorite constellations, winked down at her, bringing to mind the old legend told to her by Hawk's grandfather.

"Once upon a time, there were seven Indian maidens." A deep voice mimicked the words in her head.

Meg spun. Hawk leaned against the doorway that separated the kitchen and the porch, arms folded and one booted foot crossed over the other.

"How do you do that?"

"Do what?"

"Just appear like that?"

He shrugged. "A gift from my ancestors I guess."

"Hmph. You should cough or put jangling spurs on your boots. Something to let people know you're coming." Meg stared at him. Even from her spot by the door, she could see the carved lines around his mouth. Deceptive lines. Sometimes they accentuated a boyish grin, sometimes they added a sternness to his face. But his eyes were pure magic. They didn't just look at, they looked into and through. And if you weren't careful…they saw.

"I don't think the fact that you carry Ute blood has anything to do with the way you sneak up on me. I think you've perfected your stalking skills just to annoy me."

Hawk grinned. “Now, why would I do that?”

“I don’t know. But you and my brothers have done your best over the years.”

“To annoy you?”

“Annoy, tease, alienate.”

“Hey.” He held up his hands. “I can’t take an equal share. I haven’t been around here that long.”

“True, but you’ve made the most of it.”

Hawk joined her by the screened door. “From what I’m hearing, you won’t be staying home long enough for me or your brothers to become too annoying.”

“Home, where I belong,” she murmured.

Hawk cocked his head to one side. “Say again?”

“Ruby said something earlier about my being home where I belong.”

“And?”

“I’m just wondering. Do I?”

“You’re asking me?”

Meg stared through the screen. “Bent Fork Ranch is a working ranch, worked by every Farrell that’s ever lived here for over one hundred years, except me. Doctors decided early on that I shouldn’t be involved in the outdoor chores or overexert myself in case the activity triggered an asthma attack. I get it. I had, still have, asthma.

“My brothers had a place and a purpose. They were a part of the raising, feeding and caring for our livestock. They were a part of managing the land to keep it agreeable to our livestock. They handled the repairs of our structures and fencing and equipment. They belonged."

"You're saying you don't?"

"Not like they do. Granted, once I learned to ride, I got to exercise the horses, and I could ride out a message if cell service wasn't cooperating. But the real work, the work that makes Bent Fork a productive working ranch, wasn't available to me."

"So, you're *choosing* to leave because you haven't gotten to bale hay or feed cattle or muck a stall?"

She drew a deep breath. "No. I'm not leaving as much as I'm going to start my new job."

"At the museum in Michigan."

"Yes. A job I'm qualified for, but Professor Nelson thinks the fact that I was once his student had something to do with my getting the position." She frowned, pulling her brows down and pinching her lips in tight line. "I had the oddest conversation with him earlier."

"In my opinion, any conversation with Professor Nelson is an odd conversation."

"He's fixated on dinosaur eggs and his need to go to Canada and hold them. His going to Canada means someone needs to take on his summer geology class, and as his best and favorite student, he's selected me."

"Will you be here long enough to do that?"

"My time isn't set exactly. I have at least four weeks. Beyond that, it depends on the ongoing construction at the museum. I've been texting with

Dr. Vanover and apparently there are some delays cropping up."

"So, if you agree to take the class, you'll be staying longer?"

Did she hear a note of hopefulness in his voice? Or did she like the idea that he would want her to stay longer? "I don't know. I told Professor Nelson I'd think about it. Then, I tried to call Dr. Vanover but it went straight to voicemail." She shrugged. "Given the time change, I'll try again tomorrow."

Hawk settled himself against the doorframe. "Tell me more about the eggs in Canada."

"Are you really interested in discussing prehistoric eggs?"

"Would I be standing here asking if I weren't?"

"You're standing here hoping to avoid Diana Maine and her sign-up clipboard."

Hawk chuckled. "I won't deny it. As much as I want to help, I don't have the time I hear Mrs. Maine wants from volunteers."

"I keep trying to sneak out," Meg admitted.

Hawk nudged open the screened door. "After you."

"Meggie?" her mother called from the kitchen.

Hawk opened the door wider. "It's now or never."

"Mary Margaret, are you out there?"

Meg sighed. "Too late." She stepped away from the door and bumped the glove basket. Everything from cloth gardening gloves to rawhide workers tumbled onto the tiled floor.

Her mother's shadow fell across the spilled gloves. "There you are. The meeting is being called back to order."

Meg bent and stuffed the gloves into the basket. "We'll be there in a minute."

Hawk took the basket and set it on the bench. "I've been asking Meggie about her new job."

Joanna picked up a missed glove. "In Michigan." Her mother flipped through the basket and found the mate. She pressed them together and folded down the cuffs. "Did you check with the Museum of Nature and Science in Denver?"

Meg squared her shoulders. "I did. No openings."

"None?"

"Only volunteer work. I did check. Just for you."

"Well, maybe something special will come along before you have to leave us."

Meg gave her mother a puzzled look. "Did you talk with Professor Nelson this evening?"

"No. He left directly after talking to you. Is there a problem?"

"No. We'll be right in, Mom."

As soon as Joanna left the porch, Hawk turned to Meggie. "What's really going on with the professor?"

The tone of his voice caused her to look up. His eyes, dark to begin with, deepened even more. "Don't get all big brotherly on me. It's nothing serious. I'm just not comfortable with his assumption that I'd take the class before he asked me. I think it's something I can do for a few weeks but that's not the point. He just assumed and made his plans."

"But you're thinking of taking the class, even for a few weeks."

"I am." She reached up and touched his face. "How's the cheek?"

"Fine. Thanks for asking. I hope you noticed there's no smell of boiled bat droppings."

Meg smiled. "For that I, and everyone present, are so very grateful."

"Shall we join the throng?"

"I'd rather be lowered headfirst into a vat of boiling bat droppings." She took a deep breath. "About the dog. I think our best option is to focus on finding him a good home where he can be a loved pet."

"There's a right place for him." Hawk draped an arm around her shoulder. "You'll see."

THE MORNING HUSTLE and bustle in the kitchen put a smile on Meg's face. Breakfast at the Farrell homestead usually consisted of food, family, friends and lots of each. Noisy chatter filled the room, rising above the clink of utensils. Mounds of food covered the oak table, extra chairs surrounded the table and a body sat on every seat, including the one that was traditionally hers. Even the island and its stools were in use.

Her nieces, Molly, Caroline and Ava, the three youngest family members, perched on the swivel stools. Hair in ponytails, clad in colorful T-shirts and denim shorts with equally colorful sneakers on their feet, the girls looked like human kaleidoscopes.

The look of joy on their faces and excitement in their voices widened Meg's smile. The attentive look on Hawk's face pushed her smile to a grin.

She watched his hopeful and hungry gaze follow the dwindling platter of pancakes being passed from hand to hand. A charcoal-colored Sitting River T-shirt fit comfortably over his shoulders and torso. She couldn't see his lower half, but she knew he wore jeans. In all the years she had known him, she had seldom seen him in anything but well-worn, well-washed denims.

The platter reached his waiting hands. He stuck his fork into the stack. "Morning, Meggie."

Meg perched on the edge of the bench opposite Hawk and poured syrup over her own stack. "Good morning. What brings you to Bent Fork so early?"

"I had some papers to give to Andrew and he invited me to stay for breakfast."

The phone on the counter rang, filling the room with an ear-piercing ring that would get their attention anywhere in the huge house or on the porches.

"Who could that be so early?" Ruby rose and reached for the phone.

Meg put her fork on her plate. She knew who was calling so early. The man who thought he was going to Canada to caress prehistoric eggs.

Ruby reached the phone on the second ring.

"Hello." She nodded and held out the receiver. "For you, Meggie."

Meg hesitated. Last night she had told the professor that she would think about his "wonderful opportunity" and he'd said he would call early for her decision.

"It's Mrs. Burlew from the community college."

"Mrs. Burlew?" Meg rose and stepped to the counter. She took the phone from Ruby and turned her back to the table. "Hello."

"Hello, Meggie. Welcome back to Tyler."

"Thank you."

"I wanted to set an appointment for you to fill out some forms and collect the professor's curriculum for the class. Would Friday at nine work for you?"

"Mrs. Burlew, I'm afraid there's been a misunderstanding."

"No. Professor Nelson set everything in order before he left."

"Did you say he left?"

"I believe he was leaving early this morning. I just need you to come in and sign the forms and I'll give you the keys to his office and classroom at that time."

"We really need to have a conversation about this. The professor—"

"The professor can be a bit distracted, I know. I assure you everything is in order for you to take the class."

"This is just it. I haven't agreed. I told him I

would think about it. I'll need to get in touch with my employer in Michigan to determine exactly how much time I can spare before I can make a decision." Meg paused. "Mrs. Burlew?"

"Oh my. Yes, we definitely need to have a little chat. Will Friday still work? I'm afraid that's my earliest availability."

"Yes. Friday at nine will be fine. Goodbye."

ALL EYES WATCHED her hang up the phone. All eyes followed her back to her seat. As always, everything was everyone's business in the Farrell home. The respectful silence ended the second she dropped onto the bench.

"What did Mrs. Burlew want?" Her mother posed the first question.

"Me." Meg cleared her throat and looked around the table at the expectant faces. "It appears Tyler Community College is under the impression I'm teaching Professor Nelson's eight-week summer geology class." Slowly, in bits and pieces. That was her process. That was what made her very good at her job. The countless hours bent over a fossil slowly scraping, brushing and chipping away bit by bit eventually gave way to a dinosaur or at least a part of a dinosaur.

Her father leaned forward. "I thought you were starting work at the new museum in a few weeks."

"I am."

"I don't understand." Her mother pushed her

plate to one side and folded her hands in front of her. "Why would the community college think you're teaching a class here when you have a job in Michigan?"

"Professor Nelson, who apparently keeps up with everything happening in the field of paleontology, heard I had been hired by the museum. He called Rachael, Dr. Vanover, to congratulate her on selecting one of *his* students for the position of head of the Earth Sciences Department. He also asked if she could confirm that a site in Canada had recently uncovered nests of fossilized eggs."

"Eggs?" John clucked. "Like chicken eggs."

"Yes, only larger. Much, much larger."

Alison rubbed her very pregnant belly. "Eggs and nesting sound fascinating but what do they have to do with you teaching his geology class?"

"He wants to take his expert knowledge of dinosaur eggs to Canada and spend the summer working at the site."

"And holding eggs," Hawk added.

Meg grinned at him. "And holding eggs."

"So," John said, reaching for more biscuits, "we're back to what does a nest of big eggs in Canada have to do with you?"

"For him to take an extended leave, someone has to take over the geology class."

"Ah. That's where you come in," Andrew deduced.

Meg nodded. "Yep."

"But," her mother said with a frown, "you're already committed to the museum."

"Uh-huh."

Caroline swiveled her seat to face the table. "That's where Sue the T. rex is, isn't it, Aunt Meggie? At a museum."

"Yes, sweetie, at the Field Museum in Chicago. Sue the T. rex and a lot of other dinosaurs are there."

"Mom, can we visit Sue someday? I want to see how big she is next to me while I'm still small."

Connor rose from the table and spun his daughter's stool to face her plate. "Eat your pancakes or the only place you'll be going while you're still small is to see the doctor to find out why you're not growing."

Molly looked at her pancakes, then at her father. "Daddy, our pancakes need more curls."

"More curls, you say?"

Snatching the canister from the counter, Ruby squirted whipped cream curls across the top of the pancakes. "There you go. More curls. Now hurry or I'll leave for town without you."

"No, you won't. You want us to go to school."

Connor tugged the ponytail of each daughter. "They've got you there, Ruby."

"I said I'd drive the girls to school on the days I play bridge at the senior center until school ends. But someone else will have to pick them up and get Caroline to soccer practice. Too bad Meggie's job isn't in Tyler. It would be nice to have an extra hand around here. Especially when school starts up in the fall."

"Ruby has a point." Alison continued to massage her stomach. "I don't know when I'll be cleared to do much of anything, let alone drive. Having an extra body would be a huge help." She moaned and pressed a hand against her left side. "Golly, one of the twins is eager to join Caroline's soccer team."

Connor rubbed his wife's abdomen. "Settle down in there, kiddo, and give your mom a break. They kept us up most of the night."

"Us? I know *I* was awake most of the night. *You* snored most of the night."

"Anyway—" Connor popped a blackberry in his mouth "—it would be great to have some extra help around the ranch in general. Dad, I know you, Andrew and John are handling most things but between my full-time paying job, my job as father and husband and handling Bent Fork's paperwork, I've got a loaded plate."

Meg looked at Connor. "How about—"

"Hiring help? With the rodeo season in full swing, a lot of the younger folks are out on the circuit. Everyone is in the same boat with outdoor work piling up, and don't suggest John or Andrew take over the paperwork. We tried that. John has a head for machinery, not numbers. And Andrew..." He looked down the table at his brother. "Who knows where his head is these days. And you've never done any of the outdoor work."

"I was kept from doing outdoor work."

"Because of your asthma."

Ruby rounded the table and pulled Meg into a hug. "We've only ever done what we thought was best for you."

For a few seconds, Meg gave in to the hug, then she took a deep breath and extricated herself. "I know and I appreciate it. But I'm a part of this family and I can help in spite of my asthma. I can pick up the girls from school when needed or take Caroline to soccer practice. At least while I'm here."

"What about the professor's class?" her mother asked.

Meg bristled. So much of her life had been dictated by others. Family and doctors she understood, to a point. Professor Nelson? He'd gone too far by telling TCC she would take his class before talking with her.

She drew another breath. "Here's something all of you need to know. I can handle my own life. My health. The professor. Mrs. Burlew and TCC. And whether or not I volunteer to help with this year's Willow River Festival."

She snatched her plate, dropped it in the sink and went straight to the back door, making sure it didn't smack her behind on the way out.

# CHAPTER SIX

HAWK CAUGHT UP with her just as she dropped a saddle on Calypso's back.

"Where are you headed?"

She tightened the cinch. "Anywhere."

"Mind if I join you?"

"I thought you had to work on the storm shelter and shore up fence posts."

"That'll all keep." Lame Eagle had taught him the value of discernment. Sometimes what seemed most important could cloud the mind and harden the heart. Sometimes you needed to be still and listen. Hawk had sat and listened to the Farrell family, and he chose to put aside the work and join Meggie.

She held her arms wide. Scents of pine shavings, hay, well-oiled leather and liniment filled the area. A recently replaced stall door still carried the smell of fresh-cut lumber. Hooks, pegs and shelves on the far wall were heavy with bridles, blankets, ropes, posters of John's latest automotive fascination and her dad's collection of baseball caps. Pitchforks and shovels leaned against the wall.

Seven of the ten stalls housed horses claimed by family. The other three horses were used as needed.

"You know which ones are good to ride. Pick one."

"I rode over on Wickiup."

One foot in the stirrup, she paused. "If you're coming, you'd better get him."

Her backside had barely met the saddle when Calypso started for the stable door. He stepped back in time to avoid being trampled. Meggie rode well, but in her current mood, raw emotion appeared to have taken priority over safety.

Hawk settled onto the back of his big gelding and urged him forward. With any luck, he'd catch Meggie before she had a chance to break her pretty little neck. Lady Luck had not been around lately. If she picked this morning to pay a visit, he would gladly point her in Meggie's direction.

Ahead of him, Meggie and Calypso flew across the ground as if demons were chasing them. Maybe they were. The earlier scene in the Farrell kitchen had felt like a volcanic eruption. An outwardly dormant situation that roiled and grew below the surface until it couldn't be contained. Once unleashed, there would be no stuffing the subject back underground. Meggie's words, emotions and thoughts had spilled out and she'd have to cope with the release.

He watched her reach the hogback between Bent

Fork and Sitting River and rein in Calypso. Good. She wouldn't ride blind over the crest. He slowed Wickiup. He knew where she was going.

Fendels Creek, more river than creek this time of year, widened on the other side of the ridge and slowed its journey to join the mighty Colorado River miles away. A meadow of grasses, low scrub brush and cottonwoods spread along the river, offering creatures, human and otherwise, a place to quench a thirst, rest a tired body or think. All of which he had often done in the last year.

He spotted them under a tall cottonwood at the creek's edge. The mare's muzzle skimmed the water. Meggie stood staring out across the water to the open valley. To the casual observer, she looked like she had wandered upon a picturesque spot and decided to relax and admire the view. Hawk knew better. He knew the many moods of Meggie Farrell. The jut of her chin signaled anything but relaxed.

Once close enough to be heard, he brought Wickiup to an easy walk. "You know," he said, sliding from the saddle, "I wasn't sure I would find both of you standing."

Meg stuffed her hands in the pockets of her jeans, leaned back against the big tree.

He unhooked the canteen from the saddle horn, left Wickiup to join Calypso and offered the water to Meggie. She refused with a single shake of her head.

He drank his fill and secured the top. "You okay?"

She continued to stare into the distance. "Yes. No. I don't know."

He remained silent, letting her take her time.

"I shouldn't have taken my frustration with the professor out on them." She huffed out a heavy sigh. "You know, once in a while when everyone was occupied, I would sneak out and ride to Sitting River. With Lame Eagle I felt normal. He didn't treat me like an invalid or a nuisance. He treated me the way I like to think my grandparents would have treated me, like a cherished grandchild, not a frail mistake in the Farrell bloodline."

"Families can be complicated. At least they're there. That's more than I can say for mine."

"I'm sorry. I didn't think. How is your mom? How is her friend?"

"Mom's good. She likes living in Albuquerque with Leona. Unfortunately, Leona's cancer is getting worse, and with no family, she's glad for Mom's help."

"Do you think your mom will come home soon?"

Hawk shook his head. "They were each other's first best friends in Minnesota. Mom will stay with Leona until she isn't needed."

"What about your dad? Have you had any contact with him?"

"From a man who preferred to chase Lady Luck and easy money instead of being a husband and father?" He shifted his gaze across the valley and let it rest on the distant mountains.

Home. His home. The place in Cheyenne where he'd lived with his mother and occasionally his father had never felt like home. It had been a place for Michael Hawk to return to when Lady Luck hadn't been kind to him.

"I've only seen him once since the day he left Cheyenne promising to return with a new bike to replace the one that had 'gone missing' the last time he'd shown up.

"He came to Sitting River. I was sixteen. Mom and I had already been living with Lame Eagle for two years. Emma said he'd arrived out of the blue, had a short conversation with Lame Eagle, stormed out of Big House, hopped into his shiny new truck and left. I passed him as I came up the drive from the school bus drop-off. He didn't even slow down."

Meg ran her hand along his arm. "Here I am complaining about my family being *over*involved. I'm sorry."

He cupped her chin and tipped it up. "I'm not looking for sympathy. I'm just saying that, as an only child, I get it. So, how many times did you make your escape and roam Sitting River with Lame Eagle?"

"Enough to know what I was missing." She sighed. "I miss him and our adventures."

"What are you going to do about Nelson and his class?"

"Last night I told him I would think about it. It's an eight-week course and right now I can only agree to four weeks. I tried to get in touch with Dr. Vanover this morning to check the status of the construction and if there are any further delays."

"And?"

"My call went straight to voicemail." She bent, picked up a handful of small stones and rolled them on her palm. "He shouldn't have assumed so much." She flung one stone and then another. "Why would he do that?"

Hawk held his peace. He gave her space and time to let her thoughts settle. She had every right to be angry. He knew all too well that lies and broken promises altered one's view of people and situations. He also knew dwelling on such situations didn't change the facts.

She flung the remaining stones into the water one by one. Ripples spread in ever-widening rings, met and mingled across the clear snowmelt of the creek. When the last wavelet faded against the water's edge, she turned back to him. "He had no right to make plans regarding me without consulting me first."

Emotions played across her face. Hurt, anger, disappointment. She needed a distraction. Needed to keep unpleasant thoughts from camping in her mind and heart. Hawk gathered the horses' reins and pulled the animals away from the creek and handed Calypso's to Meggie. "I want to show you something."

"What?"

"You'll see." He swung himself onto Wickiup's back.

"I'd like a little more information."

"It's not far."

"How far is not far?"

Hawk stared down at her. "Trust me." Those were words he seldom said. Trust had been stolen from him with his father's constant broken promises. Lame Eagle had fostered honesty and nurtured truth through his words and actions, giving Hawk a chance to discern when and whom to trust. He trusted his desire to protect Meggie Farrell.

She stroked Calypso's nose, then climbed into the saddle. "Whatever it is, it had better be good."

They followed the bank of the creek for several minutes before turning toward a grove of aspen trees. Hawk stayed slightly ahead, leaving her to her own musings until the trail emerged from under the canopy of quaking aspen leaves. He paused and waited for her to catch up and pointed past a tumble of rocks and another cluster of aspens that mingled with the darker green of pines.

The trees backed against the spiny plate of Barren Ridge before making a gentle climb toward the top of the ridge. Occupying a crescent-moon-shaped clearing at the edge of the trees was a cabin.

His cabin now that his grandfather was gone.

They stopped at the foot of a wide set of steps leading to a wraparound porch. Meggie slid off Calypso's back and draped the leather reins over an old-fashioned hitching post. A brand-new old-fashioned hitching post. Hawk dismounted, tethered Wickiup and slid his palm over the smooth wood of the post, pleased with the result of his hard work.

"Lame Eagle's sanctuary," Meggie said. "He told me he came here to breathe and listen to the wisdom of the Elders."

"I think he built the cabin to find some quiet time away from my grandmother and Emma. After my grandmother passed, I think he came here to remember her."

"It's been a long time since I've been here." Meggie stood at the bottom of the steps. "Lame Eagle occasionally took me hunting for fossils and rocks and such. After a couple of hours, we'd stop here, sit on the porch swing and have lemonade. Then we'd empty our collection bag of treasures. If there were fossil bits, we'd make up stories about what the dinosaur might have looked like and sounded like." She sighed. "Lame Eagle always spoke special words over the fossils. He said creatures, even ancient ones, deserved to be remembered."

"And the treasure pieces that weren't fossilized bits?"

Meg smiled up at him. "I kept them. Mostly

rocks, feathers, unusual-looking pine cones. They're on shelves in the shed behind the hay barn. They weren't allowed in the house."

Hawk watched as she ran her hand along the wooden rail, nodding as she went up the steps. "You've made changes."

"Some. I pulled this wraparound from the original porch. The chimney shell is river rock from the creek. I widened the front windows to help lighten the inside."

"I'm glad you kept the swing."

Hawk let his gaze settle on the swing. Wooden slats formed the back and seat. Wider pieces of wood served as armrests, and links of chain hanging from the ceiling beams supported the swing and allowed for ease of movement. "Lame Eagle's listening spot. He sat out here in snowstorms, downpours and wilting heat. Just sitting and communing with the Elders." Hawk climbed the steps and stood next to the swing. "I thought about moving it down a few feet when I lengthened the porch." He thumbed his hat back a bit. "It was my grandfather's place to be. It needed to stay just where it is. For now."

He eased himself onto the swing. "I've been coming here more since his death. It started out as a way to stay connected with him. Then I started making changes. I like to think he would approve."

Meggie settled next to him. Hawk welcomed

the company. Lately it seemed he'd had too much time alone.

With one booted foot, he pushed the swing back and forth in a slow, steady movement. Meggie matched the easy swaying with the tip of her boot. He'd push, she'd push. A tranquil quiet settled around them, then he heard her sigh.

"I understand why Lame Eagle came here. Like the swing at Big House, it's a perfect spot to listen, to rest, to just be."

"The Spirits, the Elders, his own thoughts, his memories. Whomever or whatever he was listening to, he found peace here."

"What about you? What do you find here?"

"Lately, too much work. Although, the work, when I can spare the time, makes me feel like I have control over something in my life. I keep telling myself it will be worth it in the end. The structure is good. The electrical, limited as it was, needed a major overhaul to bring it up to code and to accommodate the updates I want."

"I noticed the lumber out back as we rode up. That's quite a stockpile."

"I've been storing up for some time. It should cover the additions I want. I've made changes inside, too."

"I'm glad. The last time I saw the inside it looked like a campsite with a roof. The bare wood plank flooring, mismatched chairs around the fireplace, a small card table, a camp stove in the kitchen and a cot in the bedroom." She shifted to face him. "May I see what you've done? If you don't mind."

Reluctantly, he abandoned his place on the swing and held out a hand. "Come on." She slid her hand in his. He liked how comfortably they fit together. He liked that they both had hands that bore the signs of hard work. Several small scars marked hers. He'd noticed them when she soothed the dog and again when she came at him with wet tissues to clean his cheek. Apparently paleontology inflicted its own battle wounds.

Meg stepped through the door and stopped cold. "Wow."

Hawk smiled. Lame Eagle hadn't been a man who needed or wanted material possessions. Nor was he. The cabin, while furnished, didn't bow under the burden of things. It breathed in harmony with the natural elements outside its walls.

Sunlight streamed through the long, wide windows to the right of the door, giving the space a sense of sitting in the open air. Rugs, woven in Native American designs, softened the gleaming hardwood floors. The furnishings were simple. A leather sofa and matching wingback chair flanked the stone fireplace. Strategically placed tables held lamps, and a ceiling fan offered light as well as cooling wafts of air.

Hawk remained silent as Meggie scanned the room. Her gaze lingered on the wall holding two framed photos. "I hope you're planning to hang more." She stepped to the wall and ran a finger along one frame. "This one is lovely."

Hawk joined her. "My grandparents' wedding photo. One of my favorites."

"Your grandmother was beautiful." She traced an outline around the couple. "I wish I'd known her."

Hawk nodded. "I wish I'd had the chance to save more memories of her. My father rarely brought us down from Cheyenne to visit my grandparents. I'm fortunate enough to have photos and hold stories told by those who knew her."

Meg pointed to the next photo. "Another favorite?"

"Your dad took this shortly after we came to live with Lame Eagle."

Meg leaned in for a better view. A group of people sat on the front steps of Sitting River's Big House. "There's Lame Eagle, you, your mom, my mom, the Reeds, my brothers and…" She looked closer. "And Ruby and me." She smiled at Hawk. "Family. I like this one."

He backed away and pointed to the aged rolltop desk anchoring the wall opposite the door. Large blue sheets of paper covered the desk's flat surface while pens, pencils, rulers and such filled the numerous cubbies. "Care to see my plan for the place?"

Meg joined him at the desk and studied the lines and numbers on the paper. "You designed this?"

"Yes. Well," he drawled. "I worked with an architectural firm in Denver to come up with the plan. They put my ideas on paper and signed off on the design so I can get the necessary permits."

"You're going to make all of these changes? Here?"

He nodded. "I'll continue the porch around the left side and have doors opening onto it from the kitchen and the back bedroom. Eventually I'll add another bedroom and a larger bathroom."

"Why?" She gestured around the room. "What more do you need? It's in a beautiful spot. Cozy, peaceful, has everything it needs for a getaway cabin."

"I need it to be more than a getaway."

"But you have Big House *and* Little House. Even with Larry and Emma sharing Big House with you, there's plenty of room for the three of you. It is, after all, a big house."

"But not enough room for nine, especially when four of the nine are children under the age of ten."

"What?"

"Larry and Emma's daughter, Jenna, and her family need a place to stay for a while. Maybe quite a while. Their son-in-law's job was eliminated in his company's downsizing strategy and Jenna's part-time job isn't enough to cover living costs plus special needs for one of the kids."

"You're giving them the use of Big House?"

One corner of his mouth tipped up.

"You're a generous man, Joe Hawk."

He shook his head. "I'm a selfish man. The other option is for Larry and Emma to move to North Carolina. I don't want to lose them." He glanced back at the photos. "Like you said, family."

"I thought I heard Larry mention the kids were coming. I assumed it was for a visit. But there's still Little House and it has everything you would need."

Hawk stuffed his hands into the front pockets of his jeans. "I'm renting Little House to the Romeros. Temporarily."

"Renting Little House. Why?"

"Necessity."

The cell phone in his back pocket blared a raucous tone. He pulled out the phone and pointed. "I did not choose the ringtone."

Meggie smiled. "Emma?"

He nodded and glanced at the screen and pressed the phone to his ear. "What's up, Larry?" After a handful of "right, right and right," Hawk stuffed the phone back into his pocket. "Larry needs help with the hay baler. Again. Seems like we're rebuilding that monster from scratch."

"Can't you replace it?"

"Not anytime soon." He drew down the lid of the desk. "I need to go."

Meggie followed him out onto the porch. "I guess I have to face the family sooner or later.

Mom and Ruby are going to have a million questions about the professor and TCC."

"You're welcome to stay here awhile." He touched the tip of her nose. "Or you can come with me?"

"Really?"

"If you have the time. We'll need to ride to Big House, stable the horses and find the part Larry thinks he needs. I don't know how long it will take to get the baler working, assuming we can."

"I don't care how long it takes. Working on your hay baler beats going home to make apologies for this morning's outburst and then listening to the loving women of Bent Fork discuss my future with or without my participation."

# *CHAPTER SEVEN*

MEG LEANED AGAINST the giant tire of the massive machine and pressed Hawk for an opportunity to help. "There must be something I can do."

"Got a new baler up your sleeve?"

"That bad?"

Hawk took the cloth she held out to him and wiped black smudges from his hands. "Belt keeps sliding. It could be worse."

"How's that, boss?" Larry squatted beside a narrow metal box pushing tools around until he came up with a small wrench.

"It could be raining."

The older man squinted skyward and shook his head. "Not today." He rubbed a weathered hand through the graying stubble sitting on the lower half of his face. "Might drop a little tomorrow afternoon."

Meg pushed away from the tire. "You think so?"

The Sitting River foreman rose and lifted one thin leg, rotated his foot and flexed his knee. "You wouldn't know it to look at me, but my wife and

I used to square dance. I was good. Emma was better."

Meg studied him. She had no idea of his age, somewhere between fifty and eighty, lean and wiry. His head sprouted sparse tufts of graying hair that matched his beard. Deep lines etched his leathered face. She looked at Hawk. "Is he pulling my leg?"

"I've seen them dance. I think they're still the best in the county."

"Aw." Larry grinned. "Used to be, boss. Used to be." He rotated the booted foot again. "Joints start to complain once you reach a certain age. Sooner if you've done a lot of dancing. They give me a heads-up when there's rain comin' our way."

Hawk kicked the tire nearest him. "Rain or no rain, we need to get this hunk of junk doing what it's supposed to do. If it rains hard on this hay, we'll have to kick it before we can bale. That will put us even farther behind."

"You could borrow Bent Fork's tedder. According to Andrew, that machine helps speed up the drying time." Meg rocked back on her heels. "Are you sure there isn't something I could do to help?"

Hawk reached down and rubbed the brown-, black- and gray-mottled fur of the dog sitting between him and the baler. "I forgot to set out water for Maiku. There's an aluminum bowl in the back of the truck and a jug of water. Would you please pour him a drink?"

"Sure." She gestured to the dog. "Come on, Maiku."

The dog dropped at Hawk's feet. Meg eyed the two. Man, and man's best friend. "I still think Maiku needs a buddy of the four-legged variety."

"We talked about this last night."

"I checked in with the vet's office and the shelter this morning. The dog is doing better, but no one has called about the missing beauty."

"Can't you take him, Meggie?" Larry asked.

"Pets aren't allowed on Bent Fork."

"Why's that?"

"It used to be that so much time was needed for the care of livestock that no one had proper time for pets. Then, I think the recommended level of cleanliness to help reduce my asthma issues kept pets out of the house." She drummed her fingers on her chin. "I don't see the need to be so thorough now. I'll ask about bringing him to Bent Fork while we wait for someone to claim him or until we find him the right home."

Hawk ruffled his dog's ears. "In the meantime, would you please pour this handsome beast some water?"

"Come get a drink, Maiku." Meg ambled to the pickup. Maiku followed. The bed of the pickup still held the tools she'd pushed aside yesterday to make a spot for herself and the wounded dog plus coils of rope and a cooler. No doggy bowl. A mound of folded horse blankets sat in the far corner. She felt around the blankets and uncovered a slightly dented aluminum bowl and held it up. “Eureka.”

Maiku barked. “Hold on. My assigned task isn’t completed until I’ve poured water.” She placed the bowl in the meager shade provided by the baler and filled it.

She left him lapping loudly at the tepid water and joined the men. Hawk’s legs stretched out from under the machine. Larry squatted beside the toolbox with a wrench in one hand and an oily rag in the other.

“Water-filling task accomplished. Now what?”

Hawk scooted out from underneath the baler. “Thank you.” He swiped an arm across his forehead. “I warned you this could take some time. You mentioned wanting to check out an area of crumbled cliff face we passed. Why don’t you go on and check it out.”

Meg scrutinized the valley. Beyond the hayfield, color dominated the area. Wildflowers of purple, red, yellow, white and blue peeked between clumps of gray-green sage and buffalo grass. Fendels Creek poured into the valley along the edge of the ridge before it spread out and slowed so much it looked like it decided to sit and enjoy the scenery. Past the valley’s edge, gentle slopes of aspen groves and pine forests of varying shades of green climbed and blended with the higher ridges that met snow-covered peaks. Beauty knew no limits in the Colorado high country.

"Okay if I take your pickup?"

Hawk dug the keys from his pocket and tossed them to her.

She caught them between her palms. "Thanks. I won't be long."

"Uh-huh." Hawk crawled back under the baler.

Meg climbed into the pickup, shifted into Drive and headed for the dirt track they'd used to reach the hayfield. It wasn't long before she spotted the pale sandstone cliffs, pitted and crinkled, rising from the valley floor.

Millions of years ago, the area had been pushed thousands of feet into the air. Time and nature had whittled away at the cliff, piling detritus at its feet and leaving the cliffs a fraction of their birthed size.

She stopped the pickup once she reached the boundary fence separating hay production from cattle grazing and scanned the distant layers of exposed rock looking for color changes or outlines that didn't quite fit. Possibly. She couldn't be sure from this distance and the ground was too rough to cross with a truck that wasn't hers. She parked the pickup on the edge of the track, took a water bottle from the cooler, tightened her bootlaces and set off along the fence line.

Weathered posts and rails stood as a barrier to prevent grazing cattle from wandering where they shouldn't. Meg spotted a small band of cows gathered under a stand of cottonwood flanking the once-wide riverbed. The rest grazed on nature's offerings beyond the trees.

One lone cow left the group and ambled her way. Another raised its head and followed, and then another. Meg watched their slow, purposeful plodding. She'd never thought much about cows other than the fact that they provided milk, meat, a usable hide and an income for those who chose to put up with them. Slowly they drew closer. They weren't attractive like horses, or small and cute like sheep, and they didn't appear to be smart like dogs. Whatever they were or were not in looks or intellect, they were getting too close for comfort.

She backed against the fencing, keeping both eyes on the encroaching bovine. "Shoo." She waved her hands. "Go. Shoo." They ignored her. "Go on. Go join your friends. Shoo."

Shooing didn't work. Meg scrambled over the fence. It rocked as she climbed and when she let go, it tipped toward the ground. Down the line of posts, several others leaned close to the ground. They didn't offer a clear path for lazy cattle to muster thoughts of escape, but more ambitious ones, like the three approaching her, might have other ideas. What would Hawk do if his cattle got loose? She wouldn't let that happen if she could help it. They were a valuable asset to him and his ranch.

She pulled off her hat and waved it at the cows. "Stop!" They stopped. Meg stared at them. They stared back. Then, one by one they slowly lowered their heads to chew on meadow grass.

"Really. That's all it takes." She'd have to remember that. Even if they meant no harm, the idea of being nuzzled by a one-thousand-pound, smelly, wet-nosed cow lacked appeal.

She replaced her hat and remained on the cowless side of the wobbly fence. And it did wobble. Enough so that a determined cow might get over.

Meg tugged the nearest leaning post upright in its hole and let go. It promptly tilted, pulling the rails with it. She lifted the post again and, using her right foot, nudged a rock against the base. She stomped the stone into the loose soil and stepped back. The post still leaned forward but not as far.

More rocks would offer more support. She glanced at the ground. Rocks were not a problem. How to get them embedded deeply enough to serve as an anchor? That was a problem. She needed tools. Fortunately, Hawk's truck held what she needed.

In the back of the pickup, she found heavy leather work gloves and slid them over her hands, tucked a hammer into the waistband of her khakis and pulled out the post digger and a shovel and dragged them to the sagging posts.

The repeated process of opening the digger blades, plunging the blades into the post hole, closing the blades and removing dirt had removed very little dirt and left her sweaty and frustrated. Her hands slid in the gloves and she winced as the leather chafed against the blister forming between the thumb and forefinger of her right hand.

She dropped the digger and settled the post into the hole and pushed rocks in after it until it felt solid. Then she shoveled dirt over the rocks, tamped it down, slid the rails back in place and surveyed her efforts.

Not professional by any means but it would hopefully hold until Hawk could get to it. She felt responsible for the fact that he hadn't been able to tend to the fence. His help with the dog and the time with her at Lame Eagle's cabin had kept him from his work. She wiped her forearm across her brow, heaved a long sigh and moved to the next leaning post.

"Need a hand?"

Meg shaded her eyes and looked from the man striding across the open meadow to the pickup parked on the track just in front of Hawk's. The dark green paint had long ago lost its shine. A deep dent marred the rear passenger side panel and rust had staked a claim. Pickups were as common in the high country as rocks in the Rocky Mountains, and while the townspeople of Tyler recognized most of the vehicles in their small community, she hadn't been around long enough since graduation to remain familiar.

She didn't recognize the man, either. His slightly bowed shoulders took from his height. Even so, he stood at least six feet. From head to toe, he wore typical work clothes of denims and a buttoned cotton shirt that hung loosely on his lean frame and a denim jacket. The dark hair with its streaks of gray stuck out from under a ball cap, reaching just past the collar. A pair of sunglasses hid his eyes, making an estimation of his age challenging. Given the rounded shoulders, gray in his hair and grit in his voice, she placed him close to her father's age. No name came to mind, but there was something familiar about him, something that made her think she should know him.

"Saw you working in that hole as I drove by. Thought I'd offer help." He held out a sun-browned hand. "Name's Mike."

Mike? No. She didn't recall a man of his age named Mike. He could be a recent resident. Meg removed the big work glove and shook his hand. "Help would be appreciated." She slid the gloves back in place. "Are you new to Tyler, Mike?"

"Let's say it's been so long since I've been around here that it feels like new." He picked up the post digger and stabbed it into the dirt. After a couple of spikes, he had widened another hole.

"Okay, let's drop 'er in."

They secured the post and slid in the rails. "Only three more." Meg gave him a weary smile. "If you're willing."

"I'm willing and able."

After they'd tamped dirt around the last listing post, they stepped back and surveyed their work.

"You did a fine job, ma'am."

Meg beamed at the man. "You mean we did a fine job. You don't know how long it took me to get one post in place."

"Results are the same." He pulled the cap from his head and ran a hand through his hair. "A good fence line is important on a ranch. They take a lot of work. If there's more to be done, I'd like to offer my help on a more permanent basis."

Meg shook her head. "It's not my place to accept your offer." She thought about Larry's arm resting in a sling, the nonworking hay baler, the additions Hawk wanted to make on the cabin, the needed fence-mending and smiled up at Mike. "Sitting River's owner is tinkering with a hay baler just down the track. He might be interested in your offer."

He stuck the cap back on his head and stuffed his hands into deep front pockets. "Sorry. I thought you must be the lady of the land."

Meg smiled at the phrase. Lame Eagle had referred to his wife as the lady of the land. "I'm one of the Farrells from the ranch east of here."

He inclined his head and gave the post a kick. "It'll hold." He started toward his truck and stopped. "I'll be happy to put those tools in your truck."

Meg eyed the digger, shovel and hammer, rubbed

the blister on her hand and smiled at Mike. "Thanks. That would be great."

He gathered the tools, lifted a hand in farewell and headed for the trucks. A few minutes later, Meg heard the slam of the tailgate and then the rumble of the old truck as the vehicle rattled down the track.

She found her water bottle, took a long drink and wiped her hand across her mouth. The blister begged for a Band-Aid, and her body screamed for a hot bath. The work on the fence took longer than she anticipated, even with Mike's help, but it felt good to have done it. Really good.

The afternoon sun headed for the mountain peaks. Once it dropped behind the summit, darkness would fall fast. She took another drink and glanced toward the broken and crumbled pieces of cliff face.

A promising area, but not today.

She finished the bottle of water and headed back to check the progress being made on the cantankerous hay baler by a square-dancer foreman and a stubborn rancher.

Hawk stood beside the baler wiping his hands on a well-used cloth and kicked the nearest tire.

"I take it you've had no luck in getting it working." She handed him the keys to the pickup.

He kicked the tire again. "We did but it didn't run for long. Larry's gone back to Big House to dig up another spare part or two. It's a good thing you're back. I need to go into Tyler to get a part I know Larry won't find in the garage."

"Seriously? You need more parts?"

"I knew we were headed for major repairs. I hoped it would be later. A lot later."

Meg eyed his smudged shirt, grease-stained hands and the deep frown pulling on his brows. He looked disheartened and tired. "Speaking of repairs, come see what I did."

"I don't have time to look at rocks, Meggie."

"Not rocks." She squared her shoulders. "I fixed your fence."

Hawk tossed the soiled rag onto the toolbox at his feet. "You what?"

"Well, Mike and I fixed the fence."

"Mike?"

Meg nodded. "He's looking for work. Didn't he stop by?"

"No, and just as well. I can't afford to take on an extra hand. And what do you mean you fixed my fence?"

Meg pressed her lips into a tight line. "We were just being neighborly."

"I don't have a neighbor named Mike and to the best of my knowledge, neither do you."

"You know what I mean. We just secured a few posts. Anyway, it's my fault you hadn't had a chance to repair them yet."

"Your fault?"

"You would have been out here yesterday if you

hadn't helped me with the dog. Don't you want to see what a good job we did? You can kick one if you want."

"I've kicked enough things today. Climb in. I'll take you to Big House to get Calypso."

Meg climbed in and turned to face him the second he closed his door. "I was just trying to help."

He gripped the steering wheel with both hands before turning his head in her direction. "I appreciate the help. But the fact that you felt the need to step in and make repairs on my ranch makes me more aware of how much work my ranch needs." He leaned back against the seat.

Meg slid her hand along his forearm. "We all can use a little help sometimes."

"Sometimes, some of us need more than a little." Hawk started the engine and spun the truck around. Clouds of dust billowed behind them as the pickup sped down the track. Meg pulled her seat belt a little tighter. It was going to be a fast and bumpy ride home—and a silent one given the set of Hawk's lips while he most likely dwelt on the needs of Sitting River and his aged hay baler.

# *CHAPTER EIGHT*

"WHAT TOOK YOU so long, Aunt Meggie? You're the last one down for breakfast. Here." Five-year-old Ava handed Meg a small stuffed triceratops from the basket at her feet. "You sit next to Uncle John."

Puzzled, Meg took the plush green dinosaur and obediently sat in her assigned seat. Around the table, a different stuffed animal rested in front of each occupant.

She tipped her head toward John. "Why do we have stuffed animals on our plates?"

John shrugged.

Molly trotted over to Andrew. "I found the penguin."

"A penguin? I'd prefer a polar bear."

"But you look like a penguin." She pushed the stuffed animal at him.

"I do not look like a penguin."

"Yes, you do," Caroline stated.

Connor feigned a cough. "There's a photo at home of you in your best-man tux." He reached across the table and took the stuffed penguin and held it up. "You know, I can see the resemblance."

Andrew snatched the penguin. “And what were you given, big brother?”

Connor lifted a blue octopus from his lap and set it on the table. “I’m sure there’s a good reason for the octopus.”

“I bet. Now, can we eat? I prefer my sausage, biscuits and gravy hot.”

Ruby turned from the stove with a meat-laden platter and set it in the center of the table. “Let’s say grace.”

Following the Amen, Ava asked for individual jam pots. “Can we? Please?”

“*May* we. *Can* is for capability. *May* is for permission,” Heidi corrected her daughter. “Lucky for you I filled the cups earlier. They’re in the fridge.”

Connor held up his stuffed creature. “Wait a minute. I want to know why I have a very blue octopus and John has a jaguar.”

Caroline hopped off the stool, ran to her father and hugged him. “That’s because you’ll need extra arms to hug all of us when the twins are born.”

Pulling her onto his lap, Connor hugged her tight. “You’ve got that right, kiddo. Thanks for the octopus.”

Alison smiled at the two and patted her stomach. “The twins thank you, as well. What about the jaguar for your Uncle John?”

Caroline turned to John and shook her head. The dark blond ponytail swung back and forth. “Uncle John said he would only take a stuffy if it was a stuffed car. We don't have a car stuffy, so he found the jaguar."

John gestured to the small stuffed jaguar. "Tiny animal, powerful car. Now, may we eat?"

Between bites, the girls explained that the stuffed animals were part of a math problem set to Ava by her father during their last video chat. He suggested they take the number of stuffies owned by the three girls, add the number of adults at the breakfast table and subtract the number of children at the table. While it was an interesting math problem, Meg found their choice of animal for each human more intriguing.

Ruby's turtle supported her frequent comments about not moving as fast as she used to. The hedgehog sitting in front of her sister-in-law had everything to do with Alison's prickly pregnant condition. Hawk's stuffed husky pup looked a lot like Maiku, and her triceratops...well, a paleontologist gets a dinosaur.

Meg poured coffee for those wanting a second cup and listened to the breakfast chatter that covered weather, work and a counting of stuffed animals from the girls.

"We have an answer for Daddy." Ava snatched the slip of paper from her cousin.

Caroline snatched it back, folded it and tucked it under her plate. "Everyone has to guess."

John and Andrew suddenly needed second helpings of everything and busied themselves filling their plates. Connor offered a quick, "Ninety-nine. One hundred if you count Ava's extra stuffy."

"Good observation." Meg pointed to the island counter. "I just noticed the extra stuffed friend up there."

In front of each girl sat their own favorite. Caroline's gray, once-white lop-eared rabbit, Molly's brown bear and next to Ava sat a ginger kitten and a raccoon.

Ava picked up the raccoon and held it out. "He's for Daddy since Daddy isn't here."

Heidi took the stuffed animal from her daughter. "Why a raccoon, sweetie?"

"Last time we saw Daddy on the computer he had big black eyes on his head."

"Big black eyes on his head?" Heidi shook her head. "I don't remember big black eyes."

"He put them up on his helmet."

"Oh, the night vision goggles." She handed the raccoon back to Ava. "He'd been cleaning them when we logged on and he had shown Ava how they worked. At least he was only cleaning them and not having to use them."

Lansford cleared his throat. "He'll be home soon, honey. Let's keep that thought in the forefront."

"Yes," Heidi murmured and smiled at her daughter. "Soon."

Ruby gave a loud sniff, picked up her plate and placed it in the sink. "We all have work to do and it's time we get to it. I want you girls to gather your critters together before they end up in the dishwasher with the dirty dishes."

Molly gasped. "They can't get wet, Ruby. They'll spoil."

"Then, I suggest you hop off those stools and start collecting."

MEG DROPPED TO the ground and inspected the color and texture on a foot-long stripe in the fallen chunk of cliff face. Nothing. She sat back on her haunches. She'd picked up, examined and tossed aside dozens of pieces of crumbled and broken stone. Nothing. Now, the dark and ominous morning clouds were nowhere to be seen and late afternoon sun baked everything it touched.

She pulled a water bottle from her backpack and drank deeply before dousing her bandanna. Gently she draped the damp cloth around her neck, closed her eyes and sighed.

Calypso snorted.

"Don't complain. You had your drink already and you're in the shade."

Meager stretches of shadow from the cliff covered her horse. Unfortunately, the shade did not extend to the stones at her feet, and they were too heavy to move. She wet the bandanna again, ran it over her throat and down her arms before tying it around her forehead. She selected a small brush from the array of tools laid out across the ground and carefully swept the soft bristles over the dark stripe in the stone. "There must be something here," she grumbled. "Anything. Big. Little. Anything."

"Like what?"

Meg squeezed her eyes shut, huffed and shook her head before placing the tool beside the others. She looked up at Hawk. He sat comfortably atop Wickiup. His favorite Stetson covered his head and sunglasses hid his eyes.

Hawk leaned forward in the saddle. "You get pretty occupied with rocks and forget about time." He slid out of the saddle. "Your mom called Big House. She's worried. She said you've been gone all day."

"Mom worried. There's a shocker." Meg straightened her back and rose. "I haven't been gone *all* day." She pulled her phone from a side pocket of her cargo pants. "I did try to call." She held out the phone. "No service."

He plucked the dark glasses from his face and dropped them into his shirt pocket. "Do you have any idea how long I've been looking for you?" He fixed her with a hard stare.

She returned his gaze. His voice could bite through you, but his eyes, Meg knew were the truth of Joe Hawk. She didn't see anger in his eyes, she saw concern.

"I'm fine." She reached down and picked up

one of the Bent Fork rifles. "I brought protection against mad coyotes or aggressive mountain lions."

He eyed the rifle. "Loaded?"

She gave him a saccharine smile. "Yes."

"Safety on?"

"Of course. I wouldn't want to accidentally shoot a friend sneaking up on me."

"A mountain lion wouldn't remind you to remove the safety once it's crept up on you."

"Calypso would warn me if a cat approached. Like Wickiup, she has a keen sense of smell."

"She didn't warn you Wickiup and I were coming."

"She obviously doesn't deem either of you a threat." Meg slid a glance at the mare peacefully munching on wild grass. "We may need to rethink that."

"Come on. I'll ride back to Bent Fork with you. I want to have a word with Andrew."

"Thanks, but I'm not ready to leave." She squatted beside the array of tools. "I want to search a little longer."

"For what?"

"Fossils. I told you yesterday that I wanted to come back and look around. You said it would be okay."

Hawk stepped closer and eyed the tumble of broken cliff face. "I did." He tapped the rock with his foot. "Find anything?"

Meg's shoulders sagged. "No. But I know there's

something here. Somewhere. Fossils have been found throughout Colorado." She gazed out on the valley. "Just imagine what it would have looked like or sounded like if one of the mighty beasts came stomping along chasing its dinner."

"Or being chased for dinner." He stuck the dark glasses back in place. "You may not think you've been gone all day, but it is getting late. How about we find some dinner of our own."

"I'm not hungry. I ate the peanut butter and jelly sandwich I packed. How about you find food and I keep searching."

"You can come back tomorrow. If there are any fossils around here, they're not going anywhere."

Lengthening shadows stretched into the valley as the sun began to dip behind the higher peaks. She had to admit there wouldn't be good light much longer and she'd hate to miss something. "Between the earth's orbital movement lessening my working light, nonmobile fossils, if any, and you grousing about food, I may as well call it a day. Let me pack up my tools." She scooped her brushes and picks into her backpack and strapped it onto Calypso's saddle horn.

"I'm going to miss fieldwork."

"Miss it? You can come back tomorrow."

"Not this." She gestured to the pile of rocks. "I won't be able to participate in long-range fieldwork once the museum opens. I'm looking forward to the work, don't get me wrong, but I will miss being out in the open spaces."

"You sure you need to return to Michigan? Sounds like you might be caught inside quite a bit."

She'd pondered the same thought on her ride up to the cliff. Having been kept inside so much of her early years, she reveled in the great open spaces of Colorado. "It's where the job is located." She pressed her palms to her abdomen. "You had to mention dinner. My stomach heard and wants to know when it can be sated."

"I'll remember that the next time I want to get you away from your rocks."

HAWK AND MEG hung their hats on pegs and stepped into the kitchen before dusk settled. Her father stood between the sink and dishwasher loading dinner dishes. Her mother sat at one end of the table with a cup of coffee and a stack of papers. John sat at the other end piling chicken wings and legs onto his plate before pushing the platter to Hawk, who had pulled out a chair and sat.

Caroline, Molly and Ava swiveled on their island stools taking turns adding shortbread cookies to a growing tower of sugary rounds. "We get to have all the cookies we can build into a tower."

Meg plucked an apple from the fruit bowl in the center of the island. "Where is the rest of the family?"

"Ruby is playing cards at the senior center. Alison is upstairs resting. Everyone else is out tending to one errand or another," answered her father. "And, girls, we agreed a nine-cookie tower is sufficient for dessert. That's three cookies each."

"If we can make a tower of twelve cookies, we could have four cookies each."

"The math is correct. The idea that you will be allowed extra cookies is not." Lansford handed Hawk a plate. "Help yourself, Hawk."

Joanna placed her reading glasses on the stack of papers. "Thank you for seeing Meggie home. Where did you find her?"

"I wasn't lost, Mom."

"I found her hunched over a mound of fallen cliff face waiting for it to reveal buried fossils."

"Technically, I did not throw myself over a random rock and beg for fossil locations. I noticed the area yesterday while Hawk and Larry worked on the hay baler. The eroding cliff and weathering sandstone make a promising area for fossil hunting."

Her father took his wife's empty cup, placed it in the dishwasher and closed the door. "Still having trouble with that baler?"

"That machine is nothing but trouble."

"Excuse me." Caroline cleared her throat. "Aunt Meggie, don't you fix dinosaurs?"

"I don't fix them in the sense that someone can fix a broken bike to be ridden again. I find their bones and put them together, so we know what they looked like millions of years ago."

"Oh. You look for broken dinosaurs?"

Hawk watched a smile tip the corners of Meggie's mouth.

"Well, Miss Caroline, I will happily meet you in the living room after dinner with a cup of hot chocolate and a special book of mine that explains some of the things I do with dinosaur bones after I clean them up. Okay?"

Caroline patted her hands together. "May we have whipped cream on our hot chocolate?"

"Okay with me."

Ava swiveled on her island stool. "I want whipped cream and hot chocolate, too."

"Me, too," Molly added. "I want hot chocolate and whipped cream, but I don't want to listen."

"You don't have to listen if you don't find it interesting." Meggie gently tugged her niece's ponytail. "But I hope you will."

John carried his plate to the sink. "I don't find any of this interesting. But I would like to know more about the work going on at Lame Eagle's old cabin. Meggie said you've made changes."

"My grandfather did a great job with the foundation. It has good bones, and the chimney is in good shape. I plan to expand when I can make the time."

John slapped Hawk on the back. "You know where to find me if you need a hand."

"Yes. Under the hood of your Mustang."

"John's right," Lansford said. "I hope you know we're here if you need us, son. You don't need to do it alone."

"I'll keep that in mind. The fact is, when I find the time, I'm actually enjoying doing the work on my own." The two men exchanged brief nods. "Thanks for the offers of help, though. I appreciate them. I like to think I'm getting better at accepting them." He glanced back at Meggie. "I have to be in town tomorrow. I can swing by and take you to TCC for your meeting with Mrs. Burlew. If you want."

"You sure?"

"Yep."

She gave him a grateful smile. "I'd like that."

"Walk out with me? We can discuss time."

On her way to the door, Meg kissed each niece on the top of their head. "I'll be right back, and we can have our hot chocolate and talk about dinosaurs."

"Molly thinks dinosaurs are scary and we should have our talk before it gets really dark," informed her sister.

Meg squeezed Molly in a tight hug. "Our talk won't be at all scary. I promise. Okay?"

"Okay." Molly offered a hesitant smile. "If you promise."

Meg and Hawk walked past the hooks holding hats and jackets and stepped into the deepening twilight.

"Do you really need to go into town?"

"I really need a new part or a used one if I can get it. And I really need to do this." He leaned forward and kissed her cheek. "Thank you."

Meg swallowed. "For what?"

"For mending my fence. For putting water out for my dog. For…" He paused and shoved his hands into the front pockets of his jeans. "For caring."

"Well, I—"

"Aunt Meggie!" The screened door creaked open. Ava leaned out. "We're ready for your dinosaur talk."

"I've been summoned. See you in the morning."

MEG OPENED THE passenger door of Hawk's pickup and brushed dog hair off the seat before climbing up. She dropped her backpack at her feet and clipped her seat belt in place. "I don't anticipate the meeting with Mrs. Burlew to take long. Want to meet for lunch at the Drop-By Café after?"

"Maybe."

His clipped tone held something more than uncertainty about joining her for lunch. "You need to do something besides pick up a part for the baler?"

"I have an appointment weighing on my mind."

He pulled onto the road and fixed his gaze straight ahead.

"I'll listen if you need to talk."

"Thanks, but talking won't change anything."

Meg left him to his thoughts and turned her attention to the vista that marked Colorado as one of the most unique and beautiful places in the country—the Rocky Mountains.

The rugged peaks had been thrust skyward and left to endure the whims of nature millennium after millennium. She never ceased to feel awed by them. Never took them for granted. She understood what forces of nature transpired to birth the massive mountain ranges. The movement of tectonic plates, the release of lava, the ebb and flow of inland seas. Mother Nature at her finest.

The higher peaks still carried snowpack on their shoulders. Avalanche danger hovered in areas prone to slides, and Rocky Mountain wildlife continued to thrive. Bighorn sheep, elk, mountain lions, coyote, fox, the little pika and birds of all types inhabited the mountaintops and valleys. Those were the living creatures.

Other creatures had once populated the area. Allosaurus, triceratops, stegosaurus, apatosaurus, ornithomimus, even the massive T. rex had been found in this area of the country.

Hawk slowed the truck and turned into the community college parking lot. "Where to?"

"Wow, time flies in the midst of stimulating conversation."

"Sorry."

"It must be an important meeting."

"It could be."

The redbrick buildings of TCC's small campus created a large square. A three-tiered fountain marked the center of the campus. From there four walkways sliced through the open courtyard. One of four main buildings anchored the end of each path. Closest to her sat the Science Building housing the geology department. "Here's perfect."

Meg grabbed her backpack and slid out of the pickup. "What about meeting at the café?"

"If I'm not waiting here in the parking lot, I'll meet you at the Drop-By. Good luck."

"Thanks." Meg watched him drive away. Something gnawed at him. She hoped he could get whatever it was settled quickly and to a positive end. She hoped she could do the same. She slung the backpack over her shoulder. Now to get some clarity and answers regarding the professor and his class. A simple, quick in-and-out meeting.

"YOU'RE LATE." Hawk tossed the words at the man climbing from the green pickup.

"Sorry." The man closed the door and patted the hood as he walked past. "This old thing isn't very reliable."

"Neither are you."

Michael Hawk lowered his gaze to the pea-sized gravel designating the small area as a parking lot and worked the toe of his boot into the loose layer of stones.

Hawk flicked a glance at his own worn boots.

He folded his arms across his chest. "I'm here. What do you want?"

"A chance to prove I've changed." Michael pushed more loose pebbles with his boot. A small mound of stones grew between his foot and the front tire of his pickup. "I've learned a lot over the years. I've figured out how to do as my dad told me."

"And that is?"

"Give more and take less."

"You've been taking from Sitting River."

"A few rabbits." Michael raised his head. "I've cleaned up the storm shelter in return."

"You think a tidy storm shelter is enough to warrant forgiveness."

"I think the work I've done on the shelter pays for a few rabbits."

"That's not what I meant."

"I know."

"You were on Meyer Ridge hunting rabbits a few days ago."

His father nodded.

"How long have you been trespassing on Sitting River?"

Michael smiled. A tight smile that tipped the corner of his mouth. "At least you didn't ask how long have I been trespassing on *your* ranch."

"Sitting River is *my* ranch. But you know that."

"I know Lame Eagle made sure my name was

removed and excluded from all legal documents pertaining to Sitting River and everything on it."

"Do you blame him?"

Michael lowered his gaze to the pile of stones and slowly placed his foot on top of the mound and pressed. Stones rolled from under his boot, leaving a deep impression of the worn leather sole and heel. "I blame only myself."

Hawk took in the weatherworn boots, the frayed hem of his father's jeans, the dark hair streaked with gray and in need of a cut. He slid a look at the rusted and dented pickup. Not as shiny as it had been the day Michael Hawk had driven past his son and away from Sitting River. Assuming it was the same truck.

"I don't expect you to open your arms or your ranch to me. Forgiveness has many years to climb."

"If at all," Hawk murmured. "What do you want from me?"

"I need a place to stay for a few weeks. I'd like your permission to stay at the Meyer Ridge storm shelter. In return, I'll make repairs to the chimney, and I'll cut up the area deadwood for the coming winter stockpile."

Hawk unfolded his arms and shoved his hands into the front pockets of his jeans. "That's it? No petitioning to come back to Sitting River? No pleading to be my dad?"

His father rubbed his hand over the thick stubble covering his cheeks and chin. "That's it. For now."

A harsh snort burst from Hawk. "For now. And later?"

"That's up to you." Michael pulled the baseball cap from his head, pushed his fingers through his hair and stuck the cap back in place. "I hope to earn your forgiveness, if not your respect."

"Don't hold your breath for either of those." Hawk opened his pickup door. "You have my okay to stay in the storm shelter. For now. Be mindful when and where you're hunting rabbit on my ranch." He climbed into his truck and sped off, hoping to outdistance the memories. Loss and regret flooding his mind.

## *CHAPTER NINE*

AN HOUR AND a half after Hawk had dropped her at TCC, Meg rushed into the parking lot with a thick manila folder tucked under one arm and several long tubes tucked under the other. Hawk's gray pickup sat near the end of the lot. He'd dropped the tailgate and perched on the edge talking with her brother. Andrew leaned against the back of the truck in his business clothes consisting of a crisp white button-down shirt and khaki pants instead of his usual worn jeans and T-shirt. He hadn't mentioned anything this morning about coming into town. Apparently, her business was everyone's business, but the sentiment wasn't reciprocal.

"What are you doing here, Andrew?"

"Hey, Meggie. How did it go with Mrs. Burlew? I hope they fired the professor."

"Apparently, Professor Nelson told them two weeks ago that he was taking an indefinite leave of absence and had arranged for me to teach his class until he returned."

"Wait a minute." Andrew straightened. "He told

them *two* weeks ago. You weren't even home two weeks ago."

"Someone told him I planned to be home for a lengthy visit before my job at the museum started. He told Mrs. Burlew that he'd talked with me and that I had gladly accepted the temporary position."

"He had no right," Andrew said.

Meg held up a hand. "I agree."

Hawk slid off the tailgate. "And?"

"Everything is settled. I'm not really hungry for lunch and would rather head home, if that's okay with you. Or I could ride with Andrew if you're not ready."

Hawk closed the tailgate. "I'm ready." He opened the passenger door for her and looked at Andrew. "Don't forget to check on the excavator. I walked over the area and there are a lot of large rocks to clear before we can level for the foundation fill."

"Will do." Andrew displayed a thumbs-up and strode toward Main Street.

Hawk climbed into the pickup. "Are you sure you're ready to head back to Bent Fork?"

"Yes. What's with getting an excavator?"

"Andrew and I are working on a project."

Meg made a tsking sound. "He's involved you in his new grain scheme, hasn't he?"

Hawk put the truck in Reverse. "He has a good idea."

"I hope so. Dad didn't take to the idea, and I think that disappointed Andrew."

"Andrew has worked through this more than Lansford realizes. He's determined to make it pay off."

"And you're determined to get an ancient baler pulling its weight. Did you get the part?"

"I had to order it."

"Another delay."

"That's the way it goes sometimes. We'll manage."

She studied his hands on the wheel as he maneuvered through the pedestrian traffic of campus. He had working man's hands, weathered, calloused, scarred and capable of both strength and gentleness.

Once they left the parking lot, he gave her a sideways glance. "What really happened in there?"

Meg sighed. "I intended to tell Mrs. Burlew that the professor had no right to promise anything in my name. And I planned to tell her that they needed to start looking for the replacement for his class immediately." She sighed. "That's what I had planned."

"But?"

"She was in a meeting and while I waited, I came up with two suggestions that were more kind. One, that they should cancel the class until they are able to locate an instructor to manage the full time required. The other option, which I liked more the longer I thought about it, is for me to teach the course while they search for an instructor to take the latter half of the course."

"I sense another *but*, or a *however*."

She chuckled. "Clever you. Before Mrs. Burlew's meeting ended, I received a call from my boss, Dr. Vanover. We went over the continuing construction issues and delays, the time for receiving our content for the museum, setting up exhibits, office space, the paleo lab and a host of other details. Bottom line is I can't begin to do anything at the museum until the construction is completed and it looks like that could add an additional three to four weeks."

"Giving you time to teach the entire eight weeks."

"Exactly. Things could change, necessitating my return to Michigan before the class concludes, and I explained that to Mrs. Burlew. She agreed to begin a search for another instructor just in case. So, you are looking at the temporary teacher for TCC's summer geology class."

"That explains the armful of items you carried out."

Meg adjusted the folders and charts on her lap. "Hawk, I really liked what she had to say about the program. Rachael and I have discussed holding classes at the museum and field trips. I hate admitting the professor could be right about this being a wonderful opportunity, but teaching this class could actually benefit me and the Mayfield.

"I also thought about what Alison and Heidi said last night at dinner about my passion for earth sciences and how I could offer a different perspective of the Rocky Mountains to the students. Everyone sees the beauty, the majesty, the awesomeness, but not everyone understands how they were formed. They may know the basics, but they don't truly see it." Meg paused and shifted to face him. "You know, it could be fun. At least until they find someone else to teach the class."

"How long do you think that will take?"

"I don't know. Tyler's a small community. They'll probably have to search outside the area. Maybe outside of Colorado."

"So, it could take some time."

"It could."

"There's a stop we need to make before heading home. I hope you're not in a hurry."

"I am eager to get back to the area I searched yesterday. I still think it's a good spot for hunting."

"How so?"

Meg smiled. Paleontological conversation often drew blank stares and casual nods. Rarely did someone show a true interest. Hawk had asked about her work. She didn't need to be asked again. For the next several minutes, she rambled on about the joining of geology and paleontology until Hawk stopped the truck.

"You stopped."

"You noticed."

"Am I boring you?"

"Surprisingly, no. However, we need to get the dog. I'm glad you asked about keeping him on Bent Fork."

Meg glanced at the long, low building at the end of the small parking lot. A teal-colored door, decorated with images of cats, allowed entry to one end of the building. The door at the other end, painted a bright yellow and stenciled with dogs of all sizes, welcomed clients and their canine pets.

"Me, too. It took a bit of cajoling for Mom and Ruby to agree, but they did with two conditions. The dog is not to be in the house, and I am responsible for him. The old shed behind the hay barn will work just fine. It's full of winter stuff like snowplow blades, a snowblower, bags of salt and stuff waiting to be carted off. No one goes out there this time of year. It's the perfect place while we continue looking for a good home for him."

Hawk slid out of his seat and walked behind the pickup to the passenger door and opened it. "Let's get our dog."

MEG LIFTED THE plastic jug out of the sink and screwed on the cap. Now to put fresh water in the dog's water bowl, add two cups of food to the dog's food bowl, check the bandages on the stitched wounds, make sure the cone is secure around his neck to prevent chewing on any bandaged areas and get to Chalk Meadow and continue searching for fossils.

"Where are you going with a gallon of milk?" Ruby stepped into the kitchen carrying a handful of freshly snipped herbs. "I need some of that for the girls' lunch."

"It's a jug for water, Ruby."

"Water? Why?"

"I'm going to clean Calypso's muzzle. She's been pushing dirt and mud around and her muzzle is dirty."

"Why not use the hose in the stable?"

"Calypso doesn't like the hose. It makes her skittish. I don't know why. She backs up and shakes her head and snorts. It's not easy to do a thorough job with her behaving like that."

"You be careful around that animal."

"Calypso's as gentle as they come. Except," Meg quickly added, "except when you approach her with a water hose."

"Uh-huh." Ruby glanced from the jug to Meg. "Just be careful."

Meg sidestepped to the door. "I'm also going to put fresh water out for the dog. Then, I'll be back to make a sandwich. I'm going up to Chalk Meadow to take another look around that tumble of cliff face and hopefully avoid Hawk's cows."

"Since you're heading in that direction, will you do me a favor before you go up there?"

"Of course."

Ruby dropped the herbs in a bowl and began rummaging in the drawer next to the sink. She pulled out a length of purple ribbon, snipped off several inches and handed it to Meg. "There are some columbines growing on the right side of the road just before you get to the cemetery. Would you pick a few, tie them with this and place them on Anne Hawk's grave? It's been some time since I've been over, and I'm full of remembering her today."

Meg heard the melancholy in Ruby's voice. Old memories were surfacing. She set the jug on the trestle table and waited. Ruby needed to say more about her friend.

"It's been almost twenty-four years since she passed. Today I feel like I could wander up to Big House and find her sitting on the porch swing with a basketful of apples at her feet waiting to be peeled and a pitcher of lemonade on that little wicker table."

"I have a memory, more smells than vision, of lemonade, apples and a porch full of people." Meg puckered her lips. "But maybe that was a family thing here and not at Sitting River."

"A family thing." Ruby looked around the room, ran her hand over the warm wood of the Farrells' kitchen table. "You know your grandmother Moira hired me."

Meg nodded.

"Mrs. Ruby Jean Turner, a bride of two months

and new to Colorado. She hired me to help with the house and the ranch while our husbands served their country overseas. We became great friends, family really, while the men were away, and the world felt like it was tilting.

"Well, Edward Farrell finally came home, a little worse for wear. Your grandmother worked like a hired hand out on the ranch while I, the now Widow Turner, held up the house and helped with the children.

"On Saturdays, Anne Hawk would come to visit, and we women would sit and talk for hours. Not all of our talks were easy. Michael Hawk worried his mother. He went down to the School of Mines for a few months after high school, then dropped out and got married." She snapped her fingers. "Just like that. He and Belinda stood before a judge, then went straight to Cheyenne without stopping for Anne and Lame Eagle to meet their new daughter-in-law. That hurt Anne."

Meg sat on the edge of the bench. "I don't remember Hawk's father."

"I don't think you ever met him. He and Belinda didn't often visit. In fact, Anne didn't know she had a grandson until Hawk was almost a year old. Belinda had called Sitting River one day and asked to speak to Michael. He'd told her he had to help his father with something on the ranch and would be gone a day or two. She told Anne that it had been over a week and would Anne please let Michael know his wife and baby were getting low on food. Anne didn't have the heart to tell her daughter-in-law that Michael hadn't been to Sitting River but twice since the wedding and both times he'd stayed less than thirty minutes."

"If he wasn't on Sitting River, where was he?"

"They found out later he'd gone gambling somewhere in Nevada. Anne loaded the back seat of her pickup with bags of groceries and things for the baby and asked if I would ride with her to Cheyenne. On our way out, she picked a posy of columbines and tied them with a purple ribbon. Said she wanted to give her daughter-in-law something other than necessities, something beautiful from Sitting River. She said wildflowers were gifts from heaven to please the eyes, lighten the heart and offer hope. Anne was like that, giving a body what they needed and offering a little something extra from the heart." Ruby held out the ribbon.

Meg tucked the purple strip in the front pocket of her khaki shorts and hugged Ruby. "I'll pick the prettiest columbines I can find."

With a sniff, Ruby pulled a handkerchief from her apron pocket and blew her nose. "Thank you, darlin'," she said and turned back to the sink.

Jug in hand, Meg slung her backpack over her shoulder and plucked keys from the peg. She paused at the screened door and swiped a knuckle under her eyes. The Widow Turner missed her old friend and there was nothing Meg could do to help except make sure the flowers placed on Anne Hawk's gravesite represented the beauty of the friendship the two women had shared.

Calypso greeted Meg with playful nudges and provided less resistance to having her muzzle cleaned than expected. A reward of apple pieces brought more coltish nudges from the pinto before she was returned to her stall, giving Meg an opportunity to refill the jug without interference from Calypso.

The dog welcomed her with tail wags and tried to nuzzle her knee. She removed the cone and knelt beside him. "We can't nuzzle with that thing around your neck, can we? Now, how about a short walk?" They made a quick necessity walk behind the building, giving Meg a chance to see how he moved. "Good boy. You're doing just fine. We'll get you a good home soon. I promise. Somebody must want a fella as handsome as you."

While the dog gobbled the dry food, she checked the bandages. They looked dry and relatively clean. She fluffed the fur between his ears and replaced the cone. "Sorry about that, but it's necessary for now. I'll be back to check on you later."

She returned to the kitchen. Ruby had two PBJ sandwiches tucked into a storage bag. Meg dropped the sandwiches in her backpack, kissed Ruby's cheek and left to pick columbines for Widow Ruby Jean Turner's friend.

FIRS AND PINES lined one side of the narrow lane

that led to Bellwood Cemetery. A low wall of fieldstone created a solid boundary on the other. Past an arched wrought-iron entrance, gravestones of all shapes and sizes marked the repose of deceased family and friends of Tyler, Colorado, for the last one hundred-plus years.

Except for holidays, Meg rarely encountered other visitors on her trips to sit between her grandparents' gravesites or the two times she'd sat at the foot of Lame Eagle's. Today an old green pickup chugged down the lane away from the cemetery. She maneuvered her pickup closer to the stone wall, giving the other vehicle room to pass. Columbines in one hand, and white yarrow and black-eyed Susans in the other, she threaded her way through the stones to the matching granite markers of her grandparents.

She placed the small bunch of white yarrow at the base of her grandfather's gravestone and the cluster of black-eyed Susans at her grandmother's. Edward and Moira Farrell. Pioneers made of sturdy stuff. Hardworking ranchers dedicated to family and country. Meg had been told they carried truth and humor in their front pockets and gentleness and determination in their back pockets, all ready to dole out when needed. She wished, not for the first time, that she remembered them.

Ruby's morning musings lingered with Meg. She wished she knew more about her own Farrell and Bennett families and the Hawks. One day she would pin everyone down and get details, memories, stories and the history about all of them. One day someone else might want to know.

She sat on the ground between the stones of her grandparents and chatted as if they were sitting beside her enjoying the cool breeze and quiet setting. "I have a new job in Michigan. It offers a lot of responsibility. I'll miss coming to talk with you. I'll miss the rest of the family, too. And I'll miss being here when Keith returns. And the birth of the twins. And I'll miss Bent Fork. And the Reeds. And these wonderfully awesome mountains. And the dog. And so much more."

"What about me?"

Meg gasped. "One of these days, Joe Hawk, your sneaking up on me is going to give me a heart attack or you bodily injury."

Hawk held up his hands. "I wasn't sneaking. Honest." He squatted beside her. And lifted the posy of columbines. "Pretty."

"Ruby asked me to place these by your grandmother's stone." She took the flowers. "She's missing your grandmother today."

He stood and held out a hand. "I'll walk with you. It's been a while since I've visited."

They stepped around large granite markers and small slabs all etched with names and dates until they reached the resting place of the bodies of Anne and Thomas Hawk. A bouquet of columbines held together by a strip of rawhide lay at the base of Anne's gravestone. Meg glanced at Hawk. "Did you bring these?"

Hawk shook his head. "I wasn't planning to stop but I saw the pickup and…"

"And?"

"I thought you might want some company. Maybe you don't. Or maybe you don't want my company."

She'd been in his company quite a lot the last week and she found herself looking forward to time with him. She wanted to make the most of any time with Joe Hawk before she left for Michigan.

*Why?* What could possibly come of more time with Hawk? He had Sitting River. She had a job in Michigan twelve hundred miles away. Nothing more than their continued friendship could come from more time together. Except. She felt grounded in his company. She felt cared about in a way that wasn't obligatory or familial. She looked down at the bouquet of columbines. "If you didn't bring those, I wonder who did. There was someone leaving as I came in. Maybe it was him?"

"A man?"

Meg pulled her mouth into a tight moue. "I think it was a man. Baseball cap, denim jacket." She shrugged. "But it could as easily have been a woman."

Hawk knelt and fingered the bouquet. "Anyone could have left these. Ruby wasn't my grandmother's only friend."

"No, she wasn't." Meg placed Ruby's flowers next to the others and blew a kiss. "From the Widow Turner." She moved in step with Hawk toward the arched exit. "What's waiting for you today? More work on the baler? Keeping your cattle from seeking greener pastures?"

"Wish it were that exciting." Hawk slowed and shortened his stride. "I'm replacing the upstairs toilet at Big House before Jenna and her family get here."

"When is that?"

"Not sure. Some doctor visits had to be rescheduled for their youngest."

They paused at the wrought-iron arch to make way for an elderly couple entering the cemetery. Hawk smiled and tipped his hat. "Good afternoon, Mr. Willis, Mrs. Willis." Meg bade them hello and watched the couple step carefully across the uneven ground. The gentleman carried a tote bag slung over his shoulder and the woman stabbed the ground with a walking stick every other step.

Hawk stopped under the arch. "Wait. I want to make sure they make it okay."

The couple entered a fenced plot that held a stone bench, and a grave marker of thick granite topped with a delicately carved angel. They stood in front of the marker, holding hands and in unison bent and kissed the smooth stone.

"Hawk, do you know who's buried there?"

"Their daughter, Lizzie. I've seen them here

over the years. They come, clean away any weeds and such and then sit and have lunch and tell their daughter all about their week."

"How old was she? Lizzie?"

"Eight."

"Eight." She glanced at the couple. "They've been coming here all these years. That's a long time to miss someone."

"All these years is a long time to love someone. Even if it's only the memory of someone."

"Memory of someone," Meg murmured. She would carry memories with her when she left for Michigan. Memories to draw on when life reached the extremes of overwhelming and sensory overload, or moments of loneliness. As they walked away from the cemetery, her fingers brushed against his. "I will miss you, too," she whispered.

He closed his fingers around hers. "Ditto."

# *CHAPTER TEN*

MEG SIPPED FROM her last bottle of water, closed the top and put it aside. Two empty bottles and an uneaten peanut butter and jelly sandwich lay near the backpack. A strong sun beat down as it had all afternoon. She ignored the heat, ignored the rumbling in her stomach and focused on the ground.

Selecting a small pick from the tools laid out on a strip of tan cloth beside her, she scraped around the only bit of fossil she'd found, a tooth from who knows what kind of creature. Only more exposure would tell. She picked, chipped, scratched and pushed dirt around for over an hour. She set the brush and pick aside and rose, stretched and started a precise and steady search of the jumbled detritus. Up and down, back and forth. She'd even crawled on her knees until they were surely bruised.

Nothing.

She squatted next to the rock and surveyed the color variations until everything blended together in one color. Nothing. Even the cows had stopped their mooing.

Another sound intruded on the silence. A man-made sound. Whistling. Meg lifted her gaze and blinked against the glare of a lowering sun that outlined a horse and rider. "Hawk. I should have known you'd show up."

"Better me than a hungry mountain lion or that coyote."

She watched him slide from the saddle, a man in control of every muscle and every thought. His lips formed a straight hard line. Meg stood and braced herself. The thoughts were not good. She squared her shoulders and ran a quick flick of her tongue across her dry lips. "Don't tell me my mother sent you?"

"No. I didn't think you'd still be up here. Being a responsible rancher, I decided to check." He pushed the cuff of his shirt off his wrist and glanced at his watch. "Do you have any idea of the time?"

Meg pushed back the sleeve of her own cotton work shirt. No watch. She looked back to Hawk and shrugged.

Hawk glared. "Late."

"Late is a relative time frame."

"The sun will drop behind those peaks soon and dark will fall fast."

Meg anchored her hands on her hips. "We've done this before. I don't need you coming to find me like I'm lost cattle. I'll head home soon."

He looked her up and down.

Meg shifted her weight. She knew she looked a mess. She always looked a mess when she worked in the field. Her sweat-stained shirt clung uncomfortably to her back. Her shorts were streaked down the sides with a mixture of sweat and dirt from the countless times she'd wiped her palms on them. Curls that refused to be bound by elastic bands, clips or hats hung in a wild tangle around her face. She didn't usually care about her appearance. The sweat, the dust and dirt were all a part of her job. Nothing mattered but the task at hand. Except now, the way he looked at her, it mattered. She pushed her hair under her hat and plucked at her damp shirt. "What? I'm working."

Hawk scanned the stretch of dry earth and tumbled stone surrounding her. "You really expect to find something here?"

"I've already found something." She rubbed her palms down the sides of her khaki shorts. "Want to see?"

"Have you found anything more interesting than a massive pile of dirt and rocks?"

"Yes. A small piece of a fossil. Well, a fragment really." She held up a fist-sized chunk of rock with a nearly three-inch bullet-shaped mound protruding from the stone. "It's a fossilized tooth, and by the shape and size I'd say it's a sauropod tooth."

"One tooth?"

"A sauropod tooth. Sauropods were massive with tiny heads, huge bodies, and usually had long tails."

"Okay, you found a tooth."

"A really old, fossilized tooth."

"Okay. How much longer do you plan to be out here? I'm heading home and I'd rather not have you losing track of time."

"I don't lose track of time. I get involved in my work."

"Involved to the point of forgetting to keep the rifle close enough to protect you." He pointed to the rifle leaning against her backpack.

"From what?" Meg flung her arms wide. "There's nothing around me but dirt, some sage, scrub grass, a few scrawny trees, a lot of rocks, a slow-running stream out in the valley, an even slower clump of cows, a handful of birds waiting to get the crumbs from my sandwich—" she shaded her eyes and looked up "—and some non-threatening blue Colorado sky. Not even a chance to be struck by lightning and no strikes to start a wildfire. No chance of a flash flood since we haven't had more than a few drops of rain the last five days. The only danger I see is a possible sunburn, and that's a slim chance since I slather sunscreen on every exposed bit of flesh." She patted the canvas hat covering her head. "Even my head is covered.

"I may not have worked out on the ranch day after day like most of you, but I've seen what our mountain wildlife, the feral animals, the predators can do in their effort to survive. I'm sorry a mountain lion is taking your cattle for food. I am.

I just wish you would all trust me to take care of myself. I'll head home soon. Right now, I want to keep searching for the mouth this tooth came from." She stepped back, stumbled over the array of tools and fell across an upturned pick.

"Ow." Pain radiated from her knee and ankle. Meg clutched her knee to her chest and rocked back and forth. Blood seeped between her fingers. Tears stung her eyes. "Ow, ow, ow, ow."

Hawk dropped to his knees. "Let me see." He pulled her hands away. "Do you have a first-aid kit?"

"My pack," she muttered between clenched teeth.

He snatched the pack and turned it upside down. Out tumbled a hodge-podge of items including a camera and the traditional first-aid box with its red cross. Using wipes, butterfly Band-Aids, and gauze, he deftly tended the wound.

Meg flinched and grounded her teeth as he worked.

"Sorry. I'm being as gentle as I can."

"I know." She tried not to move as he tore the strip of gauze and tied it tightly around her knee.

"There." He sat back on his heels, took her hand and slid two fingers over the vein at the base of her wrist. "How do you feel?"

"I feel like a fool. I tripped over my own tools."

"Seriously, Meggie. Dizzy? Lightheaded?"

"I'm fine except for the fact that my ankle is

throbbing like crazy and my knee has a gash the size of the Grand Canyon."

"Is your tetanus current?"

"Of course." She studied the bandaged knee. "You did a nice job."

"First aid goes hand in hand with ranching." He reached for her. "Okay, up you go."

Meg stiffened. "Wait. Go where?"

"I'm putting you up on Wickiup with me. You shouldn't ride alone."

"Hawk, it's not that bad."

"That gash needs stitches."

"Are you some expert on stitches?" Meg glanced at the wrapping around her knee. Spots of blood seeped through the gauze. Still bleeding. Not good. "What about Calypso?"

"You can hold the reins and she can run beside us. Big House is closer than Bent Fork. We'll leave her there when we get the pickup." He reached for her again.

"Wait a minute. I need to get my gear." She squirmed back and attempted to stand. Pain shot from ankle to knee. She crumpled like a puppet cut from its strings.

Hawk bent, scooped her into his arms and marched toward his horse.

"My gear. I can't leave my gear. That's my camera, my new rope, my lucky canteen, my tools and my inhaler."

He opened his mouth to protest but then closed

it and settled her on Wickiup. "Try not to bleed all over Wickiup while I get your stuff."

"Thank you." She checked the makeshift bandage. Blood saturated the cloth. "You don't need to be careful. Just shove them into my backpack."

HAWK WALKED OUT of the clinic carrying a well-worn size-seven hiking boot. Meg hobbled behind him. Aluminum crutches stuck out from under her arms and yards of white material covered her knee. A stretchy beige wrapping bound her diagnosed sprained, but thankfully not broken, ankle, making it impossible to wear her right shoe.

"Let me carry you down the steps."

"I know how to go down steps," she snapped.

"On crutches?"

Meg leaned on the crutches and sighed heavily.

He raised his hands in surrender. "I'll get the truck and then we'll get you home."

"Home." Meg stumbled backward.

Hawk steadied her. "Easy."

"You know what going home will be like?"

"Yep. Inquisition and massive amounts of hovering."

Meg moaned.

Hawk shook his head. "You're lucky Emma was out when we stopped at Big House to get the pickup."

"Or this place would be swarming with Farrells. I know."

"To be so loved." He smiled. "Just a heads-up. I called Bent Fork and left a message that you were with me and I would bring you home."

"You what? Why?"

"They were going to worry if you weren't home by dark."

"If I can get home and in bed before everyone gets back, maybe I can delay the fussing until tomorrow. Let's go."

Fortunately, only the twin lights flanking the front door shone from the Bent Fork homestead as they came up the drive. The rest of the house was dark. "Good. They're not back yet. I have a chance."

Hawk parked at the back of the house and carried her through the kitchen into the living room.

"Where are you going? My bed is upstairs."

He deposited her on the deep leather sofa. "Relax. We'll hear them in time for me to get you upstairs. I'm going to get some ice for your ankle."

"I don't want ice."

"Doctor's orders."

"I don't remember her saying anything about ice."

He looked at her knee and ankle. "That's because Lottie was talking a mile a minute using every bandage in the clinic to wrap your wounds while the on-call doctor gave the instructions for your knee and ankle. She said you were lucky you were wearing hiking boots. The added support kept you from having a worse sprain or a broken ankle. So, the crutches are to keep the weight off the ankle as you go about your life. The ice will help reduce the swelling, and with a bit of rest you'll be back on both feet in no time."

"Fine." She acquiesced and fell back against the cushions.

Hawk pulled a pillow from a nearby chair and tucked it behind her head. "How's that?"

"Fine."

"Do you need anything else? Another pillow? A blanket? How about something to eat?"

Meg snatched the pillow he held. "I need you to stop fussing."

"I'm just trying to make you comfortable."

"I am comfortable. I'm very comfortable."

"Good. I'll be right back."

A minute later, he entered the living room holding an ice pack in one hand and a piece of paper in the other. "This was on the table." He handed her the ice pack and read the note. "Your Dad, Mom, Ruby and Heidi are at a festival committee meeting at the senior center and Ava is having a sleepover at your brother's."

"What about Andrew and John?"

"No info on them. However," he continued reading, "there's lasagna in the fridge and fresh bread in the bin."

"I'm really not hungry. Maybe a cup of tea. If

you don't mind. The tea bags are in the bamboo box in the pantry. Pick any one. I don't care."

As soon as Hawk left the room, Meg leaned against the propped pillows and closed her eyes. She didn't want food. She wanted a long soak in a deep tub of hot water.

After Lottie had cleaned her gashed knee and wiped her legs, she'd handed Meg a cloth to clean her dusty face. Better than nothing. Her hair, on the other hand, had a mind of its own thanks to the genes of her grandmother Moira.

Meg had seen photos of the Scottish beauty who had arrived in the United States in the company of male relatives. A boatful of brothers, uncles, cousins, and Moira. Most of the men were very brawny, most of them very redheaded and all of them more than ready to fight their way through a day. While Moira lacked their brawn, it was said she had the same wild, thick, red hair and attitude.

Meg combed her fingers through her own hair and fished an elastic band from her pocket. She pulled her hair, more auburn than red, through the band several times. There. A mess, but a mostly contained mess.

Hawk returned carrying two cups of steaming tea. Meg took the mug he offered and sniffed. "That does not smell like tea."

"You didn't sound enthusiastic about tea. When I saw the chocolate mix next to the tea box, I opted for the chocolate. You still like hot chocolate, don't you?"

Meg sipped the rich drink. "Mmm. I think chocolate is a curative for everything that ails a body." She took another sip. "Especially hot chocolate."

She lowered the mug and looked down at her wrapped ankle and bandaged knee. "You know I'm used to dealing with asthma, but this—" she waved a hand over the leg "—this makes me feel so foolish. I fell over my own tools."

"Do you do that very often?"

"I've never tripped on my own tools before. Never."

"Anyone else's?"

"Ha, ha. No. I'm very careful on-site."

"About tools, maybe. How about managing the asthma?"

"Actually, it's been pretty good. I had a bad flare-up about a year ago. That's why I missed Lame Eagle's funeral. I was working with a cluster of duckbills in South Dakota. We were finding new pieces every day and there was so much work to do. I didn't have my inhaler on me. I kept meaning to put it in my pack, but I forgot.

"I ended up at the ER. The doctor strongly suggested I take up a new career. I told him I had no intention of doing so. He cautioned me to keep an inhaler close at hand." She patted her hip pocket. Empty.

"It's there on the table." He gestured to the rectangle coffee table. "I tucked it in my pocket when I reloaded your backpack. Just in case you needed it on our way to the clinic."

"Thanks." Meg sipped from the mug. "For everything. And thanks for the hot chocolate. It's so much better than Ruby's tonics du jour."

Hawk chucked. "I know you've sampled plenty of those over the years."

"More than I care to remember." She closed her eyes and shuddered. "I dreaded being bundled into bed and propped up with pillows and hovered over. At times, I disliked the hovering more than the labored breathing. The floating in and out of someone checking on me. The silence as they listened to my breathing.

"They would slip in and tiptoe around my bed whispering. Sometimes, in the dark hours, I'd pretend they were fairies come to take me outside to look at the stars and feel the wind." She yawned. "I'm feeling a little groggy. Did you add anything to the chocolate?"

"It's just hot chocolate."

"It's really good hot chocolate." She yawned again.

"Why don't you close your eyes? I'll stay until someone comes home."

"Thank you." Meg snuggled against the cushions and closed her eyes. "Hawk?"

"Hmm?"

"Why haven't you married?" She shifted her leg and the ice pack fell to the floor.

"Stay still. I'll get it."

Meg shivered as he replaced the cold pack. "So?"

"You were serious?" He pulled a small blanket from the end of the sofa and draped it over her.

"Yes."

She heard his heavy sigh and opened her eyes. He knelt beside the sofa and tucked the blanket under her chin.

"Because."

"Because why?"

"Because I've been waiting for you to figure out that you belong here. Waiting for you to see me. Me, more than a neighbor and big-brother figure. Now, close your eyes and rest."

She did see him as more than a neighbor and friend and she'd never seen him as a big-brother figure. She had enough of those. For her, seeing Hawk included more than her feelings. There was his ranch, his ancestral land, his family. Then there was her ranch, her asthma, her family.

She closed her eyes. "Do I belong here?"

"Only you can answer that."

"Hawk."

"Yes?"

"I think it's raining. Did you and Larry get your hay put up?"

"Ah, Meggie. You make me crazy," he murmured and pressed his lips lightly to hers.

Unexpected but welcomed, she shed doubt and complications and let herself drift into the tenderness of his kiss. She laid her fingers into the thick hair at the base of his neck. "I think—"

BOOM!

Thunder filled the room. Hawk pushed himself to a stand and crossed to the wide windows. "Finally, some much-needed rain. Not cats and dogs, but steady."

Meg closed her eyes and listened. She could hear it clearly. A soothing rhythmic patter. "Wait. Did you say cats and dogs? Hawk, I forgot to check on the dog. Hand me the crutches."

"No."

"But—"

He pressed her gently into the thick pillow. "No."

"He's my responsibility. It won't take long. I have food and water in the shed and first-aid supplies if his bandage needs changed. I'll hurry."

"You won't be hurrying anywhere on crutches. I'll go."

Meg sighed and sagged deeper into the cushion. "You will? Thank you."

He turned to leave.

Meg caught his sleeve. "He might need a walk to do his business."

"Okay. I'll walk the dog because I would want someone to do the same for Maiku if necessary and I know you. You'll go out there after I'm gone if I don't walk him."

"Thank you. Take an umbrella from the stand."

"You owe me!" he called as he headed for the back door.

Ten minutes later, he stepped barefoot into the room wiping a dish towel across his face.

"You're wet. You walked him without an umbrella."

"I couldn't walk him. He wasn't there."

"What?"

"The shed's empty. He wasn't there. I called. I whistled. I even rattled the food bowl."

"He has to be there. He was there this morning." Meg caught her breath. "What if I didn't close the door completely? What if he's out right now in the rain, wet and hungry?" She attempted to rise. "We have to look for him."

Hawk positioned himself between the sofa and the crutches. "*We* are not going out in the deep dark of a rainy night full of thunder and lightning, especially with you on crutches, to look for the dog. He's probably found a dry spot nearby."

"What if it was Maiku lost in the rain in an unfamiliar place?"

"Maiku's too smart to wander out in the rain. The dog will be fine."

"Do you really think so?"

"I do. Now sit back and relax."

"Hawk," she murmured, stifling a yawn. "I really appreciate how you've been so helpful these last few days. I feel like I've taken so much of your time. Time you needed to use for more important things. So, thank you." She pulled her lower lip between her teeth and waited. *For what?* For him to say she was more important than anything else. That he'd gladly delayed work on Sitting River to spend time with her. That he'd been looking forward to her coming home and hoped she'd stay. Wait. He did say that. Didn't he?

She rubbed her temples. "My mind's wandering out of focus."

"I'm not surprised. You're tired and maybe in a bit of shock and the pain medication must be kicking in." He smiled down at her. "And you're welcome. It has certainly been interesting having you home."

*Interesting?* Well, he could have said he would have done the same for anyone. Or, that he'd been glad to help but how soon would she be out of his hair? Or, he could have kissed her again and held her hand and assured her that first thing in the morning they would search the county together for their dog. No. Not *their* dog, as he kept reminding her. He'd reluctantly gone out in the rain to check on a dog that wasn't their dog because she'd asked him to.

*Interesting.*

# CHAPTER ELEVEN

"HERE YOU ARE, MEGGIE. Nice and hot." Ruby stepped onto the porch with a steaming cup of tea. "You just sit here and rest your leg," she said, placing the cup on the small table before pushing a stool in front of Meg's feet. "Up."

Meg eased her leg onto the stool. "Thanks." She leaned her head back and closed her eyes. She'd had a restless night, waking in the early hours, in her bed, fully clothed with her knee and ankle throbbing. Hawk must have carried her upstairs before the family could pounce.

Andrew bumped the screened door open with his hip. One hand gripped a mug of coffee, and the other held a copy of his favorite ranching magazine. "Hey, Meggie, you want to hobble out and kick cattle through the branding shoot?"

Ruby clicked her tongue. "Don't tease your sister. She's going to sit here and rest her leg like the doctor said." The housekeeper pulled a cushion from the swing and tucked it under Meg's bandaged foot. "I don't want to see you hobbling out to the storage shed again to take care of that dog.

Your brother can do that." She straightened and gave Andrew a long look.

Andrew saluted. "Yes, ma'am."

"Hmph," Ruby snorted and stepped inside.

"I wish I could help with the branding, or the baling, or the anything."

"No way. You're going to be stuck here all day under the watchful eyes of Ruby and Mom while I get to move rocks around and pound marking stakes in the hot sun with only Hawk for company." Andrew looked up from his magazine. "Speaking of Hawk." Andrew jutted his chin toward the long drive.

Hawk parked his pickup and joined them on the porch.

"Morning, Hawk. You missed breakfast," Andrew said.

"I had my fill at Big House." Hawk sat on the top step and looked at Meg. "How are you this morning?"

"I'm fine. Thanks again for helping me. I hope I wasn't too much trouble."

The screened door swung open. Caroline and Molly stepped onto the porch. Ava followed holding one end of what looked like the cloth belt from Ruby's teal bathrobe. Attached to the other end was the dog.

Andrew whistled. "Whoa, what have we here?"

Caroline grinned and patted the top of the dog's head. "We have Ava, Molly, me and Buddy."

"This must be the mutt Meggie and Hawk rescued." Andrew ruffled the thick fur around the dog's neck. "That's some bandage. Have you girls been playing veterinarian?"

The three girls shook their heads. "He came that way."

"He did come that way."

Meg looked past the girls. Standing in the doorway, behind the dog stood her sister-in-law. While Heidi Farrell looked frail, with her petite frame, white-blond hair and pale skin, Meg knew better. At breakfast, straight-backed and dry-eyed, Heidi had shared with the family that Keith's return might be delayed until December.

The family had marshaled smiles and talked excitedly about the upcoming festival while the children were at the table. Once the girls had hurried off to "take care of something," the conversation shifted to Keith.

Only then did Heidi tear up. Hugs were doled out and confident murmurs went round the table. They all believed he would come home, maybe not until December, but Keith Farrell *would* come home.

Heidi squeezed past the dog and dropped onto the swing next to Andrew. "Ava found him here on the porch last night after everyone had eaten dinner and gone. We'd stayed behind to have our video call with Keith. Ava insisted on removing the cone and bringing the dog in to show her father. Keith acknowledged him with a, 'Hello there, Buddy.'"

"I asked Daddy how he knew his name was Buddy."

Meg smiled at Ava. "Because your daddy is very smart."

Heidi stroked Buddy's ears. "Ava has been enjoying his company." She watched the girls pull cushions from the remaining chairs and lead Buddy to them. "She's not always so happy after our video chats. Keith and I try to keep the conversation light and fun but having Buddy there last night made a big difference. In fact, she insisted on taking him with her to Alison and Connor's for the sleepover."

"I'm surprised they agreed," Andrew said.

"I think they knew how much it meant to Ava at that moment."

All eyes turned to the three girls laughing and hugging the lost and wounded dog.

Meg smiled. "I brought him here yesterday to heal until someone claims him."

Heidi reached out her hand and stroked her daughter's fair hair. "I think someone already has."

HEIDI AND THE girls led the dog down the steps toward the barn. Hawk admired how Heidi carried her worry with dignity. He didn't doubt her concern for Keith weighed heavily, but she didn't let it smother her, nor did she let it spill over onto little Ava.

Since his mother's move to Albuquerque and his grandfather's passing, the Farrells and the Reeds were the closest thing he had to a family. Almost a year since Lame Eagle passed and time continued to take his grief and flip it around. Some days the loss felt as fresh as the day he'd walked into Lame Eagle's room to find Emma weeping at the bedside. He'd known in that moment Lame Eagle had gone to join the ancestors and hold his beloved Anne "Singing Bird" Hawk once again.

He'd sat with Emma and his grandfather and in the silence of grief recalled moments of laughter and great peace. Times of union he and his grandfather shared with the land. Stories his grandfather told of struggles the ancestors endured, sacrifices made to keep home and family. And Lame Eagle had asked for a promise to keep the land whole and in the care of family.

Family. He wasn't sure he'd ever have one. He had no time for dating and very little to offer if he found someone willing to share a rancher's life with him. Once upon a time, he'd hoped the woman sitting on the porch with a bandaged knee full of stitches and a wrapped ankle would be the one to share his life, be his partner in all things. He'd waited too long. His father had left him doubting his own ability to be a good husband and father, leaving him questioning his ability and confidence to commit to loving someone and starting a family.

He'd waited too long to realize the doubts he carried weren't going away. Sitting River wasn't likely to be free of debt anytime soon. Whether or not he would be a good father had less to do with Michael Hawk and more to do with himself. When and if the time came, he would draw from what he witnessed with the Farrells. Deep love and a strong familial bond. Add that to the faith and conviction Lame Eagle had shown him for family, land and a history of courage and persistence.

It didn't matter now.

Meggie Farrell had her own plans. She wanted to be independent. She wanted to find and dig up ancient bones and display them for the world to be amazed and informed. Nuggets of opportunity had fallen her way, feeding her plans. When the museum in Michigan had offered that opportunity, Meggie took it. Now, in the eight weeks before leaving for Michigan, she had taken the chance to share her geological knowledge with eager students.

And he'd waited too long.

"So, will that work for you?" Andrew nudged Hawk with the toe of his boot.

Hawk looked up from his own worn boots. Andrew and Meggie were staring at him. "What?"

Meg sat back in her chair. "By your expression, I'd say you were pondering something serious."

He didn't plan to share his thoughts. He didn't want sympathy. "Work. I was thinking about work."

"Aren't you always?" Andrew drained his coffee and set the mug on the porch rail. "I checked on renting the excavator." He pulled a paper from his pocket, unfolded it and handed it to Hawk. "Aaron said I could pick it up as soon as his brother-in-law returns it. Should be sometime this morning. I got us a good deal."

Hawk tapped the paper. "What are these?"

"Lumber costs. Assuming you're still bull-headed enough to insist on paying for the lumber."

"Lumber? What lumber?" Meggie scooted forward in her chair, trying to get a look at the paper her brother held.

"Hawk and I agreed to split expenses for the grain project. I'll provide the seed and work the acres Hawk has leased to me. At a reasonable agreement, I might add." Andrew joined his friend on the step. "Now, this stubborn Ute insists on providing the lumber for a storage barn and helping with the construction."

"The building will be on my ranch, making it an asset of Sitting River. It's only fair I help since I'll be getting the bigger, long-term benefit and I already have the lumber."

Andrew's eyes narrowed. "You have the lumber?"

Hawk nodded. "Up at Lame Eagle's old cabin."

He heard Meggie's sharp inhale and kept his eyes on his boots.

Meggie shifted forward again. "You said that lumber was for the changes you wanted to make at the cabin."

"It's for whatever has the greatest need. Right now, I need it to build a structure to store grain and equipment." Bringing in more revenue held a greater need than a second bedroom or an extended porch. The additions to the cabin would wait.

Andrew scanned the paper. "How much do you have?"

"Enough to get started. I'll worry about more if it's necessary."

"When do we want to move the lumber to the meadow?"

"After we've marked and cleared for the foundation."

"Good." Andrew folded the paper and tucked it in his back pocket. "I've got a lot to do before my date, and hauling lumber today is not on my list."

"A date?" Meg studied her brother. "You have a date? With who?"

"You don't know her. She moved to Tyler after you ran off to get a degree in dinosaur remains."

Hawk chuckled. "As much as I would like to witness the dating third degree, I have hay to drop at the Pattersons' upper pasture and then I'll check on Larry and the baler. Meet me at the barn site about noon. We'll stake off the foundation area and clear as much as we can and hopefully start grading for the fill to stabilize a foundation slab. We can work faster if you bring another shovel and a wheelbarrow."

"And me," Meggie added.

The two men turned in unison. Hawk smiled. His friend frowned. Meggie's hands rested in her lap. Her eyes were wide and hopeful.

"I'm tired of sitting here. I'll be as quiet as a mouse. You won't even know I'm there. I promise."

Her brother folded his arms across his chest. "There's nothing for you to do up there."

"I need a change of scenery. I'll take the notes Mrs. Burlew gave me for the geology class and go over them while sitting quietly and staying out of your way. If I'm stuck here Ruby, will bring me one of her special tonics sooner or later." Meg wrinkled her nose.

Andrew shook his head. "No way."

Meg turned to Hawk. "I can't drive myself or I'd be up at the base of the cliff on my hands and one knee looking for more of the sauropod already." She smiled. "I don't suppose either of you would be willing to drive up there."

"No," Hawk said.

"No," Andrew echoed.

"Then take me with you."

Hawk let the possibility of taking Meggie along swim through his mind. Inactivity often wrestled with Meggie. She'd promised she'd sit still and quiet with her class notes. A promise she would try to keep until she felt she could help. She had wanted to help with the hay baler. He hadn't given her the chance. He'd pushed her aside like the whole Farrell family tended to do. At least their motives had been grounded in keeping her healthy. His motives?

His motives had nothing to do with health issues and everything to do with how alive he felt with her near. She'd pulled him up from the pit of anxiety and doubt he'd fallen into the last few months. With Meggie, he was seeing a life, living a life, not just existing to face endless work that climbed on his back, wrapped around his mind and crouched in his gut with a weight he carried with him every day.

Meggie Farrell blew his burden away with her endless ability to give, her desire to belong and her trust in loving, unconditionally. Without knowing it, without trying to, she gave him hope.

Maybe it wasn't too late.

MEG STIFLED A YAWN, scooted back against the trunk of the cottonwood and picked up her folder of class notes and curriculum. The shade under the leaves did little to stave off the late afternoon heat. Her tank top clung to her, and perspiration dripped from every pore. Her knee and ankle felt like they were wrapped in sandpaper dipped in vinegar and tied as tight as a tourniquet. The longer she sat, the tighter the bandages felt, and no amount of scratching eased the itch. Even with Hawk's denim jacket wadded into a ball and propped under her ankle, the throbbing remained.

She opened the folder again and thumbed idly through the papers, making a few notes here and there. Professor Nelson preferred a more lecture-based curriculum. She wanted an interactive, hands-on class. The more hands-on the better, in her opinion. Participation and movement kept students interested. Being stuck in one spot allowed one's mind to wander and one's body to become restless. Her own mind and body proved the point.

She dropped the paper and pencil and shaded her eyes. Hawk and Andrew pounded stakes, strung twine, tossed rocks into wheelbarrows, dumped the contents outside the staked area and repeated the process.

They had discarded their button-up work shirts. Andrew wore under his work shirt a cotton tee that bore telltale signs of physical toil. The front of the white tee had a bright yellow smiley face winking at the world and a streak of dampness down the back. Hawk had discarded his work shirt, and the gray Sitting River logoed T-shirt underneath bore marks of perspiration. The bright red bandanna tied across his forehead looked like it could use a good wringing.

Hawk poured his heart, soul and body into making Sitting River the best it could be. More so since Lame Eagle passed, according to Andrew. She wished, not for the first time, that she could help ease his burden. Right now, all she could do was maybe ease his thirst.

Meg opened the cooler at her side, grabbed a large jug of water and lifted it high. "Hey, guys."

Andrew looked up. "What now?"

She pointed to the jug. "How about a break?"

The men dropped their shovels, tossed aside their heavy work gloves and joined Meg under the shade of the cottonwood.

Hawk squatted beside her, pulled another bandanna from his back pocket, wiped his face and picked up a plastic cup. He held it out to Meggie.

"Water or orange stuff?" she asked.

"Water. The orange stuff is a fortified fruit drink with minerals and vitamins and tastes like a mixture of colored mud and sugar. Your brother swims in it."

Meg filled a plastic cup for each. "Let me help with something besides pouring water and—" she wrinkled her nose "—orange stuff. I'm roasting alive sitting here. At least let me sweat with purpose."

"Doing what?" Andrew asked. "You're incapacitated with a stitched knee and a sprained ankle. How exactly do you expect to move rocks and dirt when you can barely move yourself?"

"Very carefully."

Hawk accepted the cup with one hand and tucked the bandanna into his pocket with the other. "Even carefully, there's nothing for you to do, Meggie, and you promised you would stay quiet and out of the way."

"I need to do something. I've been sitting here for hours, quietly I might add, watching you two sweat and heave rocks and dirt. I even sat still and quiet while you gobbled sandwiches and debated the chances of Tyler High's football team to make it to the state championship game this year. Surely that earned me something."

"My undying gratitude." Andrew pressed his empty cup into her hand and stood. "Can we get back to work now? I have dinner plans."

"Right. Big brother's focus is on living things."

Hawk drained his cup and dropped it in the cooler. "You may as well go, Andrew." He looked at the line of low clouds butting against each other above Meyer Ridge. "There's more rock clutter than I expected. We may as well save it for the excavator."

"Aaron apologized long and loud about the excavator. According to him, it's his brother-in-law's fault we can't get it until next week."

"I don't care who takes the blame as long as it gets here."

Andrew pulled keys from his front pocket. "See you in the morning."

Hawk glanced at Meggie. "Andrew, take her with you."

Meg struggled to stand. "Wait a minute." She leaned her weight on one crutch and, lifting the other, pointed it at the two men. "I am not going home. Not before five."

Andrew swatted at the rubber tip of the crutch. "That's because Mrs. Maine should be gone by then."

Hawk sighed. "Maybe it's a good thing I don't have siblings."

"What?" asked Meg.

"What?" echoed Andrew.

"There is something to be said for being an only child. Go on, Andrew. I'll take her home."

Meg let the dust settle from Andrew's rapid departure before she hobbled over to join Hawk near the growing pile of rocks. "So, this is how you start building a barn?"

"This is how *two* men start building a barn when the rented excavator didn't arrive as scheduled and you have limited manpower, limited time— " he looked up at the dark clouds "—questionable weather and a woman who refuses to sit still and be quiet as promised." He tossed another large rock aside.

Meg ignored his last comment. "How big will it be?"

"Big enough."

She pushed at one of the discarded stones with

the end of her crutch. "I know this is the Rocky Mountains, but I bet you didn't expect to find half of them right here. Couldn't you put the barn someplace else?"

"This area works because it's a sizable piece of flatland. It's near water but not threatened by a flood plain and it's not currently in use."

"But, if you—" The stone rolled, the crutch slipped and Meg quickly braced herself with the second crutch.

Hawk reached to steady her. "Meggie, please go sit down before you hurt yourself. Again."

"I want to be useful." She gave him a pleading look. "There must be something I can do."

"Hand me that crowbar."

Meg handed him the tool and watched him wedge it under a small boulder and rock the stone back and forth. Slowly the earth's grip loosened, and the boulder rolled free. Her forehead creased into thin lines as she looked at the underside of the freshly exposed rock.

No. Not rock.

A thick dull brown streak ran across the bottom of the uncovered stone. Hawk tucked the crowbar under the stone, and with a booted foot on the end of the metal bar, prepared to roll it to the roped boundary.

"Stop!" Meg waved a crutch and hopped toward him. "That's not rock. Well, it's not all rock."

She dropped the crutches and grabbed Hawk's

arm. "Help me." He helped her lower herself until her backside met the ground. Angling her bandaged leg to one side, she leaned over the exposed stone and brushed away loose dirt.

Hawk squatted beside her. "What are you doing?" Hard hands closed over her wrists. "Meggie, stop. It's a rock. The place is covered with them. We're in the middle of the Rocky Mountains."

"It's not a rock. I mean, it is a rock, it's just that it's more than a rock." She saw the skeptical glint in his eyes. "There's a fossil embedded in there." Her conviction came from a place of knowledge and knowing. She *knew*. She looked hard into his eyes, wanting him to believe her.

"Of course you think it's a fossil. There's nothing else on your mind these days but fossils."

"That's not fair." Fossils weren't all she thought about. Hawk occupied more of her mind lately than she cared to admit. Even to herself.

After her transfer from TCC to the University of Michigan, her visits home and thus her encounters with Hawk had been sporadic. Seeing him in her home or spotting him on the ranch never failed to stir butterflies in her stomach or spread a familiar warmth through her body.

This visit home, a longer visit than usual, she'd found herself frequently in Hawk's company and enjoying their time together even when they were arguing about the wounded dog and fossils. Their adventure with the dog had revealed a tender side of Hawk she knew existed but had rarely had a chance to see. He'd gone to the shed to check on their homeless canine when she couldn't and, on finding the dog missing, had looked for the pup longer than he'd admitted. She knew because he'd removed his shoes when he returned to the house and his pant legs were damp.

His narrow focus on Sitting River had shifted. She knew the ranch was in debt. He carried the debt and his promise to Lame Eagle to keep the ranch in the family without complaint. Lame Eagle's death had carved a need for more than Sitting River in Hawk's life. Somewhere in him, a willingness to open up and accept a helping hand had started to sprout. The leased acres to Andrew, the renting of Little House to the Romeros, offering Jenna and her family the opportunity to stay at Big House and giving Meggie freedom to search for fossils on Sitting River.

Hawk gave easily. Taking, on the other hand, hadn't come easily. Maybe it had more to do with accepting. Accepting blended with a need. Needs weren't easily or readily acknowledged.

"You mean you don't think about fossils?"

"Of course I think about fossils. It's my job to think about fossils. Do you think about ranching? About cattle and cutting hay?" She pointed to the overturned stone. "I'm telling you that is fossilized bone. At least part of a fossilized bone."

"A bone doesn't mean dinosaur. It could be elk or deer."

Meg tilted her head. "A fossilized bone. Do you know how long it takes for fossilization to occur? Tens of thousands of years. Do you think there are fossilized elk around here?"

He stood and folded his arms across his chest.

"Any chance you have a small pick and brush or something sharp enough to scrape away some of the stone?"

"There might be something in the toolbox in the back of the truck."

"Would you check? Please." He walked away mumbling to himself. The clatter of tools mingled with the mumbling and the mumbling grew louder. Meg alternated between brushing dirt with her fingers and blowing puffs of air to loosen soil until Hawk handed her a small chisel.

She squealed, snatched the tool and hugged it to her chest. "Thank you, thank you, thank you."

"How long is this going to take?"

"As long as it needs to take."

"Won't take long. Rain's coming."

She picked up a rock and for several minutes pounded the top of the chisel, chipping away small pieces of stone from around the fossil. Finally, she straightened and motioned to Hawk. "Come see. I don't have the correct tools to do much without fear of damage, but I think even you can differentiate between rock and bone now."

He leaned over her shoulder, resting his hand lightly against her back. “I see an odd bit of brownish rock in the middle of a bigger chunk of rock.”

“That oddly colored bit is fossilized bone millions of years old.” She ran her fingertips lightly over the exposed area. “Here.” She placed his hand at the top of the stone and led it across its width. “Feel the difference?”

He stroked the strip of rock. “There is a difference. A very subtle something.”

“Fossilized bone is smoother to the touch. There’s almost a warmth to it.”

Using the chisel, she pointed out specifics. “See how the bone is surrounded by sandstone? That will need to be very delicately chiseled away. As I work, I’ll leave it in the matrix, the encasing stone, to protect it until I can determine more of the skeletal placement.”

Ever so gently, his fingers stretched out. Just as deliberately, they closed into a loose fist. Finally, he straightened. “What is it?”

“I told you. It’s part of a fossilized bone.”

“What kind?”

Meg sighed. “There isn’t enough to say. I may never find enough to say.”

In her heart of hearts, she wanted it to be a rare dinosaur in perfect condition with all its bones present and accounted for. What was life without a few wild wishes?

“You want to keep working on this?”

She chanced a look at him. He pulled his hat from his head with one hand and yanked the bandanna from his forehead with the other. He pushed his fingers through the thick, damp hair and stared out over the valley. *His* valley. *His* land. His rock holding a millions-year-old fossilized bone of a creature that no longer existed. He had thoughts running through his head she wasn't sure she wanted to know.

She nodded.

He picked up the shovel. "On my barn site."

Meg looked directly into his eyes. They were hard, as hard as the blade of the shovel he held. "It's where the fossil is buried."

Hawk gazed into the distance. Indecision waged a battle. "My grandfather treated this land as a living entity. He told me the land spoke to him. It told him of our ancestors and how the land had chosen them to live on it. They had been grateful to have been chosen and vowed to honor the land."

Meg waited, heart pounding. Would he deny her the opportunity to dig for more of this fossil because it lay buried on Sitting River? "You're digging here, as well." The words fled her mouth before she had time to understand what she was saying. It was his ranch. He could do what he wanted.

"My ancestors honored the land and its gifts. They worked on it for the purpose of survival and for the care of the land. I'm trying to do the same.

Any digging I do on Sitting River is to plant and harvest to sustain man and beast or to provide shelter for man and beast. What will these bones do?"

"Depending on what I find, they could offer a new or better understanding of the dinosaurs that walked through here millions of years ago. And…" She hesitated, reluctant to offer hope she couldn't guarantee. "It's possible there could be some financial benefit to Sitting River."

"What can you accomplish in a few days?"

"Days? I have no idea what I'll find until I start digging. I may find nothing more than this. Plus, I'm a bit encumbered from my accident. That will slow me down. And I'll need teaching time, and possibly, once I'm cleared to drive, I might have some child chauffeuring duty."

Hawk puffed out a heavy breath. "I'll give you until the excavator arrives. Hopefully by then you should know if there's anything more buried under my barn site."

"A few days." She grabbed his arm. "You can't expect me to know everything that might be buried here and remove it in just a few days."

"I don't want you unearthing anything." He gathered his few tools and headed for the wheelbarrow. "Unless it's rocks."

"Where are you going?"

"Back to Big House. I have a never-ending list of work waiting for me." He tossed the tools into the empty wheelbarrow and covered it with a heavy tarp. "And, if you don't want to get caught in a storm, I suggest you start hobbling to the truck."

"Do you have another tarp? I know it's small, but I'd like to protect the bit of exposed fossil."

He pulled the tarp off the wheelbarrow and handed it to her. Then he dumped the tools on the ground and flipped the barrow over them.

"Thank you."

"Welcome."

She draped the tarp over the fossil, anchored it with rocks and managed to stand with the aid of the crutches. As much as she wanted to stay and work, Hawk was right. A storm gathered around them, she had no tools, no transportation. "May I come back tomorrow? Early?"

"Sure. But you'll need to find your own way."

"I can arrange that." She hoped.

Raindrops spit at her as she climbed into the pickup.

"What happens if you find something you deem worthwhile? Will you stay?"

"Stay? As in Colorado?"

"Is that an option?"

Meg shifted her gaze out the passenger window. Lowering clouds carrying much-needed moisture filled the distant view blurred by raindrops hitting the window and running in rivulets down the glass. She let the tingle of discovery, the hope of something worthwhile seep into her thoughts. What if she found something major? Would she stay? Could she stay? What about her job, a wonderful position? Would she give it up for a worthwhile find?

Puzzling emotions and questions had been nagging at her since her arrival on Bent Fork. She had yet to place them. New questions pricked. Could she give up her job for a fossil discovery on Sitting River? Could she give it up for *someone* on Sitting River?

"I can't answer that right now."

Hawk mumbled something incoherent and put the truck in gear.

# *CHAPTER TWELVE*

RAIN PUMMELED THE roof of the pickup by the time they arrived at Bent Fork. Meg reached to open the passenger door.

"Wait." Hawk turned the engine off and pulled his jacket from behind his seat. "You can use this to cover your head."

She had barely draped the jacket over her when he opened the door and scooped her into his arms. He strode to the back porch and bumped open the screened door and deposited her on the nearest bench. "I'll get your crutches."

"And my backpack."

He ran to the pickup and returned with the items.

Meg took the crutches. She positioned one under her arm but dropped the other. The aluminum crutch clanged against the wrought-iron umbrella stand before clattering onto the tiled floor.

The kitchen door swung open. Ruby stood in the doorway with a broom in her hand ready to do battle if necessary. "What's going on out here?"

"It's just us."

Ruby lowered the broom. "What happened?"

"Sorry. I'm still a little clumsy with the crutches."

"Be careful coming through the kitchen. I just finished wiping up the floor. The girls and that dog came traipsing in here with muddy shoes and dirty paws. Now they're putting on swimsuits to take a bath. Who ever heard of taking a bath wearing a swimsuit? Any news on an owner or anyone interested in the dog besides these girls?"

"Not yet," Meg said. "It's only been two days."

Hawk handed Meg the dropped crutch. "Where is he, Ruby? I'll put him out in the shed after I help Meggie inside."

"He flew upstairs with the girls."

Meg tucked the crutches under her arms.

"I can manage on my own, thank you."

"Don't fuss about what's best for you." Ruby stepped back from the door. "Help her in, Hawk. There's leftover chicken cacciatore, rice and mixed vegetables in the fridge. Hawk can use the hall bathroom to clean up and Meggie, you can use mine while I set out the leftovers."

"Don't go to any trouble, Ruby." Hawk pulled out a chair for Meggie. "I can't stay."

"It's dinnertime and you need to eat."

"Okay. I'll eat if you let me take care of getting out the leftovers."

"There's plenty. It was just me and the girls tonight." She fumbled in her apron pocket and withdrew a white handkerchief and patted her cheek and forehead. "It's been constant activity and nonstop chatter with these girls." Gentle pats across her cheeks and forehead slowed her agitation. "And I still need to oversee baths. I'm getting too old for this."

Meg glanced upward. "It's quiet now."

"Too quiet." Ruby turned and fled the room. "You girls better not have that dog in the tub!"

Meg pushed herself to a stand. "Let's clean up and eat before Ruby and whoever is in the tub come down. Check the laundry room on your way to wash up. There's probably a shirt hanging next to the dryer that will fit you." She plucked at her own dirty, sweat-stained shirt. "Will you hand me my backpack? I should have a clean tank top in there."

"Then we'll talk about how much of my ranch you want to dig up."

She took the backpack and crutches and made her way to Ruby's bathroom to clean her body as best she could and settle her mind if possible.

Hawk wanted to talk about her desire to dig on his new barn site. He didn't *want* her digging on the site of the new barn. He didn't want her digging on Sitting River. Period. But she'd found a fossil. It could be a huge find, or it could be a few scattered bones from a scavenged beast killed eons ago and left to fossilize. It didn't matter to her which one as long as she had a chance to uncover it.

To do that, given her limited mobility and teaching time, she needed more than the few days he'd given her, maybe a lot more. Meg wrinkled her nose. Would he grant her more time? All she could do was to ask and hope.

She draped the washcloth over the lip of the tub and sighed. Clean shirt, clean hands and freshly washed face left her feeling refreshed but longing for a proper bath. A long soak in a tub of hot water with both legs instead of dangling her stitched leg over the side. Soon.

“Meggie,” Hawk called from the kitchen. “Leftovers are in the microwave.”

Ignoring the crutches resting against the sink, she half hopped, half limped down the hall toward the kitchen. She reached the entryway between Ruby’s live-in residence and the kitchen and paused.

Hawk stood at the kitchen counter pouring milk into two tall glasses. Andrew’s blue work shirt fit nicely across his shoulders. He’d left the tail untucked, rolled the sleeves up to his elbows and left the top three buttons opened. He looked as appetizing as the leftovers smelled.

She pushed away from the doorframe. The muscles in her left leg bunched into a tight knot and pulled her down.

“Ow, ow.” She squeezed her eyes shut. An unfamiliar pain immobilized her and intensified with the slightest movement. Even a simple breath locked her body.

Hawk reached her side in a heartbeat. "What is it?"

She tried to speak. "Ow," she whimpered and rolled back and forth on the hardwood floor. "Cramp. Leg. Ow."

Hawk cupped his hand under her calf and with firm, soothing strokes, slid his hand over the taut muscle.

Meg clutched the fabric of her khaki shorts. Slowly his rhythmic strokes eased the knot in her leg and breathing became bearable. "In all my years of coping with asthma, I've never felt anything that intense."

"You've never had a leg cramp?"

"Never. And I never want another one."

He continued to knead the tender muscle. "Your good leg has been compensating for the other."

Meg watched his broad hands slide over calf. She didn't want him to stop.

"Feels like the knot has unraveled."

"Better?"

Hawk knelt in front of her, his hands rested on his thighs and concern etched on his face.

"Yes," she croaked. "Thank you."

He reached for her. "Let's get you to the table."

"Thank you."

"What? No 'don't treat me like an invalid' comeback?"

Meg sighed. She felt more an invalid in this moment than any other in her life. Allergies and asthma symptoms were familiar and treatable. She knew those feelings. She knew how to cope with them. But this, this tangle of emotions seeping through her, she doubted. Was it gratitude? Certainly. And not just for easing the cramp in her leg. He had come to her aid a lot over the last few days. Friendship? Yes. Her once-childish crush had evolved from butterflies and giggles to a comfortable camaraderie. Love?

"I'm trying to accept help for what it is, someone wanting to be there because they care, not because they think I'm incapable."

"Good." Hawk leaned forward, and she saw something other than pique or concern in his eyes, as her own drifted closed.

"That dog." Ruby burst into the room with an armful of towels. "I've never seen an animal shake off so much water." She stopped in her tracks and eyed Hawk and Meggie sitting on the floor. "What happened?" She dropped the towels and hurried to Meggie's side. "Are you okay? Should I call Dr. Lewis?"

"I'm fine, Ruby. I had a leg cramp, that's all." Meg paused and shifted her gaze to Hawk. He gave her a look she hadn't seen from him before. His eyes held an intensity deep and beyond familiarity. He looked as if he were searching for something. "Hawk helped me."

Together, one on either side, Ruby and Hawk

raised Meg from the floor and helped her to the table.

Hawk stepped to the door. "I appreciate the dinner offer Ruby, but I need to go."

"You sure?" Ruby cast a glance at the counter. "You've got everything out and ready."

"I'm sure. Jenna and her family arrive tomorrow, and I want to make sure everything is in order."

"Well, have Emma let me know if she needs anything."

"I will." Hawk picked up his dirty shirt. "I'll return Andrew's shirt in the next day or two."

Meg nodded. "No hurry. I doubt he'll know it's missing."

"Good night, ladies."

As soon as Hawk's pickup roared to life, she turned to Ruby. "I think I'll skip dinner. I'm too tired to eat." She didn't need food. She needed to let the emotions and thoughts crowding her mind find a place to settle. She needed to think.

HAWK STOOD IN front of Lame Eagle's old desk. His plans for the cabin lay curled in a tight roll. The lumber for the new rooms sat out back waiting to become a barn instead of an addition to the cabin. The construction would have to wait. Not only for the cabin, but now the barn site, as well. He had no idea what Meggie needed to do about the fossil she thought she'd found. He'd give her the few days it would take to get the excavator. After that? He'd wait and see.

He shoved the rolled plans into a long tube, pushed the tube back against the cubbies and pulled down the lid. Waiting didn't sit well with him. Waiting, for too long, usually meant you weren't going to get what you were waiting for. Too many times he and his mother had waited for his father to come home. Too many times hours became days and days became weeks. Eventually the man would show up with a mouthful of excuses and a pocketful of nothing.

Hawk took his coffee and his boots out to the porch.

Between sips of coffee, he wiped his boots. The worn leather kept a fair amount of dirt and dust trapped in the weathered creases. He needed new boots. He needed a new hay baler. He needed forty-eight hours in his twenty-four-hour days. He didn't need Meggie Farrell disturbing his ranch. Or his life. He blew out a heavy sigh. Too late on both accounts.

Meggie had been fated to be in his life from the moment he spied her peering at him from the Farrells' front porch. Younger than him, thin but not scrawny, she'd stood straight and steady with a rock in one hand and a notebook in the other. A bun of dark auburn hair had been piled high on her head and secured with a mechanical pencil. He'd tried not to smile when she'd pulled the pencil and released a mass of wavy hair. She'd tucked as much as she could behind her ears, sat on the top step, put the rock to one side and started to write in the notebook. He'd intended to ask her what she'd found so interesting about the stone until Andrew and John Farrell had decided Hawk should see the stables. That day had been a turning point in his life. He'd made friendships that, to this day, he believed would last a lifetime. He'd met a woman to whom he now compared all other women, smart, curious and determined to claim her independence. A woman who wanted to hunt for and dig up bones long buried on his ranch.

And he was going to let her.

Tires crunched over the gravel drive. John Farrell sped over the loose gravel in a restored Willys Jeep, screeched the vehicle to a halt and hopped out.

"Nice job on the Jeep," Hawk said.

John grinned. The youngest Farrell son resembled the only Farrell daughter more than the other boys. Both had unruly red-brown hair and an easy smile.

"Thanks. It took more time and more money than I thought I'd need but I'm happy with the results."

"You still working on that old Mustang?"

John dropped onto the step beside Hawk. "Hey, don't call my Shelby old. She's just a kid compared to my Willys and they're both classics. I'm going to get some original hubcaps for her. Once I have those, I'll paint on white lemans stripes. By the time the Willow River Festival rolls around, she'll look as beautiful as she did in '68."

"I have no hubcaps."

"No, but Meggie insists you have her camera."

"It fell out of her backpack yesterday." Hawk pointed his thumb over his shoulder. "It's on the table by the fireplace. What's Meggie planning to do with the camera?"

John shrugged. "She gave me a long explanation I didn't listen to before I dropped her at a spot of dirt she's calling a dig site."

Hawk flattened his lips. "A dig site?"

"Yep." John took the steps two at a time. "I'll get the camera. Then, I'm off to Denver to look for Shelby's hubcaps."

"I know where Meggie's digging. How about I relieve you of the camera burden?"

John leaped down the steps. "You sure?"

He was sure he wanted to see Meggie. He wanted to see her smile and see her eyes shine while she worked at her dig site searching for new bones. He wanted to watch her forehead crease and her lips pucker as she scraped at rocks. He wanted to see Meggie. He couldn't help himself.

"I want to talk to her about a few things."

"Just be careful. You might get roped into playing in the dirt with her fossils."

"Not a chance."

MEG HUNCHED OVER the ever-widening trench and slowly ran a small brush across the top of the ancient vertebrae. The number of vertebrae had increased as she chipped away at the matrix. She could now identify three. Three vertebrae of a what? Not enough to name the type of dinosaur. Her gut screamed *allosaurus*. No rhythm or reason, just a feeling. They'd been found in Colorado, Wyoming and Utah. Most of those finds were scraps of broken bones, pieces of skull, a few massive teeth and a claw or two. For Hawk's sake, she hoped this one, regardless of type, would be complete, or mostly complete or somewhat complete. At least more than a few bones. Enough for the Mayfield to purchase and create an exhibit.

"Here."

Meg glanced up from the narrow pit. Her camera dangled from its nylon strap a few inches from her face. She put out a hand. The strap snapped upward, lifting the camera out of reach. "I don't have time for games, John."

"Try again."

She tipped her head back and focused on the man holding the camera. Old denims rode low on his hips and a green plaid cotton shirt covered his upper body. The sleeves were rolled back, and several empty buttonholes left a good amount of deeply tanned throat visible. Meg swallowed.

"What are you going to do with this?" He lowered the camera.

"Gee, I think I'll do something crazy, like take pictures." Meg took the camera and placed it near her discarded sweatshirt.

"Pictures of what?"

"I'll photograph the site, mark off a grid and take photos of every stage of discovery."

"And all of this stuff?" He gestured to the supplies laid out beside the trench.

Meg scanned the items neatly displayed around her. Basic supplies for fossil hunting and excavating. Small dental tools, brushes and picks of varying sizes, a trowel, a geological hammer, a small sieve and sifting screen, notebook, sketch pad, string for marking grids and burlap bags. One bag bulged with lumps.

"What's in there?"

"Those are rocks for my class." *My class.* She liked the sound of that. It held a promise of something she couldn't quite wrap her mind around.

"Ever the rock collector."

Meg glanced from the bag of rocks to Hawk. "You don't mind if I take a few rocks, do you? Sorry. I should have asked first. I think the class will find them interesting. Well, I hope they will find them interesting. The rocks will be a simple but important beginning to the class."

Hawk hefted the bag. "That's a lot of rocks."

"And there is a purpose for each and every one of them."

"If you say so, Teacher." He placed the bag on the ground at her feet.

*Teacher.* There it was again, a feeling she tried to name. A lighthearted budding excitement for this new experience. Her tutoring and TA work at college felt more like friends studying together. With this geology class, everything fell on her shoulders to give the students information and experiences in a positive, meaningful manner. The materials for visual learners versus auditory learners and lots of hands-on activity to hopefully keep everyone interested in the topic she found fascinating.

"Meggie?"

"What?" Meg reluctantly let go of the pictures in her mind. "Sorry. What did you say?"

"How's the leg feeling? Anymore cramps bother you last night?"

"No, no cramps." A great deal of wondering about her feelings for Hawk and how they were bound to complicate her nicely laid-out future bothered her last night.

"THANK YOU FOR dropping off the camera. I appreciate you taking time away from your work. I know you have plenty to do."

"I have a few minutes to spare. Want to show me what's going on in that pit?"

Meg's eyes widened. "Really? You're interested?"

Hawk pulled his hat from his head and pushed his hand through his hair. "I want to know what you plan to do with whatever it is you hope to uncover."

"Have you ever been to the DMNS?"

"A time or two."

"Then you've noticed the Denver Museum of Nature and Science has a number of fossil exhibits."

He nodded.

"How do you think they got there? Depending on the species and the number and condition of these old bones, this could be an important find to add to a museum collection. The Mayfield, for example." She paused, waiting for a response.

Hawk looked past her. She turned. Andrew's pickup pulled to a stop beside Hawk's. Her brother hopped out, stuck his wide-brimmed felt hat on his head and joined them.

"Mind if I borrow Hawk for a few minutes?"

Meg shrugged. "That's up to him."

The two men strode over to Andrew's truck.

She watched Andrew pull papers from his pocket and spread them on the hood of the vehicle. It had to be about the grain project. It seemed to be the only thing on Andrew's mind lately. And Hawk's mind? She didn't want to know.

Hawk returned wearing a look of resignation on his face. He stopped at the edge of the pit, tugged the Stetson low over his forehead and stuffed his hands into the pockets of his jeans. "Meggie. Would you join me for dinner tonight at the cabin? I'll cook."

"Dinner? I don't know, Hawk. I'd really like to work as long as possible. Unless you're telling me I can't remove these."

"That's part of what I'd like to talk with you about."

"Oh."

"I'll be at the cabin by six." He slid a glance at the pit, turned and headed for his pickup.

Part of what he wanted to talk about. What more did he want to talk about? Meg frowned. She didn't know if she should be pleased or worried.

# CHAPTER THIRTEEN

ANDREW ARRIVED AT the dig site for pickup duty dressed in black denims and a polo shirt of soft gray.

"Nice. Is that your chauffeur's uniform?"

"I have a date."

"Another date? Same girl agreed to go out with you a second time? So soon. Interesting."

"Ha, ha."

"Give me a few minutes. I want to stake out another few feet to extend the search area for tomorrow. I'm already losing time because I'm having dinner with Hawk instead of working."

Andrew's eyebrows rose. "You have a date, too."

"It's not a date. We're meeting at Lame Eagle's cabin to discuss the excavation."

"Of our new barn or your old bones?"

Meg raised her own eyebrows. "I don't know. Probably both." Hopefully, the conversation would end in a positive light for her and her dig site. It might help to be on time. "Let's go. I can set up an extended search area tomorrow. If you will lend a hand with storing my tools and tarping the pit, we can go. Wait a minute. You've got a date and John is in Denver getting presents for his old Mustang. Who's going to drive me to the cabin?"

"Can't Hawk pick you up?"

"I could ask." She pulled her cell phone from her backpack. "No service."

Andrew rubbed his temples.

"No service is not my fault."

"I'll drop you at the cabin and let's hope Hawk can take you home because I'm not playing chauffeur tonight."

"I'm just as tired of being driven around as you and John are of driving me around. I see Dr. Lewis tomorrow afternoon. The swelling has gone down and the ankle doesn't throb as much, as long as I don't overdo and continue to follow instructions. I expect her to clear me to chauffeur myself." Meg smacked her canvas hat against her thighs, sending dust floating around her legs. "I'm a mess. I need to go home first."

"Hawk has a bathroom."

Meg sighed.

"Meggie, I don't have time to take you home and then up to the cabin."

She dusted off her shirt and khakis. "Okay. I'll make do. Since dinner is not a date."

Andrew belted out the last lines of some country tune as he pulled to a stop at the cabin's steps. "Doesn't look like Hawk's here yet. Good thing, too. You're going to need time to get ready for your date."

"It's not a date. It's a business conversation taking place over dinner."

He dropped her backpack on the porch and leaned her crutches against the railing. With a finger tap on the brim of his hat, he said, "Don't do anything I wouldn't do on your date."

"It's a business dinner." She watched the taillights disappear before easing herself down on the swing. It had been a long day and she had more to do. Work didn't stop just because the sun went down.

She'd taken necessary photos and made brief sketches. Now she wanted to flesh out her sketches, adding more depth and detail. Plus, there was the matter of class preparation and material in Professor Nelson's office she wanted to get.

She drew in a deep breath of cool evening air, sighed and, with the exhale, pushed her tired body off the swing. Time to clean up. She slung the backpack over her shoulder, thankful she'd put a fresh T-shirt in her pack, and, leaving the crutches on the porch, hobbled to the bathroom.

It took what felt like thousands of hobbling steps to reach the bathroom. She flipped on the light and gasped. A wild-haired, dirty-faced, red-eyed hag stared at her from the small mirror above the sink. Andrew had been right. She desperately needed to do something about her appearance before her date. Business meeting. Dinner. Before Hawk arrived.

Soap and water removed the dirt from her face and arms. The clean pale blue T-shirt replaced the sweat-stained tee. She combed her fingers through her hair, gathered it into a ponytail and searched her pockets for an elastic band. No luck. As soon as she released the somewhere between curly and wavy hair, it did its thing. She shrugged, propped the backpack on the edge of the pedestal sink and rummaged through the pack until her fingers found a pencil. She coiled her hair and stuck the pencil through the knot. A few wisps fell around her face and neck. The majority held.

Now to do something about the thunderous rumbling in her stomach.

Hawk had said he would be at the cabin by six. Six had come and gone. Two more minutes and six thirty would pass with no Hawk in sight. Too hungry to wait, Meg found a package of whole-grain spaghetti noodles, a jar of marinara sauce and a can of green beans. That would do. If he arrived in time, he could eat with her. If not, he could heat up leftovers.

She poured the sauce into a pot and set water to boil for the noodles. A search for a can opener started with the opening and closing of every drawer in the kitchen and ended with her staring blankly at the electrical appliance on the counter. What did people find so difficult about a manual opener that someone needed to invent electric machinery to open a can?

Meg stuck the can under the blade. Countless attempts failed to move the blade around the lip of the can. She checked the cord. It fit snuggly into the wall socket. She pulled the can out and fingered the moving parts of the opener. They moved. They just didn't open the can. "Blasted thing. Why won't you work?"

"May I help?"

Meg twisted, can in hand. Hawk leaned against the doorframe, arms folded over his chest and the ever-present Stetson pushed back off his forehead.

"What happened to knocking?"

"I live here. I don't have to knock. Even if I had, your argument with the can opener would have drowned out a knock."

"I do not argue with kitchen appliances."

"My apologies." He pointed his chin at the can. "May I?"

Meg flipped him the can. "Help yourself."

He caught it, crossed to the counter, slid the can into place and set the opener in motion. The machine whirred and spun the can. "What are we having with canned green beans?"

"I hope you don't mind that I started dinner. You weren't here to cook, and my stomach had begun to protest vigorously."

"I'm sorry I'm late. I tried to call but the battery on my cell died. A meeting went longer than planned." He looked at the can. "So, what are we having with the green beans?"

Meg held up the box of spaghetti and pointed to the pot of boiling water and noodles.

"I didn't see a vehicle. Who played chauffeur?"

"Andrew. And he made it very clear he wasn't happy about the role and equally clear that he wouldn't be the one returning for me. He said he'd leave a heads-up at home, but I should be prepared to sleep over if no one wanted the job."

"Why don't you call Bent Fork and let your folks know that I'll bring you home. Assuming you have a charge and service. First, taste and let me know if it's hot."

Meg closed her lips over the spoonful of red sauce. "Almost." She set the spoon on the counter. "Hawk, you don't need to take me home.

"I'll call Bent Fork and see if someone is able to pick me up. Assuming I have service. You've done enough." She held up the phone. "Surprise. I have a charge and service."

Hawk chuckled and plucked another noodle from the pot. "This should be ready soon."

"I'll keep it short," she said and hobbled into the living room.

A few minutes later, Hawk deposited a heaping bowl of pasta on the table. "If you'll get the wine-glasses, I'll uncork the wine."

"Dad said thanks for the offer of a ride home,

but he will pick me up in an hour or so. Where are the glasses?"

"In the cabinet left of the sink."

Meg opened the cabinet door and leaned against the counter, taking most of the weight off her ankle, and took down two glasses. "These are beautiful."

"My grandmother's. My mother and I came for a rare visit from Cheyenne and my grandmother offered me milk in one of her special glasses while she, Lame Eagle and my mother drank a deep red wine. She made me feel special. It was the last time I saw her."

"I'll be extra careful with them. Now—" she pointed to the bottle "—the cork has to come out of the bottle before we can pour the wine."

Hawk cleared his throat. "Right." He lowered the arms of the corkscrew and popped the cork.

Meg carried the glasses to the table. "How did your meeting go?"

"Which one?"

"I didn't know you had more than one."

"First meeting was with Wendell to discuss some wire fencing. The other meeting wasn't scheduled. I happened to run into someone who wanted to talk business."

"Business you don't sound pleased about."

"I don't suppose many people enjoy a talk with bankers and accountants."

"Bankers and accountants. Oh my." She grimaced and wagged her head.

Hawk chuckled. "You look like you just took a long pull from a gallon of very old milk."

"Recalling the loan application process for college."

"My sentiments exactly." He mimicked her expression.

"Bad news? And if I'm being nosy, just tell me to mind my own business, and I'll try."

"I like that you'll try." He gave her a quick smile. "I had hoped for better results."

"*Better* may yet come your way. I'm hoping there are more bones to uncover at the site. That might bring something better."

"So, you want to keep digging?"

Meg nodded. "It would be amazing if we were able to find enough to identify and assemble for a display. The Mayfield would be my first choice, obviously. So much would depend on what I find and the condition. Bits and pieces are okay for study, but a more complete skeleton offers the potential for substantial payment."

"Payment?" Hawk lowered his fork. "What kind of payment?"

"I know things are challenging for Sitting River right now. Connor says Bent Fork is struggling, as well. We'll get through this, we always do. In the meantime, Dad said Lame Eagle helped us a time or two when we needed it. I can't give you money, I don't have any to give. You wouldn't take it anyway."

"No. I wouldn't."

"I can offer you an opportunity. Possibly. If you let me continue to dig until I have to go to Michigan and if something is found, we could both benefit. If not, you've only delayed the construction of the storage barn a few weeks."

"And if you do find something more? Those bones won't magically remove themselves. Will you be here?"

"That's a difficult question to answer."

He looked at her long and hard. "Will. You. Be. Here?"

Meg swallowed. "Hawk, I can't answer that. Please. Let it be. For now."

HE FINISHED HIS PASTA, stacked the plates and took them to the sink. He needed results, not promises. He couldn't trust promises. Meggie offered him a possibility. Hope. That he could take.

"Let's finish our wine on the porch. Head on out. I'll be right behind you."

He finished clearing dishes, tucked the wine bottle under his arm, lifted the delicate glasses and pushed open the screened door. Meggie slouched in the swing with her eyes closed. A peaceful smile tugged at the corners of her mouth. She nudged the swing back and forth with her good leg while the injured one, still sporting a beige bandage around her knee, stuck out like a new fence post. Her head, like his own, too often held a hat. Tonight, she'd anchored her hair with a pencil as she'd done the day he'd met her. Memories flashed around him, and temptation took a mighty hold.

He closed the door as quietly as he could. He wanted to savor this moment, to brand his mind with the unguarded picture of Meggie Farrell sitting on his porch, on his swing, in his company.

Meg opened her eyes. Hawk held out her glass of wine. "Penny for your thoughts?" Better her thoughts than his.

"Just letting my mind wander."

"Wandering far?"

"Michigan and back."

Hawk settled on the swing next to her. "Long trip."

"Too long," she sighed. "Lame Eagle picked a perfect spot to build this cabin. It rests far enough from the creek to escape rapid snowmelt but close enough to enjoy the lullaby of the water."

Hawk scooted closer. "Lullaby?"

"Soothing. Melodic. This is one of my favorite places. The water. The way the valley looks when it's all gussied up in larkspur, paintbrush and daisies." She bobbed her head. "And the aspen and conifer climbing up the ridge carrying their varying shades of green."

He couldn't argue with her. Beauty surrounded him and it was his. It suited his needs. For now. He didn't need a space the size of Big House and the Reeds did. Once the additions were completed, the cabin would comfortably hold himself and his mother when she visited.

He set his glass on the narrow table by the swing and turned to Meggie. "I've thought about what you said. About the bone. How old it was, what it looked like and were there any more? I've taken some things for granted since Lame Eagle passed. He wouldn't have let me lessen the merit of what's around me. Living or dead."

"Sounds like you're okay with my continuing to dig."

Hawk nodded.

"Thank you. I have the names of two students from the School of Mines who live in the area and are home for the summer. They're grandchildren of a couple of Ruby's senior center friends. Anyway, they're willing to volunteer their time and help with the dig. I'm planning to ask my class if they would be interested in coming up to the ridge to view geological formations and the dig site. It would be very educational in many aspects."

"Gathering a bag of rocks for your class. Planning a field trip. You've taken quickly to the idea of teaching."

"I didn't expect the job to matter so much. I thought I'd help as long as I could and hope TCC would find a teacher before I had to leave. But…" She smiled. "I'm really looking forward to tomorrow. I have a bit of first-day jitters, but I am excited about the whole thing. I'll need your approval for the field trip. It is your property."

"Let me think about it."

"Thank you."

"I didn't say yes, yet."

She gave him a wide grin. "You said you'd think about it. That's a start."

"Hmm." Hawk took her wineglass. He set it carefully on the small table with his own. "What about you?"

"Me? I have a job, thank you."

"A job in Michigan. What about a job here, in Tyler? You just said you love it here. You have a gift, Meggie. A passion for giving to others. You're one of the most selfless people I know. But sometimes, sometimes I think you need to think about what *you* want, what you really need."

"I really love paleontology, and I really need a job."

"In Michigan?"

"That's where the job is."

"Is that where the job has to be?" He traced a line from her temple to her jaw and down the side of her neck.

Meg sucked in a breath. "Hawk?"

"Hmm?"

"What are you doing?"

"Working my way up to kissing you." He leaned closer. His breath fell across her parted lips before they touched. Soft and hesitant. With a husky mur-

mur, he wrapped his arms around her in a movement as natural as breathing. He pulled her against him, and breathing seemed unimportant.

Her fingertips splayed across his back and one hand cupped around his neck. Even as her hands moved, so did his. He unwound her arms, gently took her hands in his and held them to his heart. "I'm sorry. I shouldn't have started this. I don't have room for more distractions in my life right now and you've made it clear you're going back to Michigan."

Meg pulled her hands free. "You know, I've thought about this moment since our ride together the day you and Lame Eagle found me leading Molasses. To be kissed by you. To return the kiss. To feel bound together in a moment of time. Never once did I imagine you'd immediately tell me you regretted kissing me." She pushed off the swing and limped to the porch rail.

"Meggie." He followed her and stretched out his hand to take hers. In the deepening twilight, headlights, bright and steady, shone on the road. He lowered his hand and looked down on her. She stood on her good leg and leaned her hip against the rail looking all tilted and small. Tiny creases etched across her forehead. He wanted to smooth the crinkles and tell her he didn't regret kissing her. What he regretted was wanting more, knowing he couldn't have more. He swallowed. "Looks like your ride is here."

Meg straightened. "I need to get my backpack."

"I'll get it." He opened the screened door. "I know you're not driving yet. I'm going by the post office tomorrow to return a baler part and have a chat with Aaron about the excavator. I'd be happy to give you a ride."

She kept her back to him. "Thank you. Tomorrow should be the last time anyone has to drive me. I appreciate the neighborly offer and the brother who drew the short straw for chauffer duty will be forever grateful."

HAWK PARKED HIS pickup in Professor Nelson's reserved spot. Meg slid out and pulled the crutches from the back seat. Her knee remained a little tender, and her ankle balked at any overuse, but she hoped Dr. Lewis would clear her to abandon the crutches today. She was tired of feeling clumsy. Her underarms ached. Her shoulders ached. Her hands ached. She wanted to get back to a normal life.

"I'll take my backpack if you will bring the rocks. Please," she added politely.

The drive into town, awkwardly silent, had given her time to think more about the night before. He'd kissed her and had immediately regretted it. That had stung, deep and sharp. She'd wanted the kiss. She'd wanted their closeness. She'd wanted that moment for a long time. The few minor relationships she'd had in Michigan had started with friendly banter and common interests. Any closeness ended when she realized they weren't whom she wanted, whom she often dreamed about. They weren't Hawk.

Where did they go from here? She didn't know. What she did know was that in the early hours of the morning, she'd pushed her hurt and disappointment aside and accepted the fact that she wanted Hawk in her life.

Hawk tugged the bag off the back seat with a grunt. "Where to, Teacher?"

Meg couldn't help but smile. "You know, I like the sound of that more and more." She turned toward the four main campus buildings. "This way," she said, and began the slow trek to the nearest redbrick structure.

"Do you want these in the classroom or Nelson's office?"

"Let's go to the office first." She pulled keys from her backpack. "There are some maps I'd like to sort through before class starts."

Meg stepped into the room and perused every inch of it. Books filled the shelves. Cardboard tubes littered the floor. Posters and charts papered the walls. Miniature dinosaurs and rocks of all types and sizes covered every available space.

"I think this room deserves a lot of the credit for my decision to focus on geology and paleontology. Dad brought me here when I was six so I could ask about a unique rock I'd found."

"Was it?"

"What?"

"Unique."

"It was to me." She ran a finger over a small bronze replica of a stegosaurus. "Once I saw the maps, the books, the posters, the rocks, the dinosaurs and the fossils, I put my unique rock in my pocket and peppered Professor Emory, the geology professor at the time, with questions. Dad had to practically gag me and carry me out."

"What's that?" Hawk asked, pointing to a piece of wood with a large hook anchored to it.

"An allosaurus claw. Professor Nelson said he found it. Now, given that he's shown himself willing to lie, I'm not so sure he was the one who actually found it." She looked from desk to floor to walls and back to the desk. "If this were my office, I'd do some serious organizing. Look at this. He has topographical maps mixed with prehistoric-era charts, and look at these shelves." She shook her head. "There's no order at all to the books. I don't see how he functioned in here."

"Maybe he was too busy dreaming about eggs."

The sound of voices came from the room next door. Her students.

Meg stared at the adjoining door. A solid barrier between her and seventeen people expecting to learn about geology from her. She put a hand on her stomach. This wasn't a course for credit. It was a summer class offered by the community college for learning's sake and raising money for the college. She wasn't a professor. She had no teaching certificate. She did, however, know geology.

Hawk opened the door. "You can do this."

She swallowed and nodded. The last email from Mrs. Burlew had the names of the students who had signed up for the class. Most of the older registrants she knew personally but the few younger ones were only familiar names.

Hawk picked up the bag of rock samples.

"Wait. I'd like one of the students to do that. I want to get them involved early."

"You're a natural, Miss Farrell. Just share what you know, and you'll do fine." He leaned down and dropped a quick kiss on her cheek. "Just fine."

DONE.

Meg picked up her backpack, slung it over her shoulder and looked around the small classroom. She'd survived the first class. More than survived. She had enjoyed it. The students were attentive and had participated with enthusiasm. Their intelligent and curious questions generated ideas for future class discussions.

She locked the door, stuck a crutch under each arm, turned and nearly collided with Joe Hawk. "How do you just appear without a sound?"

"I can't help it."

"Try. Or I'm going to get the biggest cowbell I

can find and hang it around your neck. What are you doing here?"

"John called and asked if I could take you home. He's delayed in Fort Collins. How about I buy the new teacher lunch."

"What's he doing in Fort Collins?"

"My guess is he's picking up a part for his Mustang that he couldn't find in Denver. So, lunch?"

"I really can't, Hawk. I want to get to work."

He gestured back to the locked classroom. "You just finished work."

"I just finished class work. Now I want to work at the dig."

"You have to eat."

She patted her backpack. "I packed a peanut butter sandwich and an apple this morning. The time you gave me is quickly running out."

Hawk frowned.

"I'm not complaining. Honest."

"I did check on the availability of the excavator and I have a proposal."

Meg folded her arms across her chest. "What sort of a proposal?"

"I'll be honest. I'm still unsettled about the movement of fossils and what it entails."

"But?"

Hawk held up his hand. "I'll give you more time to continue your digging if you'll have lunch with me."

Meg poked his shoulder. "Aaron doesn't have the excavator back from his brother-in-law yet."

Hawk gave her a sheepish grin. "Not yet."

"So, I was going to have more time even without your offer." A smile spread across her face. "Okay. Lunch, but at a place of my choosing."

He raised one eyebrow and fixed her with a sober stare. "I'll choose. Reward for playing chauffeur again. Besides, you'd opt to sit at a fast-food spot."

She started the rhythmic movement of crutches forward, legs follow. "Okay. And just to be clear, I'd have picked a drive-through."

Hawk adjusted his stride to keep pace with her slower steps. Reaching the outer door, he stopped and held it open. She paused. "Hawk? If lunch gets me extra time, how about I cook dinner for us, and you okay my idea of bringing my class up to the site for a geological field trip with some paleontology thrown in?"

"You cook? Would an electrical appliance and a can of veggies be involved?"

"I really do know how to cook, and we have a manual opener at Bent Fork."

"I don't have one at the cabin."

"You want me to cook at the cabin? Again?"

"You call a box of pasta and canned peas cooking?"

"We satisfied our appetites, didn't we?"

He nodded. "We did satisfy our appetites for food. How about tonight?"

"Tonight?"

"It's quiet at the cabin. No Farrell family interruptions. Is that a problem?"

*A problem?* A quiet dinner with Hawk at his beautiful cabin with no family interruptions. A problem? No. Except for the fact she'd been spending more and more time with Hawk. A lot. Maybe it was a problem.

"Meggie?"

More time to dig and an opportunity to bring her class up to the site. She'd deal with thoughts of missing Hawk when the time came. She held out her hand. "It's a date. I mean it's a dinner."

# *CHAPTER FOURTEEN*

HAWK SLID INTO the last open booth and waited for Meggie to pass through the lunch crowd. The Drop-By Café brimmed with locals, including a few students from her class. Comments of "great class, Meggie" and "looking forward to the next class" were called out as she wove her way through the maze of tables.

He handed her a black-and-white laminated menu. "You've made quite an impression."

"Have I?"

"You heard them."

She glanced around the small café and spotted Nick Sauders, the youngest in the class, huddled with his friends at a corner table creating something with thick-cut fries, mustard, ketchup and salsa.

Hawk rested his forearms on the table and leaned in. "What do you think Nick's doing?"

Meg smiled. "Given our discussion in class, I'd say he's attempting to illustrate something about tectonic plate movement or volcanoes or both. At least he paid attention."

"You have a real gift, Meggie. There's excitement in your voice and your eyes go bright when you're explaining things. I noticed you use more common words around the technical terms to make sure everyone understands."

"I didn't know going in how much collective knowledge the class would have. Mr. Glenn probably knows more than I do but Nick Sauders barely knows his name and address and apparently likes to play with his food."

Hawk chuckled. "Nick may be eighteen, but there's more to him than testosterone. He helps on Sitting River from time to time. You'll find he's a quick study."

"They all are." She tapped her mouth with her index finger. "How do you know I use common words around technical terms?"

He held up his hands. "Caught. My chat with Aaron didn't take long so I came back to wait for you. The connecting door was ajar, so I listened a little."

Napkin-wrapped utensils slid across the table and brightly colored coasters followed. "Afternoon, Hawk. Meggie. Heard you were home. How long are you staying this time?"

"Hi, Angie." Hawk greeted the woman with a flash of white teeth and leaned against the back of the booth as the café owner placed glasses of water on the coasters.

She tapped the eraser end of her pencil on the table. "I'm hearing good things about your class."

"Really? The class just ended."

"A few others wanted to sign up, including me."

"Why the interest in a geology class, Angie? If you don't mind my asking?"

"Learning," came the simple reply. "A body should always be learning. I visited California once. Took part in an earthquake." Angie shuddered. "Wondered ever since what made the ground skip around like that."

Hawk saw Meggie's face pucker with thought. Something had popped into that head of hers. He hoped it wouldn't require more of his ranch.

"What will you have, sugar? My chicken potpie is fresh out of the oven."

"You mentioned there were others interested in the class." Meggie leaned her elbows on the table. "How many others?"

"Well, there's Sharon Willis and her sister Mary. They have the pottery shop next door." She rubbed the pencil against the side of her head. "And four or five others."

Meggie's head bobbed slightly. Yes, there was definitely something percolating in that pretty head of hers.

"Now." Angie collected the menus. "How about two potpies?"

"Sounds good to me." Hawk opened the wrapped utensils. "What's for dessert?"

"Leftover peach pie. It's good, but if you'll come back Saturday night, I'll make a special dessert just for the two of you."

Hawk looked across the table. "It looks like we have a date for Saturday?"

"I don't know."

Propping a fist on one hip, Angie eyed Meggie. "You'd say no to a Saturday night with this fine, handsome man?"

"No. I mean. Well, he is handsome."

"Then you're saying no to a special dessert made with my two hands from my great-grandfather's recipe?"

"No."

"Good. Two potpie specials coming up. And I'll see the two of you Saturday night."

Meggie looked at Hawk and grinned. "I guess we didn't need menus after all."

"Are you okay joining me Saturday? I guarantee you Angie's dessert will be worth it."

"I suppose."

"Some enthusiasm would be nice."

"Sorry. It's been a long day already and it's not even half over." She unrolled her utensils.

"I've been thinking," he said.

"I've been thinking," she said, at the same time.

"Sorry. Go ahead," Hawk prompted.

"No. You first."

Their laughter, like their words, met and mingled over the table. Hawk let the moment settle before gesturing her to continue.

Meggie cleared her throat. “I want to thank you. I know I’ve asked a lot of you lately and I really appreciate everything from helping with the dog, to the rides here and there and for at least thinking about the future of my work with the fossils and for agreeing to a field trip for my class up to the dig site.”

Hawk leaned back in the booth. “Did I agree?”

“Didn’t you? I thought the deal was I cook dinner and you agree to my class coming up. I think they’ll benefit from seeing the bluffs. It will give them an opportunity to observe firsthand the work that went into creating these majestic mountains we call home. For them to see, in a different light, what’s in their own backyard.”

“You mean, in my backyard.”

“And the site could be a valuable teaching tool. So much learning goes on outside of classrooms and textbooks.”

“I have a few questions.”

She rested her forearms on the table, folded her hands and leaned closer. “Okay.”

“How many will be coming? How long will they stay? What will you need from me?”

“Always the responsible rancher.”

“My ranch, my responsibility.”

“The only thing they’ll need from you is your

permission to be on Sitting River and to take away a few rocks they may find interesting."

"Or unique."

Meg smiled. "Or unique. Showing them the fossil will interject a little paleontology into the trip and will hopefully enhance the understanding of geological time."

"Do you think they would want to do any digging? Assuming they have *your* permission."

Meggie leaned back. "Wait. You're saying it's okay to bring my class up to the bluffs *and* let them dig at the site?"

He watched her eyes flash with hope. She truly lit up when she talked about her rocks and fossils. They grounded her, gave her a place to anchor her body and her mind.

"If they want and you supervise."

"Of course. I'll give a quick tutorial on proper excavation and select an area they won't do any harm but will still be helpful."

"Always the responsiblc paleontologist."

Angie stopped beside their table and placed steaming potpies and colorful salads in front of them. "Be here Saturday at seven." She winked and sashayed away.

Meggie steepled her fingers. "Why?"

"Why what?"

"Why let the class come up to the cliffs? Why encourage them to participate in the dig? I know you don't like to have too many people on the land your family has considered sacred for generations."

Hawk shrugged. "Maybe I'm getting more comfortable having people on Sitting River." With his mother's move to Albuquerque a few years ago, it had been only Lame Eagle, the Reeds and himself, plus hired hands when needed. Now his ranch was filling up with people. The Romeros had asked him to consider selling Little House to them once the rental agreement ended. Jenna, her husband and family were living in Big House with Larry and Emma. The grain project would put Andrew on the ranch more frequently, and Meggie… Meggie had become a regular presence on his ranch and in his life. A presence he found both comfortable and troublesome.

"You won't even know we're there."

He inclined his head. "You have a point about seeing the area through new eyes, your eyes. To understand how the land came to be."

Meggie grinned and lifted a finger. "Ah, there's the fallacy. The land hasn't come to be, as if it's reached its final destination. The earth is constantly changing. We don't see the transformations unless they're dramatic, but change is occurring all the time. And time is part of why we don't see the change. There's geological time and there's human time. And the two are very, very, very far apart." She pushed her plate aside. "Speaking of time, how about we get this to go?"

"You agreed to lunch with me at a place of my choosing. I chose this place and lunch isn't over." He slid the plate in front of her. "It tastes better hot."

"I will eat. Later. I have work I want to do and very little time."

"And I have a ranch to run. If I keep leaving Larry shorthanded, he'll quit. But I need to eat, and I prefer to enjoy my meal in the company of a beautiful woman sharing stimulating conversation instead of staring at the backside of a herd of mooing cattle from a moving horse, surrounded by the odor of said cattle, and listening to Larry complain about his aching joints while I try, with one hand, to shove one of Emma's fully loaded turkey sandwiches into my mouth and hold reins with the other."

Meg's cheeks warmed. He'd called her beautiful. Hawk didn't hand out compliments with ease and she usually didn't accept them with ease. A hint of a smile tugged the corners of her mouth. This one came so effortlessly. She'd receive it and move on. Meg picked up her fork. "I didn't realize a rancher's lunch could be so sensory heavy."

Hawk laughed. "That's a delicate way of saying a working lunch stinks."

MEG PUT THE food in the refrigerator and went out to the porch to wait for Hawk. She was late, he was later. She checked her phone. Nothing. She placed it on the side table and sat on the swing. Her leg ached. She'd been cleared to drive with the promise of not overdoing. The first time driving had left a dull throb in her ankle. She pushed against the smooth planks of the porch with her left foot gently rocking the swing back and forth and stretched her right leg.

The swing's momentum picked up enough for her to lift both legs and let it sway back and forth on its own. She tipped her head against the cushion, closed her eyes and listened to the sounds of hunger growling from her empty stomach loud enough to rival the distant thunder. Much-needed rain was imminent. Clouds she'd admired on her way to the cabin had thickened with moisture. She'd welcome the rain, she just didn't look forward to a drive back home in a downpour. She didn't like driving in the rain. Visibility dropped, wipers thumped, roads developed slick patches, and it all tensed her body and mind.

The swing stopped its back-and-forth swaying. Meg rose. Hawk would have to fend for himself for dinner.

She reached for her phone just as it chimed. Hawk. She swiped her finger across the screen. "It's about time. I was going to pack up the food I brought and—"

"Meggie, have you seen Ava?"

"Ava? Yes, this morning at breakfast. Why?"

"She's missing. We can't find Ava or the dog."

Meg dropped onto the swing. "What do you mean she's missing?"

"We've searched Bent Fork on foot without any sign of her or the dog. We're going out on horseback to cover as much ground as we can before dark. Your father wants you to come home along the north track and keep a look out for Ava. If we—"

"Wait. How can Ava be missing? Where would she go? Why would she leave Bent Fork? And why take Buddy?" Meg couldn't imagine Ava, sweet, loving five-year-old Ava, wandering off on her own. At least not going far. She pressed her hand to her chest, inhaled and exhaled. "She must be somewhere around the homestead. Did you check the outbuildings? The shed where we kept the dog? You said Buddy was gone. Maybe she took Buddy to the shed to get him out of Ruby's way. We all know how Ruby feels about the dog."

"We've looked everywhere there is to look around here. Head this way and keep your eyes open for any sign of Ava or the dog and let me or your parents know if you see anything. We'll do the same."

"I'm leaving now." Meg pushed off the swing. "Hawk?" Her words stopped, her mind stilled, her body froze. Images of the coyote snarling at Buddy flared in her mind. Hawk's talk of a rogue mountain lion prowling for weak livestock ran behind the image of the coyote. Either animal might attack a dog or, worse, a small child. "Hawk," she squeezed his name from her throat. "The coyote. The mountain lion. They're out there, too."

"Meggie, we'll find her. I promise."

"Heidi? She must be frantic."

"She's focused."

And more terrified than Meg. "I bet she's wishing Keith were here." That's what Meg would want. She'd want the man she'd chosen to spend her life with and have a family with to be present, to draw strength from one another. To comfort each other.

"Meggie?"

Hawk's voice seeped through her fear. He knew the land. He'd search with her family for Ava. She knew the property as well as the others. She needed to do her part. "The north track. I'm going. I'll call if I see anything."

She stuffed her phone in her back pocket and collected her backpack. While her heart wanted her to sprint to the pickup, her head and ankle urged caution. The four steps felt like four hundred and the distance to her vehicle looked miles away instead of a few yards. She tossed her pack onto the passenger seat and sped toward the north track.

The track curled west off Sitting River property and sliced between Sitting River and Bent Fork before it reached the county road. Between the two ranches, frequent travel and hard-packed dirt marked a clear track for a motorized vehicle. Meg bounced along the dirt road, hands on the wheel and her gaze flitting from one side of the road to the other.

Once past the cluster of trees near the cabin, the open valley offered a clear view of grasses, wildflowers, willows and aspen trees flanking Fendels Creek and to the peaks beyond.

No wandering little girl walking a dog.

She hadn't asked how long Ava had been missing. Even if she'd been gone for hours, the child wouldn't have gotten this far. Ava had to be hiding somewhere around the house. She, Molly and Caroline often played hide-and-seek and they had some great hiding places, inside the house and out. Had they asked Caroline and Molly about Ava's absence?

Meg pulled her phone from her pocket. No service.

She tossed the phone on the seat with her backpack and switched her gaze from the road to the sky overhead. Dark clouds sank into the valley, blocking any rays from the setting sun, and let loose their contents on everything underneath. And now, rain had a companion to impede their search—darkness. Dusk would soon be on them.

The wipers slapped back and forth while thoughts of Ava lost, frightened, wandering alone in the dark and rain ratcheted Meg's effort to cover more ground as fast as possible. She ignored the complaint from her ankle and sped over the dirt road, only slowing for the deep potholes and stopping once for a small herd of elk crossing to reach the creek.

Rain, less now than the initial downpour, hindered her field of vision and when the road curved to the west, her truck skidded and she slowed again. As the road straightened, she spotted a pickup well off the track. No lights. No exhaust that she could see. No evidence of a driver. No signs of an accident. It was battered with age but nothing recent. No tracks of another vehicle. The truck didn't belong to Bent Fork, nor did it carry the Sitting River logo that emblazoned Hawk's ranch vehicles. Still, it looked familiar.

For all of five seconds she debated continuing before pulling to a stop. Someone could be in the pickup. Someone could need help. She tugged her hat from her backpack, stuffed her phone in her pocket, leaped out of the truck and promptly slid on the wet grass. Her ankle, still weak, gave way, dropping her on her backside.

She scrambled to her feet just as Hawk and Wickiup galloped toward her.

"Are you okay?" Hawk asked, sliding from the saddle.

"Did you find Ava?" Her words were spoken before his feet hit the ground.

"Not yet." He caught her by the arms. "Are you okay?"

"I'm fine." She shook off his concern. "I thought someone would have found her by now. Where could she have gone, Hawk? Why would she have gone?"

"No one is sure. Caroline and Molly said Ava wanted to show Buddy the tire swing Keith put up for the girls before he was deployed. That was right after Ruby had gotten back from town, about two thirty. When your dad didn't find her near the swing, they started a full-scale search." He shot a glance at her pickup. "Problems?"

"No. I've got out to check that one." She pointed to the battered truck under the cottonwood.

"Did you see it go off the road?"

"No."

"I'll take a look. Why don't you get out of the rain."

"I'd rather come with you, Hawk." Her words were directed to him, but her focus narrowed in on the truck. "There's something familiar about that pickup. I can't remember where I've seen it. But I have seen it recently."

Meg gripped his arm and limped along beside him. The closer they came to the truck, the stronger her feeling of recognition. She knew it from somewhere.

Rounding the back of the truck, Hawk jerked them to a halt.

A man sat on the ground, back against the front wheel with a tarp draped over his head and shoulders. Slowly he rose and lowered the canvas covering.

"Mike." Meg stepped forward.

"Shh." Mike put a finger to his lips. "The little

one's sleeping." He tipped his head at the cab of the truck.

Hawk peered through the driver's window. "Ava."

"Oh, thank goodness." Meg sagged against Hawk. He slid an arm around her and held her to him. She inhaled deeply and slowly exhaled. "Thank goodness."

"She's okay," Mike said. "As far as I can tell. I'd parked in the shade and went to hunt for…" He slid a sideways glance at Hawk. "I wanted to snare a rabbit. When the rain started, I hiked back to the truck and found the little one curled up inside sound asleep with the dog sitting next to her."

"Buddy," Meg said.

"He wouldn't leave her. I opened the door real slow and quiet like to let him hop out for a call of nature if he needed." Mike shrugged. "Dog wouldn't budge and when I leaned in to take a closer look at the little one, he made it known my company wasn't wanted."

Meg peered into the cab. On the passenger side floor, curled into a big ball of fur, slept Buddy.

Hawk looked from the truck to the man. "Why didn't you call someone?"

"No phone."

"You could have taken her home to Bent Fork or Big House."

"I didn't know she belonged on Bent Fork or Sitting River. She was asleep and I didn't want to scare the child. I figured I'd wait out here until she woke up or until it got late. Then I'd figure out something."

Meg gave him a smile. "Thank you. That was very thoughtful. I think we should let the family know Ava is okay and get her home."

"I'll carry her to your pickup." Hawk opened the door. "Ava," he called softly. "Ava."

"Let me." Meg leaned into the cab and caressed Ava's head. "Ava. Wake up, sweetie. It's time to go home."

"Hmm," murmured Ava. "Buddy."

"Buddy's right here. It's time for him to go home, too."

"Ruby doesn't want Buddy. I heard her on the phone. She said Buddy needed to go." Ava's lower lip trembled. "I don't want Buddy to go. I want to keep Buddy forever."

Meg swallowed. "Where were you and Buddy going?"

"To Hawk so he could keep Buddy until Daddy comes home. Then we will get our own home and Buddy can come with us and not cause trouble for Ruby. Hawk likes dogs. He has Maiku. Maiku and Buddy could be friends." Ava smiled at Hawk. "Would that be okay?"

Meg grinned at Hawk. "What an excellent idea."

MIKE CLEARED HIS THROAT. "I can take him since nobody wants him. We have a lot in common. The dog and me."

Meg helped Ava from the truck. "First, we need to let the family know Ava is okay. Then, get Ava home. After that, we can decide what to do with Buddy." She checked her phone. "Still no service. I'll head home with Ava. Somewhere between here and Bent Fork, I should have service and will let the family know everything's okay."

Hawk pulled the phone from his back pocket and swiped open the screen. "Nothing. Okay. I'll meet you there." He turned to Mike. "I'd like a word with you. If you can stay a minute."

Mike nodded. "Okay by me."

"Can we drive Buddy to Hawk's? He doesn't like the rain."

"Let's take Buddy to Bent Fork for now. We can decide what's best for him tomorrow. Okay?"

Ava nodded. "Aunt Meggie, do you think Buddy knows he's not wanted in the house?"

"I think Buddy knows you want what's best for him. And I want what's best for you." She kissed Ava's forehead. "What's best is to get you both home." Meg caught the makeshift leash of frayed rope Ava must have gotten from the shed and wrapped it around her hand. "Thanks for watching over Ava, Mike."

Mike tipped his head. "My pleasure."

"I'LL NEVER FORGIVE MYSELF." Ruby wiped her face with her apron. "What if something had happened to that child?" She sniffed and dabbed a corner of the apron under her eyes. "I would have to leave Bent Fork." She choked back a sob. "It's my fault Ava ran away from home."

Lansford draped his arm around Ruby's shoulders and gently squeezed. "No one is going anywhere."

Heidi stooped in front of Ruby and took the woman's hand in hers. "Ruby, Ava didn't run away because of you. She didn't run away at all. She innocently took it upon herself to find a temporary home for the dog."

"A dog she heard me say was causing too many messes."

"You're not the only one in this house who has said, or at least thought, the same thing," Joanna pointed out. "We all want him to have a good home. I'm not sure Bent Fork is the right home."

Meg bent and ruffled the thick fur between Buddy's ears. The dog rolled to his side, giving her access for a belly rub. Meg complied. "It's not your fault, pup," she whispered. Buddy had been someone's pet. Once loved and cared for. Now he was deemed a nuisance.

Hawk pushed away from the doorjamb. "I'll take him to Sitting River. The Reeds' grandchildren are quite taken with Maiku. I'm sure they will enjoy having another dog around. If not, I'll take him up to the cabin."

Meg ruffled Buddy's ears. "Okay, if you're willing to keep him for a few weeks, I'll take him with me to Michigan when I leave."

Lansford chuckled. "First no one wanted him and now he seems much in demand."

Ruby tilted her head to one side and then the other, giving the dog a long look. "I can't have Ava lose Buddy because he's a little oversize and rambunctious. He just needs a little training." She blew her nose. "I'll look into it first thing in the morning."

"Oh, Ruby." Heidi gathered Ruby into a hug. "If the family is willing to keep Buddy, Ava and I will see about some behavior classes. I should have done something about the dog as soon as Keith saw him on our video chat and called him Buddy. Ava had already fallen for the dog, and with Keith's smile when he saw Ava's arm around Buddy and Ava grinning ear to ear, well..." She hugged Ruby again. "I think Buddy has found a home and has become my responsibility. Mine and Ava's. A responsibility we will gladly accept."

Ruby sighed. "Mine, too. I want to make sure Ava knows I am okay with having Buddy around." She tugged her apron and smoothed it over her lap before standing. "Now that that's settled, I think we're all due for drinks on the front porch. We have a little bit of everything."

"I'll help." The ringing of her phone filled the air with its shrill tone. Meg glanced at the screen. "Dr. Vanover. I need to take this."

Thirty minutes later, Meg plugged her phone into the charger and joined her family on the porch.

"Is everything okay?" her mother asked.

"Yes."

Hawk made room for her on the swing. She settled herself between him and her dad.

"You sure, honey?" Her dad patted her knee, a gesture she'd come to accept as his version of a hug. "You sound a little hesitant."

"Rachael wanted to fill me in on opening progress, or lack thereof in some aspects. She said some areas were moving along smoothly, others, not so much."

"Do you feel the need to be there? I'm sure TCC and your class would understand."

Her mother supported the need to go, if necessary, even if it wasn't what Joanna Farrell wanted for her daughter. Was it what Meg wanted? Surprisingly she wasn't missing the chaos connected to the construction or the uncertainty of when to bring in exhibit items or the need to make sure everything revolving around her paleo lab and precious fossils fell into perfect order. She had plenty to do here in Tyler.

"I don't *need* to be there. Yet. I'm basically on call."

# *CHAPTER FIFTEEN*

MEG DIRECTED HER class to gather around the trench and gestured to the helpers bent over the worksite. "Yesterday, these two wonderful volunteers from the School of Mines found something amazing. I had planned for this field trip to be mostly geology focused. However, I want to point out this working fossil site and their discovery before we venture off to study the surrounding geological formations."

She stepped into the trench and squatted beside the young man. "Matt, why don't you show the group what you uncovered."

He paused, brush in hand, and nodded. "You sure you don't want to, Meggie?"

"You found it."

"Okay." Matt cleared his throat and waved the small brush over a section of rock. "A couple of days ago, we started scraping away at a chunk of fossilized something." He pointed to a jagged piece of fossilized bone. "Meggie says it's part of a skull. A real dinosaur skull. Right here in Tyler, Colorado."

"Thanks, Matt. I know it doesn't look like much,

but this is a jawbone. The jaw is tilted downward, so we can't see teeth, assuming the jaw still holds teeth."

Ray Powers, the oldest and last to join the class, pointed at the fossil. "So, is that series of bumps a part of the same dinosaur?"

Meg smiled. "Good question. The quick and unfortunate answer is, I don't know. While the skeletal structure of a dinosaur is the same basic pattern as four-legged mammals living today, it's not often we discover a dinosaur skeleton nicely laid out with all its bones and teeth in place. Usually, we find bits and pieces scattered around. Most likely, this guy died at the edge of a river that flowed through here millions of years ago. There could have been a flash flood or maybe the river was fast flowing. Anyway, in getting washed downstream, or caught on a sandbar, the body became a jumbled mess, possibly scattered across the area, eventually covered by sand and mud and the result is the piece of skeleton you see here. Erosion often wears down the covering and exposes the fossil and our work frees the fossil."

She paused to gauge their interest. Some were nodding, some were looking into the trench and a few had their eyes on her. "It's possible the rest of this dinosaur is buried here. It's also possible, given the proximity of the eroding cliff, that the river dried up and the land lifted. Remember we discussed the process of upthrust in class. The riverbed could have been thrust upward, creating the ridge behind us, which is also the victim of weathering and erosion."

"Is it okay if we look around, Meggie?" Nick asked.

"Of course. Make sure you take water and a notebook. If you see anything of interest, don't remove it. Mark it, make notes and let me know. We can have a Q-and-A session before we leave."

She added boundary lines for sight and sent those interested in searching the area on their way. Several students stayed at the site to watch or work with the two volunteers. All in all, she was pleased so many of her class made the trip.

Hawk had yet to make an appearance. She hadn't seen or spoken to him since the night they'd found Ava and Buddy. Emotions had run high on everyone's part but Buddy's. Emotions still battled for their place in her mind and heart. She hadn't forgotten the fear that had hung on her like a heavy blanket until they'd found Ava. She hadn't forgotten the kiss she and Hawk had shared sitting on Lame Eagle's swing. Flutters erupted in her stomach every time she thought about that night, that kiss. The teenage crush hadn't gone away; it had simply gone dormant…like a volcano. Now the feelings were gathering under the surface like lava filling a magma chamber. Confusing feelings swirling around Hawk, family, friends, her job, living in Colorado versus going back to Michigan.

She blew out a heavy breath and stopped looking up at every sound.

With the class settled at the site or wandering in small groups around the area, Meg shifted her attention to a particularly weathered area of the cliff face that had eroded and carved out a small cavity. She wouldn't be able to get too close without equipment, but it was worth a glance.

The gradation went from a gentle incline to a bunny ski slope to a decent sledding run before leveling off at the cliff's plateau. It wasn't a trek for everyone.

"I'm going to walk up the ridge. Anyone want to come along? No? Okay."

MEG LEFT MATT scratching at the rock encasing the newly found jaw while those who remained peppered him with questions.

A third of the way up the slope, Meg stopped and lowered herself onto a boulder to rest her knee and ankle. Mobility improved daily but she had a tendency to overdo and end up with an aching ankle by evening. Today she meant to avoid the ache.

"Clang. Clang. Cowbell ringing."

"Hawk."

"I didn't want to startle you. Is the ankle okay?"

Hawk perched behind her on a rock twice the size of hers. His left arm rested on his drawn-up knee while he shaved slivers from the slender piece of wood he held. Had it not been for the heavy layer of dust on his jeans and boots, she'd have thought she'd interrupted a casual morning of cowboy whittling. The only thing missing was a softly whistled tune.

He tossed the wood aside, folded his knife, stuck it in his hip pocket and slid off the rock.

"I want to make amends for my inappropriate behavior and the thoughtless comments that followed the other night when I kissed you."

"I liked the kiss. A lot. And your comments were—"

"Were meant to keep me from expecting more from our friendship than either of us are able to give." He nudged aside a small stone with the toe of his boot. "I need…"

Meg contemplated Hawk's distracted pushing stones around. Embarrassment? Regret? Hesitation?

"You need?" she prompted.

With a sharp shake of his head, he shifted his gaze from the trail to the open valley. Meg waited. He needed time. That much was clear. Time to settle whatever nagged and nettled. Time to come to terms with the angst he carried from his childhood. Time to come to terms with his emotions. She didn't know what churned and burned inside him.

"So, how's Ava?" he asked.

Whatever it was that needed time, it apparently needed even more. She wanted to push him to yield and open up, but the very thought of someone trying to pull feelings from her that she wasn't ready to impart sent a shiver of annoyance through her.

Meg sighed. "Ava is fine. Resilient and already trying to teach Buddy house manners."

"House manners?"

"No taking food off the table. No jumping on furniture. The sort of manners all house dogs should know."

"Good. Buddy's a smart dog. He'll catch on quickly."

"I hope so, for everyone's sake." She gave him a quick smile. "So, what are you doing up here?"

"I tracked the cat close by, lost the tracks and decided to hang around until you and your class left."

"Being the responsible rancher." She glanced down the path. On the valley floor sat her dig site with the bones of a dinosaur coming to life in bits and pieces. She had high hopes that the discovery of the jaw would lead to something worthwhile. "We haven't talked in a few days. There's been a development with the site you should know about."

"Someone hurt?"

"No, nothing like that. It's actually good news."

"We do need to talk. Can we do that tonight at the Drop-By? If you're still willing."

"Right. Angie's special dinner and dessert."

"Seven okay?"

"Works for me. If you'll excuse me, I want to have a short Q-and-A with my class before we get off your ranch and let you get about your ranching."

HAWK SAT AT the booth sipping lukewarm coffee and glanced out the wide windows of the Drop-By Café.

Still no Meggie. Probably still working to uncover more fossils. With his luck, she'd found a veritable graveyard of dead dinosaurs by now and was setting up a permanent base.

Then what? Move Andrew's hybrid grain site and outbuilding. There were other options. Just not the best options. Move Meggie? He couldn't do that. Meggie sat where the fossils sat as solidly planted and unmovable as the dead and buried dinosaurs she fawned over.

A nagging sensation poked at him. Jealousy. Was he jealous of ancient, extinct creatures?

Angie leaned over the table and refilled his coffee cup. "Better find something else to think about before Meggie gets here. Wouldn't do for her to see such a big frown sitting so heavy on your handsome face." She patted his cheek, took her coffee pot and moved to the next booth.

Hawk sipped the coffee and focused on the activity beyond the café windows. Better to people-watch than struggle with ridiculous thoughts of jealousy over dinosaurs.

Cars and pickups filled the angled parking spaces. Some wore rust and dirt, and while they might look neglected on the outside, the inner workings received all the tender loving care a rancher could spare. One couldn't afford to be stranded in the high country.

Storefront banners and sale signs flapped in the gusts blowing off the surrounding peaks. Folks strolled past and some paused to check Angie's menu board. The three-by-five-foot board sat on an easel in one window with the day's specials printed in bold-colored chalk. The other window framed an array of posters advertising area events, lost pets…and Meggie.

She stood near the door wrestling with her hair. The ever-present backpack sat on the sidewalk at her feet. She started a search of her pockets. Whatever she needed, she didn't find it in the snug jeans. She shifted her focus to the backpack, squatted and conducted another search of pockets, pouches and netted areas before pulling a thick elastic band from the depths of the pack. Heavy hair artillery. She snagged a handful of hair and pulled it through the band multiple times. How did women do that without a mirror? Some instinct? Some skill taught and passed down?

With one hand, she tugged on the front of her emerald-green shirt and snatched up the backpack with the other. She pulled open the door and walked with only the slightest hint of a limp to the booth.

"I'm sorry I'm late." She slid into the cushioned seat opposite him. "I had something I wanted to take care of before meeting with you."

"No problem."

"I kept working at the site after the class left."

"And lost track of time." He should've known she'd stay and work with her fossils. Given the shine in her eyes and the smile that skipped around her mouth, she'd played long enough to find something that interested her.

He leaned back in the booth and waited for her revelation.

"Well, I suppose I did lose track of time. But not because I was digging. I went home to email photos of the site findings to Rachael, Dr. Vanover. She'll be the director at the museum when it opens."

Hawk pushed napkin-wrapped utensils across the table and waited.

"Thank you." She folded her hands together on the table and gave him a wide smile. "We found something the other day. Well, giving credit where credit is due, Matt found it. I took photos and sent them to Rachael. I have a gut feeling about this discovery. If Rachael can verify what I think we've found and if we can find the rest of this guy, or even most of this guy, we can create a wonderful exhibit."

"And what is it you think you've found?"

"Well, I can't say for sure until I get verification, but I think it's an allosaurus."

"A gut feeling."

Meggie grinned. "Don't dismiss my gut feelings, or intuitions, or whatever you want to call them. Your grandfather believed in his instincts and in mine."

He leaned back and folded his arms across his chest. "How much will this exploration cost me?"

"It won't cost you anything."

"Meggie, I'm—"

"Here we go." Angie lowered two plates to the table. "Two special dinners. Dig in while it's hot."

"Thanks, Angie. It looks great." Hawk eyed the plate of saffron rice, almond-crusted trout and steamed broccoli and sniffed. "Smells good, too."

Angie beamed, wished them "bon appetite" and returned to the kitchen.

Meggie blew across a forkful of trout before popping it in her mouth. "Hot." She reached for her water glass. "Heat hot, not spicy hot. I like the seasoning."

Hawk pushed his plate aside, planted his arms on the table and waited.

Meggie looked up from her plate. "You aren't eating?"

"I will as soon as I understand about the removal of the fossil and the cost that's not going to cost me."

"Well, like I said, I hope you'll let me present the bones to the Mayfield. I think the museum will make you a decent offer to be able to display them. If not, you're free to look elsewhere."

He settled back in the booth. "Hmm."

"I thought you'd be happy. The sale of the fossil could financially benefit Sitting River. Maybe a lot."

He stared past Meggie at some nonexistent place. The jumble in his mind didn't allow for focus of any kind. The only clarity he had sang to him from a memory of Lame Eagle. A memory of peace, of unity with the man who taught him about honoring the earth and his Native American heritage, about loving family despite their flaws, about being true to oneself and giving more than you receive.

Hawk pulled on another memory. The weak rise and fall of his grandfather's challenged breathing. Eyes closed and mouth barely moving, his grandfather had taken Hawk's hands and cradled them against his sunken chest and hummed an ancient tune. When the song ended, or breath gave way, Lame Eagle murmured, "All will be well. I promise."

Would all be well? *Well* didn't only apply to his hope for a debt-free ranch, sooner rather than later. *Well* needed to positively affect his hunger for a life beyond the haven of Sitting River. All being well would have him whole with the woman he loved, and a family on his debt-free ranch.

The last words his grandfather had spoken to him hung in the space between his eyes and his future. *All will be well.* He heard them now as clearly as he had that day. He wanted to believe that promise. He *needed* to believe that promise. Now more than ever.

# *CHAPTER SIXTEEN*

MEG SQUINTED AND adjusted the camera lens for the third time. *Focus.* She aimed the camera on the fossilized vertebrae, clicked and tried to push away last night's conversation with Hawk.

Over Angie's amazing cherry cobbler, she'd talked about the possibility of hiring extra help for the dig. The sooner they knew what they had to offer the Mayfield, the sooner Hawk would know what kind of money he could plan to use for Sitting River. While she had gotten more and more excited about the process, Hawk had gotten more and more quiet.

She'd expected some excitement, maybe some relief when she told him there was money to be made from the sale of the fossils. Now, looking back, she realized she had done most of the talking and most of the planning.

A gust of wind blew across her damp face, offering a brief respite from the heat. She put down the camera and sat back on her heels. Loose topsoil moved in swirls over the ground and the leaves of distant aspen trees danced. Overhead, the few scraps of gray cloud she'd seen mingling over Big

Tooth Gap had gathered speed and company. A storm was about to leap into the valley.

Meg stood and stretched aching muscles. She, Amy and Matt had started digging in the trench at seven this morning. She checked her cell phone for the time. 11:18. More than four hours bent over the fossil scraping, brushing, measuring and marking. Nick had stopped by offering a helping hand and asked if his help would count as class participation.

Meg agreed to his request for class participation and gladly accepted his help, freeing Matt to broaden their search. At one point, he'd said he was going to walk along the base of the cliff. That had been an hour ago.

"Amy, I'd like you and Nick to tarp the trench and make sure the tools are stowed and then get some lunch. That storm will open up soon and I don't want any of you out when it does."

Amy eyed Nick and grinned. "Sure thing, Meggie."

"I'm going to find Matt and send him this way."

Slinging her backpack over one shoulder and the rifle Hawk insisted she carry over the other, Meg turned toward the cliff.

High country storms carried the potential to be deadly. Rain could produce flash floods. Lightning and wildfires threatened land and anyone on it. She didn't want to be in the open, nor any of her team, when this one roared into the valley.

She found Matt on his stomach, his head missing his baseball cap and the long sleeves of his athletic shirt pushed past his elbows. He held a dental pick in his hand and scratched along a sandstone outcrop. "Find something?"

He rolled to his side. "No. I thought this discoloration might hold something." He shook his head. "Nothing. You know this paleontology stuff is more work than I thought it would be and a little monotonous. At times. You really have to get used to disappointment."

Meg chuckled. "Yes, you do. I've found patience pays off if you're patient enough. You're doing good work."

"Thanks. I'm enjoying it despite the monotony and disappointment. Hawk said paleontology is contagious."

"Hawk said that?"

"Uh-huh."

"When?"

"Maybe half an hour ago. He stopped for a few minutes, asked how things were going, then headed up that way."

"Up?"

"Yep. You know, I still think there's something here."

Meg glanced skyward. The thick dark gray clumps bumped against each other, forming an ever-widening mass. "Right now, I'd like you to mark this area and join Amy and Nick for lunch. You can wait out the storm in safety and we can start up again later after lunch."

"Sure thing, Meggie. I just want to clear a little more."

"I understand the enthusiasm, but safety comes first. I'd like you to mark the area and join Amy and Nick."

He stuck a foot-long piece of a pine branch into the ground and tied a bright red bandanna around it.

"Done." Matt stood and dusted his hands on his jeans. "I'm glad I brought my pack up with me and I'm glad I listened to you about what to stow in it."

Meg turned her gaze up the slope. Something nagged at the back of her mind. Call it a sixth sense. Call it crazy. Whatever it was, it slowly filled her body. "Did Hawk say anything about mountain lions or tracks when he came by?"

"How'd you know? He said he'd spotted tracks in the valley, and I should stay alert because this one was a mean one."

"Hmm. He's determined to get that mountain lion," she muttered.

"You coming, Meggie?"

"What?"

"Aren't you coming with us?"

"No. I need to talk to Hawk. If it becomes necessary, I can wait out the storm in my pickup. Go on. I'll see you back here after the storm passes."

HAWK STOOD ON the cliff's rim and skipped a stone into the air. It flew straight for a few seconds before falling to the valley floor.

A Steller's jay soared in a wide arc under the swelling blue-black clouds before circling back to the pines. A rumble of thunder, low and long, echoed across the valley. The bird was smart to seek shelter.

Hawk flung another stone. Then another. Thunder rumbled as he whipped yet another off the cliff. He needed to follow the jay's wisdom before the clouds decided they didn't want to carry the rain any farther.

Rain didn't bother him. He knew where it would fall—everywhere. But lightning sought a target. And he made a good one standing on the edge of the cliff with nothing but a scrawny pine to vie for the strike. The tree's roots barely clung to the topsoil. A strong gust or two birds on the same limb could topple it.

Yet, here he stood, his mind in as much turmoil as the approaching storm. He needed to focus on a plan, and he had decisions to make. His grandfather's death had left him with hundreds of acres supporting cattle, horses, hay and grain. Three habitable properties and numerous outbuildings. Two permanent employees, a handful of part-time help that had become less than part-time lately. And debt.

A ranching plan was simple. Grow it and sell it or feed it and sell it. Debt was also simple. Don't get yourself there and don't let someone else get you there. Once you do, it gets complicated. Removing debt also required a plan. He had one. Work hard and save where he could and believe Sitting River would one day be free of the debt brought on by Michael Hawk and his demands for money.

He threw another stone and watched it arc and fall. Somewhere down there, under the green tarps, sat Meggie's fossil pit. Dinosaurs discovered on his land hadn't been a part of the plan. Falling for Meggie hadn't been part of his plan, either. But, if having dinosaur bones on Sitting River kept Meggie here a little longer, he would take the complications they handed him and all the ancient bones the ground spit up.

MEG STOPPED AND shifted the rifle and backpack to her opposite shoulder. Thunder boomed across the valley. Maybe Hawk had left the area. Maybe he was on his way to the cabin. Maybe he was already at the cabin. No need to worry.

Except for the cat tracks and the squeezing in her gut.

He hadn't come down.

A growling deep in the clouds rumbled around her. She drew her elbows to her sides and hunched her shoulders up near her ears. Wind pushed at her in heavy gusts, lifting the brim of her hat. The rain wouldn't wait much longer. What was Hawk thinking to head up there with a storm imminent?

Lightning lashed out in a blinding flash. She

should turn around and get to the pickup. But her instincts rooted her. Not yet. One more turn in the switchback and she'd reach the gentle slope to the plateau. If he wasn't there, she'd hightail it back to the pickup. Pulling the hat snugly over her head, she hurried up the path.

She rounded the last bend and paused to catch her breath. The plateau stretched straight ahead with Hawk at the cliff's edge. A target for lightning bolts if ever there was one. Unless the pitiful tree next to him drew a strike first. Either way spelled disaster.

Meg cupped her hands around her mouth. Words of warning never passed her lips. Her vision narrowed, as if she looked through a small tube. On the boulder behind Hawk crouched a mass of tawny fur, sleek and muscled. A long tail swished silently. The threat of the storm vanished. The danger of lightning disappeared. Her breath caught. She opened her mouth and closed it. She couldn't risk startling the cat or Hawk.

Her knee hit the ground hard as she knelt. She shrugged off the backpack, catching it before it reached the path, and put the pack to one side. Sure. Calm. Steady. All she needed to be and none of which she felt. She slid the rifle from the other shoulder.

Mountain lions didn't typically attack humans, but this one had all the hallmarks of preparing to strike.

Hawk seemed oblivious to the cat behind him. Even as she looked from man to beast, the menacing twitch of the cat's tail stopped. Its body tensed.

Meg pressed the rifle butt tight against her shoulder. She aimed the barrel at the cat. Her finger closed on the cold trigger. She had a vision of the cat launching itself at Hawk. Claws raking Hawk's back, laying open his flesh.

Hawk turned.

Meg fired.

# *CHAPTER SEVENTEEN*

TIME AND SENSES shifted to slow motion. Her mind and body struggled to catch up. The rifle blast left her ears ringing. Pictures oozed through her brain in a series of stills. The cat dropping. Hawk stumbling back against the tree. Hawk and the tree falling over the edge.

Had she missed the cat and hit Hawk? She clutched the rifle in a death grip and bolted up the trail.

Meg kept her gaze fixed on the edge of the cliff and forced her legs to move faster. A familiar burning lanced through her lungs. *Not now*, she pleaded with her body, *not now*.

She barely registered the still form of the cat as she ran past it toward the rim of the ridge. "Hawk!"

"Meggie?"

She heard his voice. Didn't she? "Hawk?"

"Stop! Stay back from the edge. It's unstable."

He sounded close. She dropped to the ground and crept on all fours nearer to the spot where Hawk and the tree once stood. "Where are you? Are you okay?"

"Are you crazy? Get back and stay back."

Heart pounding and blood racing, she eased her body flat on the ground and army-crawled to the very edge. Loose soil drifted down, and small clumps gave way as she reached the rim and peered over.

Hawk looked up at her. Scratches and traces of blood and dirt splattered across his face. His hat was gone, and bits of debris littered his thick hair. He perched on a sliver of an overhang about ten feet below with his back pressed against the cliff wall cradling his left arm to his chest. Below him, the old tree lay splintered on the valley floor.

Disbelief clouded her mind. "I thought you'd be lying down there in a mangled heap with that tree."

"Sorry to disappoint." He spit out flecks of dirt and wiped his mouth with the back of his hand.

Relief and anger hit. "What were you doing standing out in the open with a storm coming? And you call me crazy."

"What are you doing up here?"

"Saving your hide."

"From what?"

"Cat. I saw it crouched behind you ready to spring."

He spit more dirt. "I thought I heard a shot. Did you get it?"

She glanced behind her. For one horrible moment, she imagined the animal rising and pouncing on her with extended claws and large teeth bared and ready to tear into her flesh. She shuddered hard. It lay in the same position. No movement. No breathing. "Yes."

Lightning flashed over the valley and thunder took its turn roaring behind. Heavy clouds had clamored over the peaks and spilled into the valley. Rain bulged in the dark clumps. Rain and lightning. She and Hawk were sitting ducks.

"Hawk, we need to get out of here."

"Got a ladder in your backpack?"

"No, but I have a rope." Meg scooted back from the edge, stood and nearly dropped to her knees. Lightheaded and trembling, she braced her palms on her knees and drew shallow breaths. *Breathe. In. Out.* Her chest, already tight, squeezed her lungs. She needed her rope and her inhaler.

Sucking in another thin breath, she smacked at her pockets. No inhaler. Nothing but a dirty bandanna. If the apparatus didn't bulge from one pocket or another, it sat in her backpack. With the rope. And she'd left her pack down the trail. "I'll be right back." She edged away from the rim, turned and sprinted toward what she hoped could save Hawk and her.

The olive-green bundle sat at the side of the narrow path. She fell on it, yanked the zipper open and turned the pack upside down. Items fell in a heap. She dug through the pile until her fingers closed over the inhaler. A quick puff and in seconds her breathing eased. She drew in several precious breaths, grabbed the rope and, ignoring the ache blooming in her ankle, dashed back up the trail.

"Meggie. Meggie, are you up there?"

"I'm here. I'm going to tie my rope around a tree."

"Make sure it's well anchored. The tree that is. I'd hate to have another one fall around me."

Meg tugged on the rope. The knot held. The pine stood firm. Inch by inch, she crept to the lip of the cliff. Squalls of wind-whipped topsoil peppered her bare limbs and face. She squinted against the blowing dirt and looked over the edge to gauge a spot to play out the rope. "Here, tie it around you and climb. And hurry!"

Hawk tilted his head to look up. "I can't climb. I think I've pulled a muscle in my shoulder and I'm a little leery about the condition of a rib or two and my ankle."

Lightning streaked overhead, followed by an ominous boom. Time was running out.

"You have to try, Hawk. I can't pull you up by myself."

She felt a tug on the rope. His sharp yelp of pain settled it. No help from his end.

"Can't. Not one-handed."

Meg rolled her fingers into a tight fist. "Okay. Stay put. I'll climb down and help you up."

"No! There isn't room for two of us."

"Well, I can't leave you sitting there to get zapped by lightning." She glanced around her for something, anything that might help get him to safety. "Think, think, think."

"I am thinking."

"I was talking to myself. But, if you come up with anything, I'm all ears."

"What about your volunteers?"

"I sent them to get lunch and wait out the storm." Another streak of lightning crackled and flashed. Meg jumped. "That was close."

"Meggie. Go find shelter. We'll figure out how to get me off here after the storm passes. It won't last long."

"No. I'm not driving off and leaving you here." Meg froze. Driving. "Hawk, I have my pickup."

"So go."

"No, I mean I have my pickup. Start tying the rope around you. And, if you're not secure by the time I get back, I'll climb down there and kick you off that ledge." She turned, and for the second time sprinted down the trail.

Her breath came in labored gasps by the time she reached the pickup. She steadied herself and drew several ragged breaths before sliding behind the wheel.

She navigated the switchback turns as fast as she dared around large rocks and bounced over tree roots. The truck climbed steadily upward, throwing out a plume of dust in its wake. Perspiration and powdery grit stung her eyes. "Almost there."

She took the last bend too fast, slid and slammed

on the brakes. The pickup lurched to a stop and stalled.

"No! Don't you dare quit on me." She turned the key. "Come on. Start or I'll sell you for scrap." She cranked the starter again and again. Nothing.

Meg slumped back in the seat and squeezed her eyes shut. For a few seconds, she let defeat wash through her, then sat straight in her seat. "Get it together, Farrell." She smacked the steering wheel with the heel of her hand. "Start!"

One more turn and the abused vehicle chugged, sputtered and started. Meg shoved it into gear and forced it forward, slowing when she crested the plateau just as teasing spits of rain hit the windshield. In short, tight turns, she maneuvered the truck around and backed it as close to the precipice as she dared.

She leaped from the pickup and plucked the nylon cord from the tree. Back to the truck, she squatted and planted a foot on the rope to make sure it didn't slither over the edge while she tied it to the tow hitch.

"What are you doing up there?"

"Just a second." Her fingers twisted, slipped and pulled at the cord until she trusted it to hold. She slid her hands along the rope as she sidestepped close to the edge. "Is your end secure?"

Another flash of lightning zigzagged over the valley. Thunder roared loud and long.

"What?"

"Are you tied in?" Drizzles of rain morphed into fat drops. "We've got to go, Hawk."

"Are you sure you know what you're doing?"

Meg dropped to her knees, then to her stomach and pulled herself to the rim of the plateau. "I know what I'm *trying* to do. Ready?"

He nodded. "Slowly. Very slowly."

She smiled down at him. He looked pitiful, but hopeful. She gave him a thumbs-up.

Lightning and thunder erupted in an ear-splitting scream of force. Meg squealed. "Hawk?"

"Go!"

Hunched against the heavy splats of rain, she darted to the pickup and slid inside. The engine started with the first turn. She put it in Neutral, letting the incline roll her forward inch by agonizing inch. Every few seconds, she peered over her shoulder hoping to see Hawk's dark head rise above the rim of the cliff. *Please let this work.*

A few feet more and she looked back again. Her breath caught. Hawk's right hand clawed at the loose soil. She hit the brake and leaned her head out the window. "Hawk!"

"Keep going!"

Meg eased off the brake and the truck crept forward. One foot. Two feet. Three feet. She gently pressed the brake and glanced back. Hawk's right arm and head cleared the edge.

"A little more!"

Another foot. Two. Three.

"Stop!"

She held the brake and twisted in the seat. Hawk dug his elbow into the dirt and dragged himself over the top. Meg jerked up the emergency brake, hopped out and ran.

He lay on his stomach, feet and legs still hanging over the rim. She reached under his right arm and tugged him away from the edge. Once she felt they were on solid ground, she knelt beside him and rolled him onto his back.

"Are you okay?" she asked through a mouth as dry as dirt.

He slid his good arm around her neck and pulled her to him. "Shh. I've just gone from hell to heaven. Let me enjoy the moment."

"I know what you mean but we need to—"

"Shh." He brushed her lips with his, pulled back enough for breath, then touched his mouth to hers again.

This kiss held everything from gratitude to passion and then some. They clung together, letting the tension in their bodies move from survival to desire.

A throaty groan from Hawk forced Meg to shift her weight. "I'm hurting you."

"I'm not complaining." He pressed his cheek against her temple. "Not one bit."

Lightning cut open the clouds and the rain poured in earnest. It fell in a straight, heavy sheet, soaking them in seconds. Meg pushed to her knees. “Come on. We need to get you to the clinic.”

“I’d rather stay right here.”

“A nice idea. A better idea is to get you to a doctor. I don’t like the looks of that gash on the side of your head. And if your ribs are hurt, you might have internal injuries.” She shuddered and pushed that thought from her mind.

Hawk reached out and brushed wet hair from her face before pressing his palm against her cheek.

She covered his hand with hers. His skin, while wet, held the warmth of life. He lived. She wanted to keep him that way.

“Come on.” Meg slid her arm under his right shoulder. “Up you go.”

“Meggie.” Hawk stroked her cheek with the back of his fingers. “Don’t go.”

“I’m not going anywhere without you.” She pulled him against her. “Upsy-daisy.”

“Don’t go back to Michigan.”

“What?” She pressed her fingers to his mouth. “We are not having this conversation right now. Come on.”

“I mean it. You can search for bones here. You’ve already found a graveyard of bones. I want you to stay.”

“And I want you to go to the clinic. You’re talking crazy. Head trauma will do that. We’ll talk later.”

“I’ve been saving too many things for later.”

"Later. I promise. Come on. Lean on me."

Once he was on his feet, they staggered to the pickup. Meg yanked the passenger door open. "In you go." He didn't move. "What do I have to do? Hit you over the head with the jawbone of an allosaurus? Get in the truck."

Hawk looked behind them, lips pressed into a thin line. Meg followed his gaze. The mountain lion lay in a heap. Rain pelted its hide. Even with its sleek fur dark and matted, it was a beautiful animal. Meg sighed. "I had no choice, Hawk. It was a heartbeat away from attacking you."

He turned to her. "Good shot."

Rain pounded them and beat on the pickup. Thunder and lightning chased each other across the valley. Echoes chased after them. Meg shivered and practically shoved him into the pickup. She closed the door behind him and ran to the other side and slid into the driver's seat. Hawk leaned back in the seat and winced.

"Give me your bandanna." She pulled hers from her pocket and knotted them together into a makeshift sling. "There. That should help until we get to the clinic." She flipped on the wipers, reached for the stick shift and paused. Her new rope dangled from the tow hitch. She hopped out, pulled it into a bundle and tossed the bulk into the open truck bed.

Taking in a deep breath, she ran to the cat and lifted the front right paw. It bore a slight mound of skin from an old would. She lowered the paw, raced back to the pickup and climbed inside.

"You can stop tracking that mountain lion. Now, cowboy, let's get you to a doctor."

SITTING IN THE SMALL, sterile waiting room while Hawk had X-rays taken, gash stitched, shoulder and ankle assessed, upped the intensity of the headache camping behind her eyes. Waiting left her nothing to do—but wait. She read and reread every posted notice. She memorized the details of every painting in the room. She counted ceiling tiles and floor tiles. Anything to keep from replaying Hawk's fall off the cliff again and again. Anything to keep from thinking the same horrific thought. *He could have died.*

Meg leaned back in the padded chair and let her eyes drift closed. A light, like the bright beam of a lighthouse, flashed through her mind and shone on her thoughts.

He lived.

He would carry on the quiet pride he held for his Native American heritage. His passion for Sitting River. The friendship he had for the Reeds and her own family. His generous spirit would endure. His right eyebrow would continue to lift, heavy with skepticism. Meg chuckled softly. Even the way he crept up on her without making a sound would go on. He lived.

Her heart ached. Her brain felt numb. She didn't

want to think any more and she certainly didn't want to think about his inane babble on the cliff. He had obviously been delirious or concussed or both.

Still, the memory of his words, his gentle touch and the heated kiss claimed her tired mind. She sighed, drew her knees to her chest, wrapped her arms around them and gave the memories freedom to roam.

Dr. Spencer's tap on her shoulder scattered all thoughts but one. Meg leaped from her seat. "Is he okay? Please tell me he's okay."

"He's fine, Meggie. He's also very fortunate. He's strained a muscle in his shoulder. There are some bruises and minor scratches and he'll need to take it easy on the ankle for a few days. The cut on his head is the only real concern I have. He said he didn't hit his head, but I'd like him to stay overnight as a precaution. Now I want to take a look at your knees."

Meg followed his gaze. "My knees?" Dirt and spots of blood covered the light bandage around her right knee. Her left carried its share of scrapes and specks of blood. "I hadn't noticed."

"Love will do that. Now, after I take care of those knees, I want you to go home and rest. I mean it, Meggie. Hawk is sleeping peacefully, and I want you to do the same. Go home and rest. There's nothing for you to do here."

*Except see Hawk.*

Dr. Spencer treated her knees, patted her shoulder and walked away. As soon as he was out of sight, Meg peeked into Hawk's room. In the dim glow of multiple machine lights, she scanned the room from wall to bed to window to chair to monitors. Memories of her own hospital visits rushed at her. The faint glow of lights, the constant hum and beeps of machines. The whispered voices of staff and family. The feeling of confinement.

She had wanted to breathe during those moments. Not just to draw breath and have her lungs push oxygen through her body, she had wanted freedom. To feel the wind and her body greet each other in wide-open spaces. To feel the wind part and move around her. She'd wanted to be away from all the low lights, the incessant and monotonous humming of equipment, the whispers and squeaky shoes.

She tiptoed to the side of the bed. His eyes were closed in recuperative sleep. A wide bandage covered the cut on his temple and head. A sling kept his left arm pinned in place. She stretched out her hand and lightly traced the pale line along his jaw. The scratch was fading nicely. "Sorry about that," she whispered.

The even rise and fall of breath soothed her anxious mind. He survived. Now she could breathe.

Stress ebbed, leaving her limp and empty. She needed to follow Dr. Spencer's advice and head straight home and straight to bed.

Straight to bed was not going to happen. Bent Fork blazed with light. The facts she'd phoned in from the clinic obviously hadn't satisfied the Farrell clan. Fortunately for her throbbing head, her mother stepped in after the initial bombardment of questions and ushered her upstairs.

Meg settled under the covers and closed her eyes. A hiss of rainfall pecked at the windows. Its steady rhythm blended with the dull thumping behind her eyes. She rolled to her side, pulled the comforter up to her chin and waited for sleep to push the doctor's words from her mind. *Love will do that.* Unfortunately, sleep took its own sweet time finding her.

THE SMELL OF breakfast greeted Meg before she got to the bottom of the back stairs. Ruby pushed open the swinging door just as Meg reached it.

"Morning, Ruby."

"We didn't expect you up so early. Guess you didn't need as much sleep as we thought. Come on." She held the door. "Everyone is down, and food is still hot."

Meg closed her eyes and sniffed. "Did you add mint jelly to the scrambled eggs?"

The older woman smiled broadly. "You know I did."

She followed Ruby into the kitchen. Chatting ceased. Utensils stilled. All eyes turned to Meg.

John grinned. "Hawk's been telling us about yesterday."

"Hawk?" She slid a glance down the table. Hawk occupied her father's seat at the end of the table. His left arm rested in a navy sling and the large bandage still stuck to his temple and forehead.

Meg folded her arms across her chest and glared at him. "What are you doing here?"

"Having breakfast."

"You know what I mean. You should be at the clinic."

"I decided it wasn't necessary."

"You decided."

Hawk nodded.

"How did you get here?"

Andrew leaned forward. "He called me at dawn and said he'd deed Sitting River over to me if I'd come and get him."

Meg smacked her brother on the top of his head. "After a statement like that you didn't think he needed to stay put? There's no way Hawk would say such a thing if he were in his right mind." She gave Hawk a long look. "He tends to say things that make no sense when he isn't in his right mind."

"That's what I thought, too. So, I declined the offer of the ranch and told him he could buy me a beer."

"And then you went and got him."

Andrew shrugged.

Ruby placed a platter of pancakes in front of

Andrew and added her own tap to his head. "Slide down and give Meggie a seat."

Meg settled onto the narrow space her brother left at the end of the bench next to Hawk. "Why didn't you call me?"

"Would you have come to get me?"

"No."

"That's why I called Andrew."

Andrew stabbed two pancakes and passed the platter. "It felt like a jailbreak."

Meg glared at her brother. "It's not funny. You didn't see him clinging to the side of the cliff with blood on his face, arm clutched to his chest, lightning and thunder all around."

"No, it's not funny." Lansford looked down the table at his daughter. "And it could have been a far worse situation had you not been there and acted so quickly."

Taking two pancakes of his own, John dropped them on his plate and reached for the maple syrup. "Hawk told us you threatened to shimmy down the rope and kick him off the ledge."

"You told them that?"

Hawk grinned.

"He also said you shot a mountain lion. And you got the truck up to the plateau."

Joanna Farrell held up a hand. "Enough, John. I don't think Hawk or Meggie want to revisit the incident."

"Sorry, Mom," John mumbled around a mouthful of pancake. "So, Hawk, what are you going to do about the dead cat? Was it the one that's been at your livestock?"

Hawk glanced at Meg. "Yes. Thanks to Meggie, I don't have to worry about that one anymore." He touched a fingertip to the bandage on his forehead and winced.

Meg leaned close. "Are you okay?"

"I'm fine. Just a little ache here and there."

Ruby rose and went to the stove. "How about some of my special tea? My tea is good for everything."

"I really appreciate the thought, Ruby, but I, ah..."

"I think Hawk needs rest more than tea." Meg winked at Hawk. "Right?"

"Right," Hawk agreed. "Rest, lots of rest."

"Good. As soon as you've finished breakfast, I'll drive you up to the cabin."

"The cabin?" Hawk shook his head. "I appreciate the ride, but make that Big House. I've work to do."

Meg glared at him. "We're ranchers. There's always work to do, and it will be there once you're able to get around. I'm sure Larry, Emma, Jenna and Mark can handle most things for a few days." She glanced at the sling. "Or longer."

"Larry did okay with one arm in a sling. I'll manage."

Meg stood. "You'll manage better after more

rest. Come on. Or do you want to stay here and drink Ruby's tea?"

Ruby pushed back from the table. "I'll send John along later with some tea and chili. What about tomorrow?"

"I'll take care of today and tomorrow." Meg snatched a pancake from the platter and nodded for Hawk to move. "I'm going to get him settled at the cabin and go back as soon as my class is over. Don't wait dinner for me."

# CHAPTER EIGHTEEN

MEGGIE'S HUMMING DRIFTED in from the kitchen. Hawk didn't recognize the tune, but he liked the happy sound. It soothed far better than her demands to stay put and rest. Or Ruby's special cure-all tea.

He wrestled the sofa for a comfortable position and shifted to his right side to take the pressure off his injured shoulder. His head throbbed and places he didn't realize he'd bruised were tender.

First-aid supplies sat on the ottoman. Gauze, ointment, scissors, pain reliever and a glass of water. He didn't want someone taking care of him. He'd taken care of himself for as long as he could remember and then his mother after Michael Hawk had ridden off to play games with the family's meager income. Between his mother's job at the law office and his odd jobs around the trailer park, they'd managed week to week. Then, Lame Eagle came for them and moved them to Sitting River and he'd had to let someone else help with the caring for him and his mother.

Life had changed and continued to change. That

was something Lame Eagle had taught him in the first days on Sitting River. Life changed and we had to learn how to change with it. It was true then and just as true now.

"What's on your mind?" Meggie stood in the doorway holding a laden tray. "You look so serious."

He pointed to the tray. "What is that?"

"Hot water with lemon and a snack to tide you over until I get back."

"You're leaving?"

"Only for a bit. I want to see how things are progressing at the site and ask Matt if he'd take charge for a few days."

"You're willing to leave your precious fossils in someone else's hands?"

"It's only for a day or two. He's quick, thorough and the others will follow his leadership. I can hand over the site but I can't abandon my class. Promise me you'll rest."

"Don't worry. I'm fine."

"You are not fine." She paused and swallowed. "Do you realize how lucky you are to be sitting here instead of lying in a broken, battered and probably dead heap at the bottom of the cliff with that scrawny tree?"

He smiled. "Where you threatened to send me."

She shivered.

"I'm sorry, Meggie. I wish I could erase the

memories. Well, most of them. I like remembering how glad you were to see me in one piece."

Meg draped a blanket over him. "Stay put."

"Oh, he'll stay put all right," boomed a voice. Emma opened the screened door and stepped inside. She carried a casserole dish in one hand, a tote bag in the other, and had a thick brown folder tucked under her left arm.

"Let me take that, Emma." Meggie held out her hands for the covered dish. "Should it go in the fridge?"

"Yes." Emma handed Meg the casserole and tossed the folder on the chair before turning to Hawk. With fisted hands on her wide hips, she gave him a slow appraisal.

Hawk shrank against the sofa pillows. He would rather face a dozen angry mountain lions and a herd of stampeding cows than the critical assessment of Emma Reed. The woman oozed disappointment and motherly love all in one deep "hmph."

"So. You go wandering off by yourself knowing there's been a crazy cat out there scratching and chewing on living things and a storm backing up against the peaks all morning. What were you thinking?"

"I was being a responsible rancher checking on the people crawling around my ranch with a storm brewing."

"Hmph." Emma sniffed and picked up the folder. "So, what are we doing with this?"

"We?" Hawk asked.

Meg chuckled and slung her backpack over her shoulder. "I'll be back in time to get his dinner."

"Don't rush." Emma put a hand over her heart and swallowed. "Fortunately, we have time. And while he rests—" she pulled the folder out of his reach "—and he will rest, I'll put up a pie." She hefted the tote bag. "Apple."

"Thanks, Emma." Meg popped a quick kiss on Emma's cheek, and with a promise to hurry back thrown over her shoulder, left the cabin.

MEG RETURNED TO find Hawk stretched out on the sofa and Emma ensconced in the chair beside him. "Yum. Smells fantastic in here."

Hawk dropped his pen on the stack of papers spread over his lap and flexed his fingers. "I'll never hold reins again."

The wingback chair creaked as Emma rocked out of it. "You're a rancher. You'll hold reins with your teeth if you have to. There's my beef stew in the fridge and John dropped off chili and bread and I'll leave the pie. That should take care of dinner."

Meg closed the door and took the seat Emma had vacated. "Have a good visit?"

Hawk groaned.

"Emma cares about you. She needed to see with her own eyes that you're okay."

"Well—" he shifted himself into a more upright position "—I'm fine. I even managed to get some work done."

Meg gathered the papers and put them in the rolltop desk and pulled down the lid. "Enough work. I'm starving. Any requests from the patient? There's beef stew or chili."

"Whatever. Mix them together. Just don't forget the bread."

Meg looked at him. He slumped against the cushions and stretched the blanket across his legs. The spark of self-reliance had faded. Maybe the discomfort or pain from his injuries was wearing on him. Maybe he was just hungry. She forced a wide smile across her face. "Comfort food coming up."

The food disappeared quickly, dishes were cleaned and put away and the smell of hot chocolate drifted from the kitchen.

"How about hot chocolate out on the swing or by the fireplace if you'd rather not get up?"

"Fireplace."

She brought two mugs of hot chocolate and set them on the ottoman tray. He took his and held it. Meg leaned back in the chair, sipped hers and waited. Silence settled around them and she let it linger. Physical discomfort aside, something weighed on his mind and had her wondering what the papers Emma brought had contained.

The long low howl of a wolf pierced the silence

and somewhere on the rocky slope behind the cabin a bugling elk made itself known.

"Did you hear that? Amazing. In Michigan, I'd hear crickets, birds, chipmunk chatters and plenty of man-made noises. I got so tired of the blare from car radios, engines, horns and the roar of missing mufflers. It's different here. Peaceful and beautiful. There's magic in the mountains."

"Meggie, I appreciate what you're trying to do. Honestly, I'm fine." He leaned his head back and closed his eyes.

She waited.

He blew out a long breath and sat up. "I've worked Sitting River the best I know how. It doesn't seem to be enough. I went through countless papers after Lame Eagle died trying to get a true grasp of Sitting River's financial situation. I knew there was some debt. I knew a lot of the debt had to do with money Lame Eagle gave my father. I didn't know how much or why.

"While cleaning out some of Lame Eagle's things, Emma found some folders. In one of the folders, I found evidence that Lame Eagle had been giving my father money, a substantial amount of money on a regular basis from the time Mom and I came to live with him until I turned eighteen. The checks became less frequent after that but still substantial."

Meg lowered her mug. "What?"

"I knew Lame Eagle gave money to my dad.

I didn't know how much or why. Until now." He lifted his gaze to her, his eyes heavy with pain under brows drawn together in an I-can't-begin-to-comprehend-this V. "My father threatened to take me from Sitting River if Lame Eagle didn't give him money."

Meg turned to face him. "Are you sure?"

"There were notes demanding checks be sent to a post office box in Nevada or he'd come and take me away."

"But he couldn't have done that. Your mother wouldn't have stood for it. Neither would Lame Eagle."

"I don't think Lame Eagle wanted Mom to know. I think he believed it was his responsibility to take care of us since his son wouldn't." Hawk gripped the mug, swirled the dark liquid and watched it slow. "Lame Eagle risked losing Sitting River for me and I've let him down."

Meg set her mug aside and cupped his face in her palms. "Your ranch will weather the ups and downs of ranching. Sitting River and Bent Fork will survive because we're strong and determined and resilient and downright stubborn. You've not disappointed Lame Eagle. Your grandfather beamed when he talked about you. He constantly bragged, in the most sensitive way, about any and every challenge you faced and bested. From the first cow you tagged to the first time you drove that ancient tractor and baler and dropped a roll of hay. He loved you and was proud of you."

Hawk turned away. "And I'm still driving the same derelict tractor because I can't make enough money to replace it."

"Don't you dare start feeling sorry for yourself. Lame Eagle knowingly put Sitting River in debt by giving his son money, probably knowing the money wouldn't be repaid. He could have told your father to take a hike. Maybe he did. Maybe he tried to help his son. The one thing there is no *maybe* about is the fact that your grandfather loved you and was so proud of you."

Hawk put his cup down and reached for her hands. He lifted them and pressed them to his chest. She watched his eyes, his mouth and felt the beat of his heart. While the truth about the money Lame Eagle had paid his son in return for keeping Hawk had startled her, it must have rocked Hawk to the core.

Meg closed her eyes and leaned her head against his shoulder. "I'm so sorry."

"Me, too."

MORNING LIGHT TOUCHED Meg's eyelids. She opened one eye and peeked at the clock on her nightstand. 7:02. Oh no. She'd promised to relieve Andrew by seven. He was not going to be happy. Hopefully, Hawk still slept.

A knock followed by Ruby's request to enter

sent Meg to her feet. She slipped into her terry robe. "Come in."

Ruby flung the door open. "Good, you're up. Alison's gone into labor. Your mom and dad are on their way to the hospital to get the girls and bring the girls back here."

"Labor! It's too early. The babies aren't due until—"

"Babies come when they're ready, not when it's convenient."

"But the babies are only…" Meg held her hands out and wiggled her fingers. "Not enough weeks?"

Ruby caught Meg's hands between her own. "They're coming early but not so early that they can't survive. They may need to be in the hospital a bit longer, but they'll be just fine."

"But—"

Ruby let go of Meg's hands. "Now, get dressed. I need you to stay with Ava and get her some breakfast. Andrew's still with Hawk. John's gone to pick up Alison's mother. Heidi left her phone so I'm going to drop it at the clinic and let her know what's going on. She'd already left for work when Connor called. Then, I'm going to stop by Sandra Maine's and give her New York cousin Diana a piece of my mind while I'm stressed enough not to care what words I spew in her direction. Then I'm going to the hospital."

"What did Mrs. Maine do?"

"Get dressed and get Ava her breakfast." Ruby started down the stairs.

"Ruby. What did Mrs. Maine do?"

"She ruined Tyler's annual Willow River Festival."

"THEY'RE SO TINY," Meg whispered.

Connor smiled. "You don't have to whisper."

Meg looked around the isolation unit. Dim lights shone overhead, and one bright light focused on the ICU nurse's stand. She returned her gaze to the incubators close to the glass. Each held a tiny human being attached to a feeding tube and monitors of one kind or another. Her nephews. "When can they come home?"

"Once their bilirubin count is acceptable and the feeding tubes can be removed and no complications of any kind manifest." Connor put his palms against the glass in front of each incubator. "Their weight isn't bad for preemies. That's a real plus. Dr. Spencer said it helped that Alison stayed off her feet as much as she did the last few weeks." He spread his fingers wide and slid them to the right and then to the left, as if he was stroking the babies' tiny bodies.

Meg put an arm around her brother's shoulders and squeezed. "They're awesome."

The phone in Meg's back pocket vibrated. She tugged it free and checked the caller. "Ruby."

"You're supposed to turn that off when you enter the hospital."

"It's on silent." She pushed the phone back in her pocket. "Give my nephews a kiss for me and hug Alison and tell her I think she's amazing."

"How did I get so lucky?"

"You chose wisely."

He turned to face her. "What about you? Are you going to choose wisely?"

"I don't have a selection from which to choose."

"I'm not just talking about a future spouse. What about your future in general? You have more options than you realize."

Meg sighed and looked at the floor, the ceiling, the two newborns and back to Connor. "I know I need to figure out a few things. Things like, where do I want to spend the next fifty or sixty years and with whom and doing what and do I need to do that right now."

Her phone buzzed again. "I've to go. Apparently, Mrs. Maine has ruined the Willow River Festival."

Connor gave her a hug. "Have fun. Give my beautiful girls a hug for me. Tell them I miss them, and I'll be there tonight to tuck them in, and I'll bring their favorite stuffies from home."

She chuckled softly. Her big brother thinking about stuffies. Her phone buzzed again. "Gotta go." She blew kisses to the babies, one to her brother and pushed through the double doors.

Connor was right. She had options. She just didn't have time to think about them.

"IT CAN'T BE that bad." Meg took her mother by the shoulders and gently sat her on the sofa.

"Not that bad?" Her mother stared at the clipboard in her hands. "She's gone. She left and nothing is ready. The plans, the contacts, the supplies. All the promises to use her connections and make this year's festival spectacular."

Meg took the clipboard and flipped to a clean piece of paper. "Let's start from the beginning. Rationally and calmly."

"You can forget calm." Ruby shook her finger. "I won't see calm until I give that woman a chunk of my mind."

"Aside from yelling at Diana Maine, who is on her way to New York, what other options do we have?" Pencil poised, Meg looked from Ruby to her mother.

Her mother sighed. "This is all my fault. I handed the festival planning over to Diana Maine. I wanted to be more available to help with the girls and Alison and Heidi and Ava while Keith is away."

Meg caught her mother's hand and squeezed. "And you're doing a great job with all of that. Alison is fine, the twins are really healthy for preemies, the girls are happy, Heidi's able to work without worrying about Ava. Things are running as smoothly as ever on Bent Fork."

Ruby huffed. "That woman never listened to a word your mother had to say. She went on and on about living in New York and watching the big parades when she was young and then working on the parades, organizing floats and bands and fireworks. She talked like she'd managed all the parades for the whole state of New York all by herself."

Meg scanned another page on the clipboard. "It's not like she took money and skipped." Meg swallowed. "Did she?"

"No." Her mother shook her head. "The committee had funds from last year to apply to this year's event. She used some to pay for a few things that have been ordered and have arrived already. They just cost more than we anticipated."

Meg raised the clipboard. "Do you mind if I look through these papers and see if I can make sense of anything."

Joanna patted Meg's knee. "I hope you can."

"I'll put on some coffee." Ruby rose and glared at the clipboard. "Hope you can read and understand that woman's city gibberish."

Meg carried the papers to the bank of windows covering the front of the house and settled on the window seat. Side notes, long and short, were sprinkled on nearly every of piece of paper.

Mostly a name, a request, a mention of this or that. None of it connected to make sense.

One page had a list in her mother's handwriting. A primary focus of the event and the division of active categories of food, music, crafts, contests, animals, activities, setup, cleanup and so on. Focused. Step by step. Lay it all out and then delegate. *That* made sense.

"Mom. I think we need to start at the beginning using your template from last year."

"Knock, knock." Hawk stood in the wide arched doorway between the living room and the dining room. "Mind if I join you?"

"What are you doing here? You're supposed to be resting." She cringed as he rolled his shoulder and shifted the sling strap around his neck. He tugged the hem of his button-down shirt. No sweat, no grime, no creases marred the crisp cotton. Even his boots lacked the usual evidence of a rancher's work. "How are you feeling?"

He eased himself onto the window seat close enough for their thighs to touch. "Better. I've missed having you at the cabin," he whispered.

His words fell through her, stirring thoughts and emotions. *Focus.* Don't think about the fact that their bodies were touching. Don't think about the kiss. Don't think about his fall. Don't think about his babbling on the cliff asking her to stay in Colorado. Don't think about how much she was going to miss everyone.

The bond of family tugged at her. And while the *feeling* was familiar, the *need* was new.

"So, are we going to have you around for the festival?"

"I should be here. The festival is two weeks away and I haven't heard anything to indicate I'm needed at the museum before then."

Her mother set the coffee carafe on the table and went back to the kitchen for cups. Her steps had slowed. Her shoulders sagged. Festival plans needed to be unraveled and put into action. Meg wasn't about to let her mother try to manage it alone.

Joanna returned with cups and creamer, added them to the tray and sat. "Well?"

Meg slid off the window seat and dropped onto the sofa next to her mother. "We will use your template and do our festival the Tyler, Colorado, way, just as they did on Tyler's inaugural day, with all hands on deck, doing the best we can with what we have. We're going to need help. Lots of help." She tapped the clipboard. "Given the amount of meetings and planning, I'm surprised these aren't more thorough."

Her mother took the clipboard, placed it beside her and hugged Meg. "Yes. We are most definitely going to need a lot of help. I'll make calls and see if I can gather a few of the committee members. Hawk, would you like coffee or something else?"

Hawk limped to the sofa, sat and shifted his

shoulder against the back cushion. “Coffee. Thank you. Emma’s had me sipping special tea that makes Ruby’s taste like the nectar of the Gods. Emma thinks it has medicinal powers. I hope it does. If not, I’ve been drinking the nasty stuff for nothing.”

“Not for nothing?” Joanna handed him a cup of coffee. “Even if it has no special properties, Emma believes she’s helping you. And that, Joe Hawk, is worth something.”

Hawk smiled. “I’ll be sure to accept the next cup with gratitude.”

Meg poked his right shoulder. “And try not to grimace as you swallow.”

Joanna took a sip of coffee, picked up the clip-board and glanced at Meg. “Shall we get started?”

# *CHAPTER NINETEEN*

MORE VOLUNTEERS ARRIVED and everyone participated with enthusiasm, offering bits of helpful information and interesting ideas. Andrew brought pizza and somewhere in the midst of listing what needed to be done and how it could be accomplished, the numerous jobs were divided into manageable tasks.

"So." Joanna placed the clipboard on her lap. "Are we all okay on our plans so far?"

Meg stretched her arms above her head and flexed her fingers. "I'll start on my list first thing tomorrow morning. I'd like to put the girls to work on a project that will be fun for them and will hopefully keep them out of everyone's hair."

"Thank you, honey." Ruby waved her stack of papers. "I'll have enough to do without minding what those young ones get into at the drop of a hat." She turned to the woman beside her, "Emma, since Diana didn't order the table coverings, how about we take any leftover fabric from last year's school play. We can take the red and blue remnants and add it to my few yards of white. I'll give the fabric to my bridge club. They'll gladly cut and sew pieces into runners for the food tables."

Emma bobbed her head. "We could add some red and blue bandannas in the mix for a little variety and to extend the amount of fabric."

"What about the floats?"

All eyes turned to Ed Ball. He sat upright in the cushioned side chair, elbows resting on the rounded chair arms, fingers steepled in front of him.

"Floats?" Larry looked at Ed as if the man had suggested they make spaceships and flying saucers. "You wanna do floats?"

Ed nodded. "We've always had floats."

Meg picked up her clipboard and flipped through the pages. "I don't recall anything about floats in Mrs. Maine's notes."

"Diana said she would line up the necessary vehicles for the floats and order the materials needed for creating what she said would be masterpieces."

"And?"

Her mother's eyebrows lifted. "All we have are boxes of crepe paper rosettes stored at Wendell's Hardware store."

Ruby turned to Ed. "You want floats. Fine. You're now in charge of floats."

"I don't want to be in *charge*. But I'll help. I think floats in a parade make it really grand. Plus, townsfolk use the floats to advertise."

"I get it." Larry poked his pizza slice toward Ed. "You want to advertise your bowling alley."

Meg jotted a quick note on the paper. "I think it's a great idea, Ed. Tomorrow, will you ask around town for advertising donations? We'll take any kind, vehicles to use as floats, materials, money, whatever someone is willing to give, we'll take. Then, they can publicize their company or whatever on the floats with banners, products, posters or bullhorns."

Emma took Larry's hand. "We can announce our intentions of starting a square dance club."

"Exactly," Meg encouraged. "That's the sort of thing that will engage our community beyond the festival."

Ed smacked his hands together. "You know, I think it's gonna work. We don't need Mrs. Maine's highfalutin ideas to make Tyler's Willow River Festival a great celebration."

Excited chatter filled the room. Hawk leaned close to Meg and whispered, "Sounds like you're in pretty deep."

Meg squared her shoulders and looked straight into his dark eyes. "It's going to be the best Willow River Festival ever. I promise."

MEG HUNG UP the kitchen phone. "We have one more tractor and one more small flatbed. Mr. Hinde sounded pleased that Ed asked for his help and will gladly drive his tractor down Main Street pulling whatever we choose to put on the flatbed." She dropped onto the bench. "That makes three."

"Three is good. We don't need a long train of highly decorated floats gliding down Main Street." She nodded. "Three is good."

"Yes, but it would be great to have more community involvement. What about adding wagons, big and small, even a group of kids pulling wagons all decked out with their own decorations. It would be fun to see what they come up with, and the Lander boys could do a side by side with their motorcycles carrying the welcome banner between them." Meg plucked a biscuit from the platter, pulled it apart and slathered it with blackberry jam. "I hope Ruby's planning to put this in the jelly and jam contest."

Joanna reached across the table and patted her daughter's hand. "I've just been thinking how lovely it is having you at home."

"Thanks, Mom. It's been good to be home."

Her mother folded and refolded her napkin. "I've been trying not to ask but do you really have to go back to Michigan?"

Meg paused, biscuit halfway to her mouth, and looked at her mother. Joanna Farrell, no longer a young woman, carried a beauty about her due more to contentment than cosmetics. Her work on Bent Fork kept her body toned and healthy. But the heart and mind of her mother focused on family first and foremost.

"Not for a few more weeks. Unless the pace of the construction picks up. If so, I may need to be in Michigan sooner to help set up display areas and exhibit pieces. It's my job, Mom."

"You have a job in Tyler."

"A temporary job that's almost over."

"A job I've heard you do very well. I've also heard Professor Nelson will not be returning. The community college will need a permanent replacement."

Meg put the biscuit on her plate and rubbed her napkin over her fingers. "He's not coming back. Wow. He didn't want to teach geology anyway and TCC deserves better. The students deserve to be taught by someone who *wants* to teach."

"I'm just saying, you might want to consider what your head says you *want* versus what your heart knows you *need*." She leaned forward and patted Meg's hand again. "Just think about it."

She had been thinking about it. From the moment she and Hawk had rescued Buddy, she'd known questions of staying had set up camp in the back of her mind. Could she be happy living again among these majestic Colorado mountains? Could she be happy teaching at TCC? Could she be happy looking for fossils in her free time instead of as part of her chosen career? Could she be happy living so close to her family? Could she feel whole?

She didn't have an absolute answer for the

questions that swirled and nagged at her. They needed to be answered, sooner or later. One question plagued more than the others, one question haunted her before falling asleep, one question jostled her day and night, one question needed an answer—if she left, could she be happy without Joe Hawk in her life?

*Just think about it.* Not today. The only thing on her mind today was how to make this year's festival the best ever because she wanted it to be the best. For her mother, her family and her town. And she wanted to help make it happen.

She loaded the dishwasher and rounded up Caroline, Molly and Ava. No easy task since the girls decided playing hide-and-seek was more fun than helping clear away breakfast dishes.

"Remember last night we talked about everyone chipping in to make the festival amazing? I have an idea for the three of you. What do you think about decorating rocks to sell at one of the craft booths?"

Molly cocked her head to one side. "We'd need a lot of paint, Aunt Meggie."

"How will we get our rocks to the booth?" Ava asked. "They're heavy."

"I'm thinking egg-sized stones. Maybe some smaller, some larger. You could paint whatever you want on them."

"Butterflies?" Molly asked.

Ava clapped her hands. "And puppies and kittens?"

"Whatever your heart desires. We can sell them as a fundraiser for next year's celebration." Meg smiled down at them. "What do you think?"

"We'll need help selling them, Aunt Meggie." Caroline looked at the two younger girls. "I understand counting money, but they don't. Someone older will need to help us."

"I'll be right there with all my fingers and toes for counting."

Ava shook her head. "Aunt Meggie, we don't use our fingers and toes anymore. We use our heads."

"Fingers, toes, heads, calculators, whatever it takes. I'll be right there with you, and we'll make it work."

"Can we start now?"

"I think Ruby has a few chores for you to do first. After they're done, if it's okay with Ruby and your grandmother, you'll be free to search for suitable rocks. Okay?"

Molly tugged Meg's shirt. "Will you help us look for them?"

Meg's heart swelled with love for her nieces. They were funny, clever, loving and willing to help with anything that didn't smack of a chore. Today they were eager to help with the town's Willow River Festival by painting rocks for sentimental and generous individuals to purchase in efforts to support next year's festival.

Meg pictured her rock collection in the shed. Just rocks, but they meant something special to her. She'd learned long ago that the composition of the earth was different in different places. She didn't understand why at that time. She only knew they fascinated her and she'd saved those that had fascinated her the most. Unique to her. Others were special because she'd found them on her treks with Lame Eagle. He'd spoken with a quietness and an awareness that made everything he said sound like a story, ancient and true. She'd learned a lot from him. Not only about their surroundings, both animate and inanimate, but also about friendship, truth and promises.

The rocks had been special to her. Now they could be special to someone else.

"Actually, I know where we can find some rocks for painting. We'll collect them as soon as you finish your chores. In the meantime, I'll put a plastic sheet outside with paint supplies and paint so you can get started while I tend to a chore of my own."

"Okay, Aunt Meggie." Ava turned to her cousins. "What chores were we supposed to do?"

Caroline took her sister's hand. "Let's find Grandma. Her chores aren't as hard as Ruby's."

Meg watched her nieces leave the kitchen in search of their grandmother in hopes of easy tasks. She went in search of a tarp large enough to contain the mess the girls were bound to make and found Ruby elbow-deep in a plastic tub full of fabric.

"Any chance there's something in there that the girls can set paint on and not matter if it gets splattered?"

Ruby rocked back on her heels. "There's everything in here. Mostly excess Halloween stuff." She pulled out several yards of an orange plastic sheet. "Here. Won't matter what they do to this. We can throw it away when they're finished."

Meg tucked the sheet under her arm. "Thanks. I'll set up everything out back before I go."

"Where're you going?"

"To Wendell's Hardware to pick up the crepe paper rosettes and drop them at the senior center and then over to TCC to collect some class material. I won't be long."

"You might stop by and peek in on the babies and Alison."

"Already on my list."

MEG PERCHED ON the tailgate of the pickup and waited. And waited. Wendell had promised to have the boxes of rosettes brought out as soon as his grandson could load them. That had been more than thirty minutes and she still sat on the tailgate waiting. Not a good thing right now. Waiting gave her time to think, and she didn't want to think.

She needed to, she knew that, but the thoughts

brought about too much confusion and too many questions she didn't have answers for.

Connor had said she had options. She did. She had a commitment to the Mayfield. She needed to be there to construct exhibits and set up the viewing area for ongoing fossil restoration, not to mention the lab itself.

On the other hand, she'd told Hawk she'd stay until she had clarity about the fossil and its potential for exhibition at the Mayfield.

She plucked long strands of loose hay from the open bed, remnants from the last time the truck had been used for hauling bales, and aimlessly rolled them between her palms. Inhale. Exhale.

And she'd just told the girls she would help sell their painted rocks. How could she do any of that if she was setting up exhibits in Michigan?

So many promises to keep. Inhale. Exhale.

Soon she'd have to say goodbye to everyone, including her tiny newborn nephews she'd just visited and had yet to hold. Saying goodbye presented major challenges. Mainly, she didn't want to say goodbye.

She tossed the hay onto the ground and shook her head. "What am I going to do?"

"About what?"

Meg gasped and stared at Hawk. He stood in front of her holding a large bag in his right hand. "I'm getting you a cowbell."

He shrugged. "Sorry. I thought you saw me coming."

Meg raised her eyebrows. "Really?"

"You were looking right at me."

"I wasn't looking at anyone or anything. I was thinking."

"About what to do?"

She sighed and lowered her gaze to the mangled straw at her feet and nudged the pieces away. "Yes."

"Okay if I put this in the truck? Emma mentioned bandannas last night. I picked up some."

She gestured to the bed of the truck. "Help yourself."

Hawk placed the bag beside her and leaned his hip against the tailgate.

Meg pointed to his arm. "Where's your sling?"

"Don't need it if I'm cautious."

"Don't need it or don't want it?" She knew the difference. She'd dismissed the crutches as quickly as she could.

"Everything's fine. Just no heavy lifting for a few more days, go easy on the ankle, and before you ask, the head is fine. I just came from seeing Dr. Lewis. He changed the bandage and declared me fit. So, what is it you need to do something about?"

"Whether or not to let Tim load those boxes by himself since he kept me waiting so long." Meg pointed to a young man headed their way pushing a flat cart stacked with boxes. "I didn't realize there were so many." She slid off the tailgate and wagged a finger at Hawk. "Don't even think about it."

"About what?"

"Helping with the boxes. Tim and I can manage and then I'll drive them to the senior center so the folks there can work their magic with them. Just one of the million tasks on my plate for today."

"Big plate."

"Tell me about it."

The boxes were quickly tucked away. Meg closed the tailgate and pulled keys from the front pocket of her khaki shorts. "I'm hoping to hear soon from Dr. Vanover about displaying your fossils in the Mayfield. Even if there's nothing more substantial than what we've already uncovered, they will make a fine exhibit."

"When are you leaving?"

"I don't have a definite date yet. The construction delays are still causing problems."

"Hmm," he murmured. "The last time you were here for a visit, you had your departure timed down to the minute."

Meg chuckled. "Well, you know the challenges of being around my family."

"Not so challenging this trip?"

She lifted her gaze to meet his. "Still challenging, but in different ways. Honestly, this whole visit has been challenging in many ways."

"Challenges often lead you to a better place." Hawk cleared his throat and smiled. "That's what Lame Eagle would tell me when I sought clarity about a particular problem."

"I wonder what he would tell me about my challenges."

Hawk tucked his forefinger under her chin and tipped it up. "He would tell you to listen to the wisdom of the Elders."

"Right. And just where am I supposed to find this wisdom? And don't tell I need to commune with the water or the wind or the trees or the ground."

Hawk put a finger to her lips. "If you don't stop and listen, you won't hear what you need to hear."

"And what do I need to hear?"

"What your heart is whispering to you."

# CHAPTER TWENTY

"SORRY I TOOK so long. I stopped by the dig site. Matt has everything under control. They're going slowly and I appreciate their cautiousness. Hawk sent these." Meg dropped the bag of bandannas on the trestle table. "Where are the girls?"

Ruby wiped her hands on a dish towel and pointed to the window. "Out back finding rocks."

"More?"

"They came in here and asked where to find rocks. I looked them in their little mischievous eyes and reminded them that they lived in the Rocky Mountains and if they couldn't find rocks to paint, then they could come inside and help me sweep floors and scrub potatoes."

Meg chuckled. "I'll check on them."

Meg found the girls stationed on the orange tarp surrounded by a mass of paint-filled bowls and an array of colorfully painted rocks.

"Aunt Meggie! Aunt Meggie!" Caroline waved with both hands. "Come see! We've painted your rocks and we found more to paint."

Molly held a small stone splattered with red

and blue paint quickly running to purple. “Look at mine first.”

Ava squealed as Buddy snatched the paper towel from her hand and dashed toward the shed. Given the amount of shredded paper towel littering the lawn, Buddy had been playing snatch and run with the absorbent sheets for some time.

Meg approached the plastic sheet. Each child held a stone and a brush heavy with paint. Buddy loped back to his spot on the grass and waited for another paper towel to become available.

“See, Aunt Meggie. Look how hard we’ve worked.” Ava pointed to the creatively painted stones.

“Wow. You three have done an amazing job.”

“I’m glad you’ll help us at the booth, Aunt Meggie,” Caroline said. “Everyone else will be very busy.”

“Maybe Buddy could be at the booth with us?” Ava suggested.

Meg chuckled and slid a glance at the dog. Despite posters and notices around the area, no one had come for him. It was just as well since Ava had laid claim to the furry beast.

Ava tugged Meg’s sleeve. “We’ve decided to put up a picture of Buddy so his owner might see him and want him back.” Ava glanced at Buddy, who’d given up waiting for loose paper towels and slept with his head draped over one outstretched front leg. “I’ll miss Buddy if his owner wants him back.”

Meg enveloped her niece in a big hug. “We’ll all miss Buddy if his owner claims him.”

Caroline shook her head. "Not Grandma and Ruby."

"Actually—" Meg looked over her shoulder to the house and back to the girls and lowered her voice "—I saw Ruby pat Buddy on the head yesterday. Granted, that was just before she shooed him outside, but it was a friendly gesture."

"Meggie!"

Meg glanced up. Her mother stood in the doorway of the back porch waving a cell phone. "You have a call. The screen says Dr. Vanover."

She leaped to her feet. "Answer it."

"What?"

"Answer it!"

Meg reached the back porch in time to hear her mother assuring Dr. Vanover that her daughter would be right there. "Here she is."

Meg mouthed a thank-you and put the phone to her ear. "Hello, Rachael. Sorry. I was outside with my nieces and—" She stopped and listened.

Her mother caught her eye. "Is everything okay?" she whispered.

Meg shook her head. "Rachael, I didn't receive one. I'll check my email while you check with Kathy," she said as she headed up the stairs two at a time.

FORTY MINUTES LATER, Meg slid the phone into the back pocket of her jeans and returned to the kitchen. Her mother sat at the table flipping through stacks of papers.

"Ed gave me the layout for the booth placements, and I can't find it."

Meg stopped behind her mother, leaned down and wrapped her arms around her for a long hug. "I'm sure they're in there somewhere."

"There it is." Joanna held up a sheet of paper littered with squares and tiny printing. "Everything settled with Dr. Vanover?"

Meg sighed. "I have to go."

"Will you be back for dinner?"

Meg shook her head. "No."

Her mother placed the papers on the table and folded her hands. "The museum?"

"Uh-huh. Dr. Vanover said she was surprised I wasn't already there. Kathy, the new office manager, supposedly sent an email explaining that the construction had wrapped up enough for materials and items to be delivered and I needed to be on-site ASAP." Meg drew a breath and slowly exhaled. "I didn't get the email. I check my email every morning. No email from Kathy. I checked just now. I even checked spam. Nothing."

"What happened?"

Meg lifted her hands and shrugged. "I don't know."

"I hope Dr. Vanover isn't upset with you."

"No, but she is eager to get everything in order as quickly as possible."

"So, you won't be home for tonight's dinner, or any dinner for some time."

Meg shook her head. "I'm sorry, Mom. I really am."

"What about your class and the festival?"

"I talked with Mrs. Burlew. She's agreed to get an emergency substitute. We're nearly through anyway and I don't think the class will object. As for the festival." Taking her mother's hands in hers, Meg squeezed. "You've got this. You know what needs to be done better than anyone."

"Well, thanks to you, things are at least in some order."

"I made flight reservations as soon as I got off the phone with Rachael and I packed a few things. Will you give my goodbyes to everyone?"

"Are you sure you know what you're doing?"

"Yes. I do. I really do." Meg hugged her mother, slung the backpack over her shoulder, picked up her duffel bag and grabbed the handle of the hard-shelled roller bag that held several well-wrapped fossils from the site for Rachael to inspect.

After a last long look out the window to where her nieces painted with joyful abandon, Meg left.

THE OLD SEDAN hit a series of potholes a few miles up the county road. The last one left the car listing. Meg pulled off the road. The front passenger tire barely clung to the rim. She checked the time and kicked the pile of useless rubber. "I don't have time for this."

She'd selected the oldest and least used vehicle on Bent Fork with the plan to get a rental in town for the drive down to Denver and leave the car for John or Andrew to claim later. Now she wasn't sure she would even get to town.

"Okay, tire-changing tools." She took the functional spare tire, a jack and an iron bar from the storage well and placed them on the ground near the worthless tire, rolled the sleeves of her teal linen shirt past her elbows and squatted in front of the shapeless rubber. "Now what?"

The car guy she dated in Ann Arbor had taught her a great deal about the parts and the workings of engines but nothing about changing a flat tire. She knew she needed a lug wrench. What she held didn't look like a wrench, but it fit over the bolts holding the rim in place. She put the tool over a bolt and tugged. No amount of her elbow grease moved the bolt even a fraction. "New name for the tool—slug wrench."

Meg tossed the heavy bar aside and sat. Inhale. Exhale. She pulled out her phone and stared at the screen. Precious time ticked by. The plane was not going to wait for Meg Farrell.

Inhale. Exhale.

She tugged and pushed again on every bolt. Not one of them budged. "You're useless, utterly and absolutely useless." She stood and flung the wrench into the roadside brush.

"That's no way to treat valuable equipment."

Meg spun and clapped her hands as Hawk climbed from his pickup and strode toward her. From the Stetson to the navy T-shirt displaying the Sitting River logo, to faded denims and his broken-down boots, he was every bit her hero. A man with strength. A man with know-how. A man who could change a tire. Or at the very least, loosen the bolts.

"Thank goodness." She pointed to the flat tire. "Will you do something about that?"

He tipped his head in the direction of the brush. "Only after you find that very necessary tool you just tossed away."

"Don't you have one in your truck?"

"I do. Every vehicle should have one, including that one." He jerked his thumb at the sedan.

"What's the point of having one if you can't use it?" she called over her shoulder as she jumped the shallow ditch and, using feet and hands, pushed aside long grass and lifted scrub brush. Sweat stung her eyes and thicker brush pricked her bare arms. She straightened, swiped the back of her hand across her forehead and looked back at the incapacitated car. Gauging the trajectory of her toss, she moved a few feet to her left and started a search grid. Slow and steady.

"Eureka!" She held up the lug wrench and waved it at Hawk.

"It only works when it's attached to the nut."

Meg folded her arms. "It didn't work for me." She stepped through the brush, leaped over the ditch and handed Hawk the iron bar. "Okay, use your magic or muscle or whatever. Just make the car movable."

"In a hurry?"

"Yes."

"Not to dig in your fossil pit. You're not wearing your fossil-digging clothes."

Meg tugged on her wrinkled shirt and shrugged. Pointless. Linen wrinkled if you just looked at it and no amount of tugging on her part would smooth the fabric. "No. I'm not going to the fossil site," she said softly.

Hawk's eyes met hers and lingered. Meg pulled her lower lip between her teeth and shifted her gaze to the tire.

"I see."

The two words reached her, heavy and cold. His voice flat, and hollow. "Hawk, I—"

"I'll take care of the tire so you can be on your way." He squatted next to the flat and struggled briefly with the bolts, freed them, slid the damaged tire off, the new one on and secured it. "There." He stood. "You're free to go."

"Thank you. I…" Her voice lost strength to go on.

"I'll put the tools away."

He stored the tools and dropped the mat over the

storage well, revealing her duffel bag and hard-shelled case. "Luggage."

"Yes."

"Flying somewhere?"

"Yes." The single word, more an utterance of sound than speech, filled the distance between them, thick and impenetrable.

"Given the direction you're headed, you weren't coming to explain or say goodbye." He pulled the Stetson from his head and pushed fingers through his hair. "I wondered how long you'd last this time." He settled the hat low on his forehead. "Don't let me keep you."

"It's not like that."

"Not like what? Not like you're going back to Michigan without saying goodbye."

"That's because it isn't goodbye."

He looked at the luggage and closed the trunk. "Yes, Meggie. It is."

## *CHAPTER TWENTY-ONE*

MEG CLOSED HER eyes as the tram sped from her arrival terminal at the Denver International Airport to baggage claim. She'd stayed in Michigan a few days longer than she'd wanted but had left confident the exhibits and displays would be set up and in proper order. As soon as she'd handed the final supply list for the paleo lab to Rachael with the promise to come back in two weeks and assist with putting the lab together, Meg had dashed to the airport hoping for a standby seat to get her home in time for the Willow River Festival opening parade.

Exiting the tram with her backpack over her shoulder, she joined the mass of people headed for the baggage carousels. With only her duffel bag and hard-shelled case to collect, she just might make it. And if she didn't?

She'd tried to pull details in order after Mrs. Maine dumped the event and flew back to New York. Her mother, Ruby and Emma knew what needed to be accomplished. Most of the town had gotten involved in various aspects of the festival.

They only needed a little focus to get everything done in time and if not, the day would still arrive with the sunrise. It would still be the day to celebrate Tyler's survival and inauguration. Maybe not with the promises of Diana Maine for fancy floats, extravagant decorations, giant balloons, spectacular fireworks or the big-name band, but it would still be a special event in Tyler, Colorado.

The best ever? She couldn't say.

Meg scanned the bags circling in front of her for the worn duffel and maroon case. Most were black, most were roller bags, none were hers. She checked the time and grimaced. The kickoff for the celebration started in just over four hours. Maybe she could still make it if the car rental shuttle sat outside and if the rental line for a car, any car, was short.

She checked her watch once more and kicked the carousel. "Two measly bags. Come on, spit 'em out."

"You do have issues with mechanical equipment."

"Hawk!" Her smile froze before it reached her eyes. Meg pressed her feet hard against the floor to keep from flying into his arms. A shield hovered between them. He wore the same Stetson that covered most of his dark hair. The same work clothes of denim and cotton covered his frame. The same worn boots he needed to replace anchored him. But his eyes. His eyes held a vastness she couldn't imagine crossing and all the words she'd wanted to say to him fell away. Words she'd hoped would soften the disappointment she'd seen in his eyes when he'd spied her luggage. Words she'd hoped would soothe the rejection she'd heard when he'd believed her departure meant goodbye.

She wiped her palms down the sides of her khakis. "How did you know I'd be here? I didn't even know if I'd make the flight."

"I'm not here for you. I didn't expect you back at all."

Meg blinked, stung not only by the words but by the flat delivery of them. She pulled in a deep breath and exhaled. "If you'd waited a few seconds longer after changing the tire you would have heard me explain that I wasn't leaving. Not for good."

"I didn't need an explanation. You made it clear what you wanted and where you wanted to be. It wasn't Colorado." He snagged the maroon case as it passed her and set it at her feet. "I think this is yours."

Her hand covered his around the handle. The warmth, the strength of him seeped into her before he eased his hand away. Meg glanced at the case and back to Hawk. He straightened and squared his shoulders. His shield still held. "Have you ever wondered why you're working so hard to fulfill a dead man's dream and rectify your selfish father's mistakes? What about your own dreams? What you want? I thought you were finally beginning see that there is life beyond Sitting River, beyond the land, beyond the past."

"Don't talk to me about not seeing. You've never faced your own life. You've attached yourself to rocks and dead creatures because they don't ask anything of you. Have you ever questioned why you've chosen to work with things instead of people?"

Tears pricked behind her eyes. She blinked and lowered her head.

"Ah, Meggie. You make me crazy." Hawk slid his index finger along her jawbone to her chin and tipped her head up. "I'm sorry. I wish I had more to offer you. Maybe then—"

"Hey, how about a welcome home, soldier."

Meg spun. "Keith!" She dropped her backpack and flung her arms around her brother's neck. "You're home!"

He hugged her tightly. "Looks that way."

Meg stepped back. Tears she'd held from Hawk fell as she looked into eyes so similar to her own. "You're really home." Meg scanned the baggage area. "Where are Heidi and Ava?" She turned to Hawk. "Did you bring them?"

Hawk stepped forward and extended a hand. "Welcome home, soldier. Good to see you in one piece."

Keith ignored the hand and pulled Hawk into a brotherly embrace. "I'm fortunate to be one piece."

Meg hooked an arm through her brother's and squeezed. "Where's Heidi?"

Keith smiled. “I wanted to surprise everyone.” He tugged on a loose curl framing her face. “You know I love surprises. So, while I waited in New York for my connecting flight, I called Hawk and asked him to pick me up. It will give me some time to catch up on what my beautiful wife omits in our video chats.”

Hawk retrieved the duffel his friend had dropped. “Ready?”

“More than ready. That pickup of yours can’t go fast enough to suit me.” Keith reached for Meg’s luggage. “Let me take that.”

Meg looked from her brother to Hawk. “Hawk’s here for you. Not me.”

“I’m sure he has room.”

Meg watched Hawk’s dark eyes narrow before he pulled his Stetson low. He didn’t want to take her, but he would.

Hawk shrugged. “She’s your sister.”

“Thanks, but apparently nonliving things are more to my liking. So, the drive home with just the inanimate car will be paradise for me. Go on. I’ll see you at home.”

“Huh?” Keith gave her a puzzled look and shrugged. “To each his own. Right now, my idea of paradise is wrapping my arms around two very special girls as soon as heavenly possible.”

Hawk leaned against the float, careful not to crush the crepe paper rosettes covering the sides of the large flatbed trailer. Bales of hay, stacked for seating purposes, filled the bed. Volunteers darted from float to float adjusting signs and anchoring banners. He contemplated going to the cabin and leaving the festivalgoers to their merrymaking. A festive mood did not sit with him.

Seeing Meggie at the airport had cracked the shield he'd erected the day he'd changed her flat tire. The day she'd made it clear she was leaving. The flat tire had slowed her departure. Had he not come along, she might have missed her flight. It wouldn't have mattered. She wanted to leave, and she would have found a way, with or without his help.

The crack continued to splinter and web its way around him, bringing down his stoic facade bit by bit. He'd learned early to assemble a barrier around his feelings. He'd gotten good at placing buffers between himself and the potential for hurt and disappointment, except when it came to Meggie Farrell.

*Why is she back?*

Fossils. Her return had to have something to do with her fossils. *Her* fossils on *his* land. Land he hoped to live on for the rest of his life. Land he hoped to share with a wife and children. Right now, all he could promise a woman was a day full of hard work and a handful of debt. No moon, no stars. No guarantee for a happily-ever-after. He wanted a woman who would be willing to stand beside him every day, even if the next day could be the day you lose it all.

His father had regularly promised his mother the moon and the stars and everything in between. Belinda Hawk had finally scattered her husband's empty promises over the miles between Cheyenne and Sitting River, where she began to place her trust in herself, her son, Lame Eagle and her chosen friends. Hawk needed to do the same. He needed to let the shield fall and trust himself to build a future around people, not just Sitting River. And he knew where he wanted to place the first foundation stone.

He moved away from the float, making room for Ed Ball to add a sign advertising new hours and discounts for the bowling lanes. Keith stood behind the float conversing with two men in uniforms representing past military conflicts. Keith caught his attention.

"So, what's going on between you and my sister?" Keith asked.

"Your sister wants to dig up and display any ancient bone she can find buried on my land."

Keith shook his head. "No, there's more than that. There's always been something between you and Meggie. I've wondered when the two of you would realize that fact and do something about it."

Hawk folded his arms across his chest. "Right now, what's between me and Meggie is nearly twelve hundred miles and a museum full of dinosaurs."

"So." Keith clapped a hand on Hawk's shoulder. "What's your plan?"

"Plan?"

"You need a plan. Best-case scenario. Worst-case scenario. And you need to know you can cope with both."

Hawk returned the brotherly gesture. "I'm glad you're home, Keith."

Keith chuckled. "You're avoiding."

"Not avoiding. I'm trusting."

"Trusting what? Or whom?"

"Lame Eagle. He told me, just before he died, that all would be well. I'm trusting him." Hawk nudged his Stetson off his forehead. "I am glad you're home."

"No one is happier for me to be home than yours truly." Keith grinned. "It's going to be the best festival ever."

"That's what your sister said. I'm not so sure."

Hawk scanned the area, taking in the colorful floats in line to move down Main Street, the Tyler High marching band tuning their instruments, the pens of sheep, pigs and cattle waiting to be judged, and at the edge of the festival grounds, an old green pickup.

"Hey, I need to talk with someone. Good luck finding your family in this crowd."

"Oh, I'll find them. My senses are on high alert for a beautiful woman and a lovable five-year-old."

MEG PULLED INTO the parking lot behind Wendell's Hardware store that served as the staging area for the floats. Keith stood next to a flatbed loaded with hay bales talking with Wendell.

She ran to her brother and hugged him again. "I thought you'd be at Bent Fork."

"Hawk convinced me everyone would be here for the start of the parade. Made sense. Why drive up to Bent Fork just to turn around and drive back here."

Meg squeezed her brother's arm. "How do you plan to surprise Heidi?"

"I don't know."

"You haven't seen that wife of yours yet?" Wendell held out his cell phone. "Here, call her?"

"Thanks, but I'd really like to surprise her in person."

Meg glanced at the slew of helpers of all ages running from one decorated vehicle to the next tucking colored crepe paper into place, tying on balloons, shifting bales of hay on the flatbeds, straightening flags, grooming horses and adjusting costumes. She grinned and rubbed her hands together. "I have an idea."

Twenty minutes later, Meg stood back and looked down Main Street as the floats began their journey. Throngs of people, many of them dressed in red, white and blue, gathered along the sidewalks. Folding chairs, strollers, cushions and blankets littered every free space between the curb and storefronts.

In line before the first float came John Farrell's newly restored, highly polished Shelby Mustang convertible. John sat proudly in the driver's seat with the mayor and this year's Tyler High valedictorian sitting behind.

Next came a flatbed pulled by a team of draft horses with Larry Reed, minus sling, holding the reins. Bales of hay filled the flatbed. Some were stacked to create seats while others had dozens of small flags sticking out like spines. A large flag formed a backdrop at the very back of the bales.

Perched on the seats were representatives of the military branches of service from the Revolutionary War, the Civil War, to the WWI air force, and Angie Wayman's brother Damian sat in his wheelchair in the uniform he'd worn in Vietnam. Angie stood next to him in her mother's patched WWII uniform. Front and center, Keith Farrell perched on a hay bale wearing his fatigues and scanning the crowds on each side of the street for his wife and daughter.

Beth Lawrence sat on a large riding mower towing a small flatbed trailer holding a canoe. Signs of all kinds and sizes stuck to the sides of the canoe, advertising festival booths. The canoe also carried two of Beth's nephews, each holding a bag full of candies to toss to the crowd Mardi Gras–style.

Behind the canoe came a Girl Scout troop on bicycles with gold-colored streamers dripping from the handlebars and stars painted on their cheeks.

The Tyler Elementary School PTA came after them pulling red wagons or pushing strollers and beyond the PTA the Tyler High band stood in formation tuning their instruments.

"Meggie! Meggie!"

Meg swiveled from the group of high schoolers and their various instruments creating raucous, grating and groaning sounds to see her mother trotting toward her.

"You made it!" Joanna Farrell pulled her daughter into a tight embrace.

Meg returned the hug and stepped back. Her mother's cheeks were damp and the smile on her face brilliant. "You've seen Keith."

"Did you know he was coming home so early?"

"No. I ran into him at the airport. You know Keith and his love of surprises."

"Well, he certainly surprised me. I nearly fainted when I saw him."

"He still hasn't seen Heidi or Ava."

"They were driving down behind me and Ruby. Ava insisted on putting a red, white and blue bandanna on Buddy before they got in the car. Unfortunately, Buddy wasn't cooperating." Joanna pressed her hand to her heart and smiled. "They're going to be so surprised. He looks good. Don't you think?"

"Yes. We had a few words at the airport before he and Hawk headed out. He seems just fine. Eager to see his wife and daughter."

"You didn't ride up with them?"

"As I said last night, I wasn't sure I'd get the flight. Standbys can be risky."

"You're here. That's what matters." Joanna clapped her hands and grinned. "Let's see if we can find Heidi and Ava. I'd like to be there for the reunion."

Meg looked over her mother's shoulder at the thickening crowd. "Where do we begin?"

A loud barking erupted among the chatter of those gathered along the street. "Buddy?" Joanna asked.

"Sounds like him. If that's the case, we know where to find Ava. Follow that bark."

They threaded their way down the block issuing a constant string of "excuse me" and "pardon me" and "sorry" before Meg spied Buddy and his colored bandanna running and barking nonstop alongside the flatbed float bearing the servicemen.

"Buddy! Get away from there!" Meg yelled.

The dog continued to jump and bark at the float. Meg elbowed her way into the street and reached for the leash trailing behind Buddy.

From atop the float her brother commanded, "Buddy, sit!"

Buddy sat.

Keith leaped from the flatbed, bent and ruffled the dog's ears before gathering the leash. "Anyone want to claim this rowdy mutt?"

"Buddy! Buddy!" Ava burst from the crowd. She ran to the dog and with one hand on her hip shook a finger at Buddy. "Bad dog!" The stance and tone mimicked what Meg had seen and heard many times from Ruby.

Buddy continued to sit with tail thumping and tongue lolling. Her brother knelt before his daughter with eyes full of love and a smile stretched across his face. How he kept from scooping her into his arms was beyond Meg.

"Here you go." He held out the leash.

Ava reached for the leash and stopped, hand in midair, and stared. Then, with a squeal, she flung herself into her father's arms. "Daddy!"

Keith stood and swung her around. "How's my sweet girl?"

"Ava! Come back here!" Heidi stepped around a stroller holding a toddler with a red-, white- and blue-striped bottle and a woman gripping a wagon full of blankets, a cooler and two more children. She spotted her daughter. "Ava!"

From her vantage point near the float, Meg saw Heidi freeze. Keith stopped his twirling and faced his wife. Holding Ava with his right arm, he held out his left. Heidi took a small step, then two, then ran.

Wild cheers and clapping erupted from the

crowd up and down the street. The floats had halted. Horns blew and the Tyler High band began playing "The Star-Spangled Banner."

Meg hugged her mother, both of them weeping openly at the sight of their family reunited. Connor joined them, holding aloft his cell phone.

Meg gave him a puzzled look. "What are you doing?"

"Giving my wife a front-row seat to the reunion."

Meg pulled his phone level with her face and waved at a beaming Alison.

"Did you know about this?" Alison asked.

"Nope. How are my precious nephews?"

Alison swung her phone around to show the twins swaddled in cozy blankets of green and white geometric patterns nestled side by side on the sofa. "Fortunately, sleeping. Give my brother-in-law a welcome-home hug when you can pry him away from Heidi."

"I will. See you soon." Meg blew her a kiss and hugged her brother. "The boys are adorable. I'm so glad they're home."

"*You* can say that. You're not changing forty-eight diapers in eight hours or burping them constantly or rocking, walking or singing to them constantly, or—"

"And you love every minute of it."

Connor gave her a big smile. "Yep. Every minute."

"Every minute of what?"

Meg turned. Her father and mother stepped toward them arms linked and happy smiles on their faces. "Connor admits he likes changing diapers and burping babies."

"I should hope so." Her mother patted Connor's cheek. "He's going to be doing that for quite some time."

"Oh, Alison and I plan to let the rest of the family have lots of opportunities to do the same. On a regular basis."

"Family gets an opportunity to do what?" Ruby joined the group with Caroline and Molly in tow.

Connor stooped beside his daughters. "The family wants to help change diapers and burp your brothers."

"Ew." Caroline groaned. "Why? Their diapers are yucky."

"Really yucky." Molly pinched her nose.

"Looks like I might need replacements for these odor-sensitive girls of mine."

"How about their Aunt Heidi and Uncle Keith?"

Connor handed his phone to Meg and gave his brother a bear hug. "Welcome home."

"It's good to be home. I'm eager to see those nephews of mine." Keeping Heidi close to his side, he took the phone from Meg and grinned at the image of his sister-in-law. "Hi, Alison. How are you feeling?"

Meg stepped back from the congregation of family and breathed. In and out. In and out. Peaceful breaths. Easy breaths.

"Some gathering."

Meg flinched. "I'm so happy right now, I don't mind that you sneak up on me." She gave him a long look. His lips sat in a flat line. No curve of a smile, no tip of amusement moved them. His eyes were dark and guarded. The brim of his hat sat low on his forehead. Tired? No. She'd seen him tired. This look, this was a look of wariness.

"You okay?"

He glanced up Main Street. "Will be. You?"

She smiled at the group in front of her. Family. People she loved dearly. Her parents stood arm in arm talking with Ruby, Larry and Emma. Connor chatted through the phone with Alison while his daughters tugged him toward the food truck. Heidi and Keith walked hand in hand behind Ava, who followed Buddy toward the taco truck. At the end of the street, John set Beth on the hood of his Shelby and waved.

"Am I okay? I'm more than okay. I'm home."

"What?"

Meg breathed in deeply and blew it out slowly, then glanced at Hawk. "It's the best Willow River Festival since the very first one. Don't you think?"

"Not yet." Hawk took her hand and led her up Main Street away from the crowds to an old green pickup parked in front of the Drop-By Café. "I'd like you to meet someone. He's going to be working around Sitting River."

Meg smiled at the man leaning against the truck. “Hello, Mike.”

“Ma’am.”

Meg extended a hand. “I hope you’ll like working on Sitting River. Hawk is the best there is when it comes to caring for a ranch.”

Mike nodded. “I believe I have a lot to learn about caring and not just for the land.” He extended his hand to Hawk. “I need to get on the road if I’m going to make Albuquerque today. I’ll be back tomorrow, or not, depending on my reception.”

Hawk clasped the hand. “Give her my love.”

Mike turned to Meggie. “I think you learned from him, too. Remember his words.”

Meg watched Mike climb into the rusted truck and pull away. “He’s going to Albuquerque?”

“Yes.”

She pointed to the truck as it turned onto Canyon Road. “That was…was that…?”

“Michael Hawk. He’s the one who placed the other bouquet of columbines on my grandmother’s grave.”

“But, your father? When? Why?” She paused and cocked her head to one side. “You knew the day we found Ava in his truck?”

Hawk nodded.

“You didn’t say anything.”

“He left a note on my pickup the day before you met with Mrs. Burlew asking if he could talk with me. I met with him while you were at TCC trying not to become the summer geology teacher. He'd been staying in the Meyer Ridge storm shelter and asked if he could continue to stay there. I agreed. He says he'll make some repairs and clean up the place." Hawk caught sight of his father's pickup as it turned and headed toward Belinda Hawk. "He's the one who fired the shots we heard the day we found the dog. Said he was hunting dinner."

"You doubt him?"

"I've every reason to doubt everything my father says."

Meg nodded. "I'm sorry. I—"

"We'll work it out." Hawk shrugged. "In time."

"Did he explain why he's here now?"

"You mean did we reminisce about the good old days? Did he ask for forgiveness?" Hawk tapped his boot against the curb. Puffs of dust flew off the leather and floated to the ground. "He said, if I wasn't too proud to let him, he'd like to earn my forgiveness, if not my respect. He also said he was willing and able to work for nothing, if I wasn't too proud to let him." A kick of the other boot dislodged a clump of dirt. Hawk pushed the clod aside. "Said it was the only way he could free himself from a burden he carried."

"So?"

"So." Hawk nudged his Stetson back from his forehead. "Sitting River has a new hand who doesn't want to be paid for his hard work. I may have a father in my life after all these years. My mother may have her husband back in her life, if she wants him. Jenna and Mark are staying on with Larry and Emma. Jenna will take over the bookkeeping for the ranch, freeing some of my time. And Mark will help out while he finishes an online marketing program."

Meg planted her hands on her hips. "I'm stunned."

"I'm proud. Maybe too proud. Lame Eagle cautioned me over the years. A proud man can be a lonely man if his pride is misplaced. I'm going to make Sitting River something to be proud of. Not just for the memory of Lame Eagle, but because Sitting River is my home."

Meg grinned. "Admit it. It is the best Willow River Festival ever."

"Not yet."

Meg tilted her head. "What's missing? Keith is home, the twins and Alison are home, you might be reconnecting with your father, you have more help with the ranch, the Reeds have their family together and I haven't told you yet." She gave him a wide grin. "Rachael wants the fossils for an exhibit at the Mayfield."

"I need to know something."

"You should get enough money to replace that old hay baler or tractor or both."

He didn't need to know about money. "Are you going back to Michigan?"

Meg took a deep breath. "Yes."

Hawk nodded. "I see."

"I don't think you do."

"You've found your place, Meggie. I'm glad for you."

"I tried to tell you the day you fixed my flat, but you took off and I didn't have the time to follow and explain. Not then." She put her hand on his chest. "You mentioned being too proud. I get that. I think I've been dealing with the same issue but didn't recognize it until recently. It's not easy for me to let go of certain memories, certain thoughts, and let new ones in, but I'm learning. Now, will you just stand still and listen to me for a minute?"

"I'm listening."

"I am going back to Michigan. I promised Rachael I would fly back shortly after I've completed my obligation to the geology class to help get the Mayfield in top order for the grand opening. Then, I will continue to work with the Mayfield as a part-time staff member."

"Part-time?"

"Correct. I'll go back and forth as Rachael and I agree there's a need, like setting up a Sitting River fossil exhibit at the Mayfield. That is if you will allow me to continue to dig and if you're willing to offer the fossils I find to the Mayfield before going elsewhere with them. Rachael agreed the fossils will make a good addition to the Mayfield and a profitable bonus for Sitting River."

Hawk dipped his head in a curt nod. "Given

your knack for finding these prehistoric bones, you could be doing a lot of flying to Michigan."

"In that case, I'll also be doing a lot of flying back home." Meg looked past him, to the peaks rising beyond Tyler. "This is where I am who I'm meant to be. It's where I want to be. I want the wide-open spaces. I want to be near my family. I want to do the work I love and to share it with others. I want to be needed. And I want someone in my life who will share my life with me." Meg shrugged. "I guess I want it all. Most of all—I want you. The day Lame Eagle brought you to Bent Fork, I knew you were significant. You stood grounded in worn boots wearing a Stetson too big for you, a braid that labeled you unique and with eyes as magical as our mountains. They looked at and through and still do."

She sighed and rested her gaze on him. "Eyes that hopefully see how much I love you. I loved you when we rode two-up after Molasses went lame. I loved you when I came home during school breaks and hoped I'd bump into you every time I went for a ride or drove into town. I loved you when you helped us find Ava in the rain. I loved you when you let me dig on your ranch and I loved you when I flew back to Michigan." She traced her finger along the fading scratch along his cheek. "I loved you before I knew what love was. And I still do."

Hawk stared down at her. "Meggie." He stroked her cheek with the back of his fingers. "I'm part

Ute and part Minnesotan and proud to be both. I am also a part of Sitting River. I want to do the work I love. I want a family. I want someone in my life who will share in all the parts of me, the good, the bad and the new when it comes along."

"I—"

Hawk pressed his finger to her lips. "I've tried to tell you, to show you where I stand."

"Just so you know, I'm not good with subtle," she mumbled past his finger.

His lips twitched. "How about this." He squared his shoulders. "I love you, Meggie Farrell. I loved you when I saw you study a rock, then pull a pencil from your hair and make notes. I loved you when you defended Buddy from the coyote and from me—" he traced the healing scratch on his cheek "—even though I hadn't done anything. I loved you when you walked out of TCC as their temporary teacher. I loved seeing the fascination on your face and hearing the awe in your voice when you found fossils on my ranch. I'm still a little unsure about how a relationship should work. I need… I need to learn to trust. Not only others but myself as well and I'm willing to try because—" he cupped her face between his palms "—I love you, Meggie Farrell."

"Your dad said to remember Lame Eagle's words. I do. Your grandfather asked me, just before I left for U of M, to promise I would come back home. The promise seemed important to him, like he was passing to me some intimate knowledge I couldn't quite grasp—until now. He'd said it was good to fly away and learn but to remember I am whole here and to promise him I would fly home." Meg tugged Hawk's Stetson low on his forehead. "He was right. It may not make sense but I've come to realize the family didn't keep me from belonging. I had to make something more of me, for me, before I could accept that I belong here."

"So, Meg Farrell, how about flying home?" Hawk placed the palm of his right hand against his stomach and the back of his left hand against hers, measuring the distance between them. "It's not too far to fly. Is it?" He held out his arms.

Meg leaped. Hawk caught her and held her close. "Not far at all," she whispered against his neck.

"Hey, what's going on here?"

Hawk set Meg on her feet. She nestled close to his side and smiled as her family approached holding tacos, cotton candy and plastic cups filled with assorted drinks.

Connor turned his cell phone toward Hawk and Meggie. "Looks like we may have extra hands to help with the boys' diapers and burping."

Meg turned to Hawk. "How are you at cuddling babies?"

"I've cuddled calves, lambs, puppies, kittens, an occasional owl and a deer. I've even cuddled a woman on my porch swing." He winked. "I have never cuddled a baby. But I'm willing to try something new."

Ava tugged on Hawk's hand. "Now that Daddy's home, I'll cuddle with him, and you can practice with my stuffy."

"Thank you, Ava. That will be very helpful."

"All right, family. Let's join the parade." Lansford Farrell motioned toward the line of Tyler residents following the floats.

They moved as one. Connor raised his phone aloft as Molly tugged him forward. Caroline walked with Jenna and her youngest daughter. Ruby, Emma and Joanna chatted and pointed as they merged with the crowd. Lansford and Andrew passed by John's Mustang. John helped Beth off the hood of the car and, hand in hand, they joined the group. Keith, Heidi and Ava lagged behind, still holding on to each another and Buddy.

Meg and Hawk brought up the rear. Laughter, chatter and singing echoed around them. Meg smiled up at Hawk. "Well, it seems like everyone is enjoying the celebration."

"In fact, I'd say it's a pretty good Willow River Festival."

Hawk stopped. He put his finger under her chin and tipped her face up. Slowly he lowered his mouth to hers. A kiss, sweet and soft with a promise of more to come.

He raised his head and smiled down at her. "Now it's the *best* Willow River Festival ever."

* * * * *